BEASTS OF THE SEA

STELLER'S SEA-COW, RHYTINA GIGAS.

PLATE XXVI. Found alive by Steller at Behring's Island. Length 19 feet 6 inches.

Drawing of Steller's Sea Cow from *Extinct Monsters: A Popular Account of Some of the Larger Forms of Ancient Animal Life* by H.N. Hutchinson, illustrations by Joseph Smit (London: Chapman & Hall, 1896)

BEASTS OF THE SEA

A Novel

IIDA TURPEINEN

Translated by David Hackston

Little, Brown and Company
New York Boston London

The characters and events in this book are fictitious. Any similarity to real persons, living or dead, is coincidental and not intended by the author.

Little, Brown and Company
Hachette Book Group
1290 Avenue of the Americas, New York, NY 10104
littlebrown.com

First North American edition: November 2025

Originally published in Finland as *Elolliset* by Iida Turpeinen © Schildts & Söderströms, 2023

ISBN 9780316585835
LCCN is available at the Library of Congress.

1 2025

MRQ-T

Printed in Canada

As long as things escape us and perish unknown with our consent, and through our silence are counted as fabulous – things which may be seen with little labour in the very land where we, with all our inquisitiveness, live – it is not strange that these things, which we are prevented from observing by the great sea that lies between, have remained to the present time unknown and unexplored.

Georg Wilhelm Steller, 1742

60°10'16"N, 24°55'52"E

NATURAL HISTORY MUSEUM

HELSINKI

To begin with, you have to walk past the African elephant and step in through the door at the back. Hanging on the walls are the flayed bodies of fish, frogs and birds. The room can feel ghostly, but visitors wander through the space, attentive and carefree, walking from one display case to the next, examining bones and info labels, and their attention is eventually drawn to it.

First, visitors see the horses, the bears, the seals and snakes, beast upon beast, their brittle bones carefully, imperceptibly attached to one another to form the contours of recognisable creatures familiar from books and zoos, and then they are confronted with this animal and its altogether different remains.

The other skeletons displayed in the room are white and neat; nothing about them reminds us of the bloody, messy work that unveiling the bones from within a living body requires. But this one's surface is rough and worn, yellowed like an old newspaper abandoned in the attic; its ribs and vertebrae are adorned with a filigree of cracks and fractures, and in the places where a bone is broken, its darkened surface reveals the gleam of something lighter and porous underneath.

The bones are scarred and battered. Two sets of numbers have been marked on the ribs, one written neatly in ink and the other sketched in pencil, allowing us to discern nineteen arched pairs. The ribs have been numbered in a delicate hand, but the order of the vertebrae has been daubed on the bones in thick, brash felt tip. In addition, there is a tag attached to the atlas vertebra, a faded archive label, and to see it you have to crouch down and risk catching the attention of the museum's security guard, but from this position it is possible to read, in robust typewritten letters, the words RHYTINA STELLERI and the year 1960. But the most arresting thing about this creature is not the marks left by human hand, but its size.

Stripped of its flesh, a bear is nothing but a scrawny, pitiful dog, a horse shrinks to the size of a pony, but even without its hide and blubber this animal makes the other skeletons gathered in the room look like flimsy little toys. If we continue into the next gallery, we see that its sturdy bones stand comparison even with the monumental frame of the humpback whale. Its sheer size commands our attention. Children run up to it shouting "dinosaur!", because that is what they are most excited to see, but their parents hesitate. They have read the museum's floor plan, and they know that the prehistoric creatures are on the third floor, not here, so they lean closer and read the words on the label to their offspring:

STELLER'S SEA COW, HYDRODAMALIS GIGAS

Imagine the Bering Sea, that great expanse of water between Siberia and Alaska, the Pacific Ocean and the Arctic Ocean. Imagine the Bering Sea in 1741.

BEASTS OF THE SEA

I

[…] *all these treasures of nature so artfully contrived, so wonderfully propagated, so providentially supported throughout her three kingdoms, seem intended by the Creator for the sake of man. Every thing may be made subservient to his use, if not immediately, yet mediately, not so to that of other animals. By the help of reason man tames the fiercest animals, pursues and catches the swiftest, nay he is able to reach even those which lye hid in the bottom of the sea.*

Carl von Linnaeus, *Oeconomy of Nature*, 1749

53°3'55"N, 158°37'32"E

KAMCHATKA PENINSULA

RUSSIAN FAR EAST

1741

All expeditions begin with a cup of tea. Captain Commander Vitus Bering pours it, and from it drinks one Georg Wilhelm Steller, a theologian, naturalist, and curious man. The captain fills the cup to the brim because he has a mission. It was the *imperator* Peter the Great himself who had first encouraged Bering to find a seaway, to chart a route from Asia to the Americas, and Bering had duly set off. In fact, he had set off twenty years ago, left the coastline and sailed north into uncharted waters, but the fog was continuous, the weather atrocious, and with his ship's reserves of fresh water already depleted, the expedition had eventually decided to turn back. Bering returned with a more detailed map of the Kamchatka Peninsula, but the upper corner of the atlas remained empty, and the *imperator* departed this world without ever finding out where the edge of the New World is drawn.

The *imperator* may have died, but the thought itself has not. One must try again, try better and harder. The Tzarina Anna has given the order, and now another two ships float in the waters at Avacha Bay: the *Sviatoi Piotr* and the *Sviatoi Pavel,* St Peter and St Paul. Between them they carry a hundred men, a full twenty are needed to hoist their sails alone, and around them a whole harbour springs up with barracks, workshops, hurriedly erected lodgings, and everything save the ships is small, dirty and cold.

Three scientists were selected to join the Great Northern Expedition, respected learned men from the newly opened Academy of Sciences in St Petersburg. No expense was spared in equipping the entourage. The scientists were accompanied by six assistants, six surveyors, two draughtsmen and thirteen soldiers, an interpreter, a physician, a technician, a drummer, as well as guides, rowers and bearers. With them, they carried a scientific library comprising hundreds of volumes, nine carts of instruments, four telescopes, five astrolabes, twenty thermometers, twenty-seven barometers, two hundred and sixteen horses and many barrels of fine Rhenish wine. They set off from the capital to great pomp and ceremony, with eight thousand kilometres of Siberia and an unknown sea ahead of them.

By the time the professors arrive in Yeniseysk, they have already been travelling for many years, many long, arduous years, and yet they are not even halfway to their destination. In Yakutsk a fire breaks out in their lodgings, destroying all their notes and samples. Years of work goes up in smoke, and everyone has reached the end of their tether. The astronomer falls out with the ethnographer; the further east they travel, the worse things get, and eventually they reach a decision. The professors write to the Academy to ask to be relieved of their duties, and without waiting for an answer they turn their horses and head westwards again.

The captain's naturalists have set off home, but on their travels, they encounter a researcher who appears wholly unaffected by the misery of Siberia. This peculiar man does not care for powder and wigs, he drinks his beer and mead from the same tankard, but he is good at his work and speaks with great authority about grasses and birds that can withstand the Siberian cold. Professor Gmelin recommends that this man replace them, and Bering yields to the inevitable. He pens a friendly but assertive letter inviting this Georg Wilhelm Steller to be his guest at the harbour in Avacha Bay.

The theologian, naturalist, and curious man Georg Wilhelm Steller sits upright in his chair. He is wearing his best clothes, but that isn't saying much; four years in Siberia will eventually take its toll on anyone's sense of style. He has arrived on a dog-sled and tries not to show how good it feels to be indoors in the dry with a cup of strong, warm tea. The Academy of Sciences had charged Steller with documenting the flora, fauna and precious rocks of the Kamchatka Peninsula, but while he was in the east a flame ignited within him. He has seen the steppes and the mountains, rowed across Lake Baikal, and now he wishes to travel even further and has requested permission to sail all the way to Japan. One expedition is much like another, isn't that right, the captain laughs, fills the scientist's glass, and Steller raises it to his lips and glugs.

Steller gathers his equipment ready for departure, but delays and unexpected obstacles lie ahead. Replenishing the ship's food stocks takes longer than expected: the crew's biscuits disappear on their way to the harbour, and the batch made to replace them never arrives either, and the Koryaks in charge of the deliveries rise up in protest – delivering something to the furthest corner of Siberia takes time, and Kolyesov, the commanding officer responsible for the shipments, does nothing to make the job any easier. He is a man who does everything tomorrow, for today he can raise a glass, and Steller waits, curses, waits some more, and in the meantime compiles a study of the local fish.

Steller waits five months, twenty slow and sluggish weeks that he could have spent studying the novel species of Nippon, but eventually the long-awaited day arrives. Some of the provisions are still missing, but the expedition can wait no longer, it is time to leave so that they can return before the autumn storms, and on the twenty-ninth day of May the ships lower their anchors in the bay to wait for clement weather. On the fourth day of June there is a favourable wind, and *St Peter* and *St Paul* finally begin their journey to Alaska.

The commanding officers crack open bottles of champagne. The cadets' cheeks burn with an enthusiasm that Bering remembers on his own face when he set off on his previous expedition two decades earlier. Young men's imaginations brim with the riches of far-away lands, islands, bays and mountains that will soon be named after them, the respect and admiration in the eyes of the aristocrats' daughters, perhaps even of the Tzarina herself upon hearing of their adventures, but Bering is reminded of the monotonous days ahead, the dwindling food reserves and squalling nights when the men will pray for the salvation of their souls in the face of what seems like certain perdition. Back then, he was a man in his prime, but now he feels every one of his six decades; the young make merry, but Bering notes a shadow in the eyes of Khitrov, the fleet master. He too was on the expedition twenty years ago, and he knows what lies in store for them.

Bering leaves the celebrations. He is in no mood to raise a glass; he yearns for the wind and the sea, and he climbs up on deck. By now he can only barely make out the harbour, and behind that the summit of Avachinskaya Sopka rising up above the bay in all its tremendous grandeur. The sight is imposing, the sunset beautiful, but he turns his back to it and resolves to spend the rest of his days in warm, comfortable rooms.

Steller is a learned naturalist, but a gentleman he is not. The son of a lowly Nuremburg cantor, he is not invited to share the champagne, and instead immerses himself in work, noting down the seabirds and plants carried on the waves. He spends his time examining the currents and making all manner of calculations, and when he next sees Bering, he rushes to his side and explains he has worked out that it would be best to steer the ship a few degrees to the north-west, but the captain commander simply gazes out at the slowly disappearing land as if he has not heard Steller's words at all.

They leave the coastline, and the ship is shrouded in an impenetrable fog. All that cuts through it is the call of a passing seabird, drizzle wets the deck and the sails, the men's clothes cling to their bodies, damp and heavy, and nothing can keep them warm. Seven days of a wet impermeable dim, until eventually a wind picks up from the south-east and the fog disperses. The men climb up on deck to see the sun, but their stomachs become knotted in anguish, for opening out in front of them is the wide, empty sea. The expedition's two ships have drifted apart in the heavy fog. For days they search for the *St Paul*, but in vain. One of the saints is gone, taking with it half of the Great Northern Expedition's provisions.

There is much to observe. The waves carry plants that only thrive in shallow waters. Steller watches sea creatures and birds that never venture far from the shore. Again, he describes his observations to the ship's command and urges them to change course, but the officers merely raise an eyebrow and shrug their shoulders. How can a man under sail for the first time think he knows the seas better than they do? The captain commander takes no part in the dispute. He has no desire to upset the officers; they have friends in St Petersburg.

Steller looks on as two officers plot the ship's course on a map of the world and place them in the wrong ocean, locating the ship in the Atlantic instead of the Pacific, but nobody corrects their mistake.

Then an animal rises to the surface, and he remembers why he agreed to this bothersome journey in the first place. The creature is approximately two cubits long. Its hide is covered in red fur and its head recalls that of a dog. It has alert, pointed ears and bulging eyes, long dangling whiskers that resemble the learned men of the Orient, but its behaviour is like that of a boisterous child. It frolics, dives underwater then returns to the surface with a tuft of seagrass in its mouth, tosses the grass into the air and snatches it again between its teeth. The crew gather to watch, and they clap their hands at the creature, but Steller summons the best sniper on the ship, a Cossack by the name of Toma Lepekhin, and instructs him to shoot the animal. Lepekhin takes a shot, but the bullet misses the heart, it pierces the skin but does not take the creature's life. It dives back into the depths, but this time it does not return to the surface.

Steller is well acquainted with all the studies and travelogues, the catalogues of known animals stored in university libraries, but this animal he does not know. Weeks of nothing but seagulls and guillemots, and he lets the first interesting creature they encounter slip between his fingers. This simply won't do, and he thinks his way through all the most bizarre shelves in all the cabinets of curiosity until, lying in his berth that evening, he finally hits upon what it is. He had to look far back in history, but there it is, *Historia Animalium,* Gessner's great bestiary, and the Danish Sea Ape, *Simia marina Danica,* with its snakelike tail, its four wing-like fins, knobbly head and peculiar, playful character, everything fits, and now he can sleep, his mind content. His knowledge has not failed him; he is still able to classify the world.

In Gessner's bestiary, the real and the imagined come together: tigers, dogs and rhinoceroses frolic alongside unicorns and satyrs. The sea ape belongs to the latter group. It is a creature unknown to science, a so-called *animal paradoxum*. The sea ape never became as infamous as the yeti or the scintillating snake residing in Loch Ness, but Steller's observation does not go unnoticed, and future generations still pore over his words. It has been suggested that the creature Steller encountered, with its fins and other features, was in fact a deformed fur seal, but this is hard to believe. Steller was well acquainted with seals, and by his own account he was able to observe the animal long enough that it would have been curious indeed had he been unable to correctly identify a species with which he was so familiar. It has also been suggested that the sea ape was not an animal at all but a caricature of none other than Captain Commander Vitus Bering, a frustrated researcher's mischief at the expense of his own captain, but if it were merely a joke, why did Steller not make it more explicit? Why depict the creature's fins and tail if it were not in fact an animal at all but a jibe at a living person? Did Steller see an animal we know by another name? Or did he encounter a species that fell into extinction before its body could be preserved in solvent and transported back to the academies of the world for identification? Or did the weary naturalist simply sketch the creature in his diary for his own amusement, to beguile those who came after him? We shall never know.

Every morning the navigator drops the plumb into the water, and every morning the line remains taut. The weight does not reach the seabed but cuts through 180 feet of black water; there is no ridge rising out of the sea into an inviting, verdant land in front of them. The crew knew to prepare themselves for a long journey, but the north-west coast of America remains further away than any of them had predicted. They have been sailing for six weeks, their freshwater reserves are beginning to dwindle, and the officers come to a decision: if they do not reach land within the next two weeks, the expedition will be abandoned. On the twentieth day of July, the *St Peter* turns and heads home.

The Cossack Toma Lepekhin knocks on the door. Steller is sitting in his cabin writing up his notes, and upon seeing the Cossack he smiles and offers him some tea, but Lepekhin declines. Word is spreading on deck: the lookout believes he has spotted land. This is as yet unconfirmed, the horizon is shrouded in mist, it might be nothing but a rain front in the distance, but the lookout thinks he has seen a dark shadow in the sea, and with that Steller forgets all about the tea. They hurry up on deck and train their eyes on the horizon, an unbearable wait, the waves heave up and down, then the lookout shouts, yells so loudly that he is startled at his own voice: *Terra firma! Terra firma!*

The officers are enjoying dinner. The captain is not eating with them. He has been feeling tired and prefers to eat alone in his cabin, so Khitrov, the fleet master, is hosting the men. When Steller enters the room, their conversation dries up. The naturalist will not take no for an answer but continues raving about the ocean currents and pieces of seaweed to anyone who will listen to him, and he does not fall silent though he knows that the officers do not share his assessment of the situation. Khitrov has begun to suspect that Steller is adapting the laws of nature and the ocean currents at will simply in order to prove his superiors wrong, and now he has the nerve to interrupt their meal, he neither greets them nor deigns to remove his cap in their presence but gabbles at them, pleading with them to change course, until Khitrov informs him that he will check this observation himself once he has eaten. During the main course, rain starts to fall from the heavens. After the punch, their visibility is further impaired, and they must wait for a clearer day as the fleet master will not believe it before he sees it with his own eyes, no, and certainly not when the wrong man is trying to twist his arm.

The rain abates and the rising sun reveals the islands' black shadows. Bering congratulates Khitrov, though in truth he could almost weep. He sees the men's childish glee, the way they laugh and celebrate without sparing a thought for how far this new land is from any civilisation, or for all the dangers and delays that lie in wait for them as they chart this new coastline. They do not know the winds in this sea, winds that for all they know might blow them eastwards and prevent them from ever returning home. What a cruel twist of fate. They have already sailed far enough that no-one in St Petersburg would berate them; they could have returned home and proved that the journey is quite simply impossible. Four days more and they would have turned back, but now, to his great chagrin, they have discovered America.

On St Elias' Day, the *St Peter* lowers anchor off the coast of this green island. For two days they edge closer to the shore. Progress is slow, as the coastal waters are dotted with rocks and sandbanks, but the mood is buoyant. Weeks of nothing but the vast expanse of the sea, and suddenly an unknown land appears in front of them, a scintillating row of wooded islands and, beyond them, an alien shore. The world expands before their very eyes, they fill their glasses and their maps, and Khotyaintsov the underskipper adds ink to the places where until now there was nothing.

They name the island Cape St Elias, but Steller objects. The word "cape" denotes a strip of land stretching out from the coastline, and an island cannot be a cape, but the officers tell him to keep his mouth shut, and this name is duly added to the map.

The captain commander does not go ashore. His head is aching, he needs to remain on the ship and rest, so the fleet master assumes leadership of the expedition. He selects the men who will go ashore, but there is no room for the naturalist in his boat. Steller asks Khitrov to explain how he can possibly examine the island's terrain, the plants sprouting from the soil and the animals walking on its surface from the deck of the ship. Of course, he is excellent at his work, but even for his considerable skills this is one challenge too many. Until now, he has accepted the officers' disdain without complaint, but he will not agree to this; he cannot agree to this. He joined this expedition in order to serve the Tzarina, the Academy, in the service of science no less, and now the fleet master is preventing him from doing his work. This simply will not do, he shall report the matter to St Petersburg, to the Academy, to the Tzarina herself! Bering is summoned on deck – why are they bothering me with these childish disputes? Let the naturalist go ashore with the dinghy sent to replenish the ship's freshwater supplies. Steller clambers into the dinghy. The trumpeter sends him off with a mocking fanfare, and Khitrov bows to Steller from the prow of his boat and laughs.

Steller is allowed to take one assistant with him, and he chooses Toma Lepekhin. The Cossack tries his best to calm the doctor, who looks so angry he could kill a man, but as they approach the shore, Steller forgets all his woes. He jumps out of the dinghy and almost trips and falls into the waves, his boots touch solid ground, but his head is still spinning, and he is forced to grip the side of the vessel to stay upright. How intriguing – he knows that seasickness can be alleviated with a tea steeped from bishopwort, but he wants to know what causes the phenomenon in the first place, that and why his body can remember the movements of the sea though the ground beneath his feet is solid. The seamen begin rolling water barrels ashore, Steller steels himself and strides off towards the edge of the forest, muttering the names of birds and trees under his breath. Lepekhin hurries after him. They have come ashore on a strange island in a strange continent, they have no notion of what beasts and souls might be concealed in these forests, and he decides to keep his rifle at the ready.

Steller's foul disposition has vanished. A short walk around the vicinity and he has already encountered several new species, the Cossack has shot some birds for him, and he has found evidence of human settlement, a path leading to the mouth of what might once have been a root cellar. Inside he found carefully preserved berries, fish, and sundry supplies, and he takes with him an arrow, a flintstone and a strap braided from seagrass. He presents these items to the sailors, and they search their belongings, rummage through their pockets and find pieces of green glass, a knife, a string of pearls and two pipes, which Steller leaves in place of the items he has taken, then he asks for more men to row ashore. He needs a draughtsman, assistants to string up a net for the birds, scouts to search for the island's inhabitants, but the dinghy brings him a brusque reply instead. The barrels have been refilled, and if Steller does not return to the ship immediately, he will be left on the shore. He has no option but to comply, but that evening he writes a bitter entry in his diary: it seems we have undertaken this journey merely to carry water from America back to Asia.

Bering, however, has no interest in the scruffy birds or the natives' trinkets. No, they shall begin their return journey that same evening. The crew shall store as much water in the cargo as will be needed for their journey home, a full six weeks at sea, and with that they hoist the sails, and Steller's worst fears are realised. They try to sail out towards the open sea, but a stubborn wind keeps pushing them off course. Weeks of nothing but the empty sea, and now they cannot leave land behind them; they have reached the Catherine Archipelago and a merciless wind keeps pushing them back towards the row of two hundred volcanic islands.

Steller argues his case, but Bering is adamant. The expedition will not go ashore on these islands, and neither will the ship stop to chart or examine them. Steller can no longer claim that they are preventing him from doing his work, and he will have to make do with the birds and grasses he has collected from Cape St Elias. Their mission is complete, they have located the American coastline, and now they can return home. For twenty years, Bering has watched his colleagues surpass him, he has had nightmares about the expedition that claimed the lives of five of his children. He will not wait any longer: he will return to St Petersburg and leave his detractors red-faced.

Steller slits open the blue jay's chest, taking pains not to damage its plumage, removes its inner organs, and casts them over the rail and into the water. He watches as the seabirds gobble up everything he throws them and wonders whether the gulls realise they are eating one of their own kind or whether they gulp down their prey unaware that this is an act of cannibalism.

He peels off the skin, removes the rest of the innards, then drops the flayed body into a vat of water, and the process of decomposition begins. Every morning, he changes the water and removes small pieces of flesh loosened from the bones, until all that is left are the bones. Reconstructing a bird's skeleton requires dexterity, precision and patience, but on this expedition he has no shortage of time – what a laughable scientist he is, examining the new world from his cabin, where all he can do is imagine the contents of these islands. He brushes the skin with preserving solution. Some scientists preserve birds by submerging them in fluid, locking them in barrels, drowned in alcohol, but this method quickly causes the feathers to lose their lustre: blackcurrant-blue, deer-brown, chantarelle-yellow and heather-red fade into a single soggy colour, and all too often the collector opens up the barrel only to discover that the alcohol has evaporated and all that remains of the birds is a foul-smelling sludge. By using glass vessels, one can observe the birds' state, but glass is always at risk of smashing. At the university, his teachers had suggested using spices, they filled the birds' stomachs with alum, ginger, pepper, myrrh and cinnamon. The smell of these collections recalled the birds' exotic origins, but despite their expensive innards, they too soon succumbed to fleas and their colour lost its brilliance.

Steller believes neither in alcohol nor spices. Once long ago he came across a trusted recipe: five ounces of camphor, two pounds of arsenic, two pounds of soap, twelve ounces of potash, four ounces of quicklime, and the decomposition process stops altogether; this tincture he spreads on the skins, and with that the bird is beyond the reach of death.

He has no eyes. He will have to order some from St Petersburg, where the master glassblower will fill their eye sockets with small pearls, each complete with a tiny round oculus.

He attaches labels to their stiff legs, gives names to those that lack one, and arranges the birds in neat rows. The seamen are horrified at his collection. Blind birds, their eye sockets gaping and empty, but Steller simply laughs – these are nothing but lifeless, hollow skins. He does not tell them that as darkness descends he too hears the flapping, the fluttering of dead birds on his shelves. It must be this ship, causing an incessant superstition to spread from one man to the next like a plague.

A storm is coming in. They can sense it, there is a heaviness in the air, and rolling clouds begin to gather along the horizon like a great reef. They decide to guide the ship towards the shore of a nearby island and anchor the *St Peter* in a secluded cove. The crew takes advantage of the stop, sends a dinghy ashore to exchange stale drinking water for fresh, and the captain relents before an argument can get underway. Steller is allowed to accompany the water-bearers, and he examines the shoreline, the creatures living in its sands. At the edge of a small woodland, he finds a spring, a deep pool with clear water, where he washes his face and drinks. After weeks of stuffy water, stagnant in its barrels, this tastes more magnificent than any wine or mead, and he drinks his fill, hurries back to the water-bearers and tells them he has discovered the best water on earth. But the seamen have already filled the barrels, lowered them into a rippling rockpool near where they came ashore and let them bubble until they are full.

Steller is horrified. Can't you see? The surface of the pool is rising and falling with the waves! That means the two are connected somehow, that somewhere at the bottom the seawater and the rainwater mix together. He orders them to light a fire, he takes a pot and fills it with water from the pool, boils the water in the pot and shows the men the sediment gathered at the bottom, the salt and limescale, but the rowers are tired. They have no desire to start their task over again, and they ask the officers to make the final decision, which comes as no surprise to anyone. The officers side with the sailors and dismiss the naturalist's objections: water is water, regardless of where it comes from, and with that Steller fills his waterskin from the spring, his pockets with berries growing along the shoreline, and decides not to assist when Khitrov's gums begin to bleed and his teeth start to fall out.

The wind dies down, and it is time to hoist the sails. Before their departure, the navigator says he wants to measure the depth of the water by the shore, to mark it on the map to help the ships of the future, but the plumb slips from his hands. The string slithers from between his fingers and spins down into the depths, and silence descends upon the deck. Dropping the plumb is the worst of all omens. They hoist the sails in silence, avoiding one another's eyes, and the *St Peter* glides glumly on its way.

Steller writes up his notes, cleans and catalogues his instruments. Four times a day he notes down the prevailing weather conditions, the forms and colours of the clouds, anything to take his mind off the sediment at the bottom of the barrels, and he gazes at the night sky, eager to know why it is that when one trains one's eyes into the darkness, what at first looks empty eventually reveals tiny specks of light. He asks the navigator to teach him the constellations, and he studies the sky, practises identifying the bears, unicorns, foxes and ravens that live there, Ursa Major, Monoceros, Vulpecula and Corvus. To him, they do not look like animals, and he would gladly suggest some improvements to the system.

Back in Kamchatka, a local cooper had fashioned wooden hoops for their water barrels. They had been expecting metal ones, but the metal never reached the harbour, it must have been forgotten about, or stolen and sold on, and now the hoops holding the barrels together are beginning to rot and fall apart in the ship's damp hold. The wood gives way and the water seeps through the gaps in the barrels.

Before long, the crew is running low on food, and they institute a system of rationing. Each man is given his daily allowance first thing in the morning. They wet the pieces of rusk with spittle, chew the floury mush first in one cheek then the other, swallow, and feel an instant pang of guilt: how had this mouthful disappeared so quickly? Hadn't he resolved to savour it a moment longer?

They had intended to return to Avacha Bay by the end of September to avoid the autumn storms, but as the weeks pass, the wind obstinately refuses to turn in their favour, and a sea dotted with islands can be treacherous. Their progress is painfully slow. The end of September comes and goes, they are nowhere near the harbour, and then the gales start to pick up.

Khitrov closes the door behind him, and Bering slumps into his berth. These days the fleet master reports directly to the captain's quarters. This is handy. Sitting by his desk, he can make a note of what he hears right away, and they can scrutinise the maps and decide upon the best route to keep the ship as secluded as possible in winds becoming more ferocious by the day. If truth be told, the reason Bering does not climb the steps onto the deck is because the exertion makes him catch his breath, and on deck he stares at the fleet master's lips without understanding a word he says. A little rest is all he needs, a few days without exerting himself, then he will be himself again, but the tip of his tongue keeps prodding the gap between his front teeth and his tooth suddenly moves, his tongue touches the tooth, and the tooth and the root holding it in place give way, and Bering catches the taste of blood in his mouth. He pulls his tongue away in horror. This cannot be real, he must be mistaken, he just needs some rest, a few days in bed and he will be on his feet again. He stares at Khitrov and nods, hopes he is nearing the end of his monologue, and when the door finally shuts, he staggers to his berth, careful not to touch his teeth, and finds oblivion in sleep.

Able seaman Nikita Shumagin dies in the early-morning dim. The crew wraps him in a sheet and buries his body on the shore of a nearby island, they dig a pitiful, shallow grave in the sand and name his resting place in his memory. But Shumagin is merely the first of many. Initially the men begin to feel weak and drowsy, then pale blotches appear on their skin, and they lose control of their limbs. After this, it is not long until they stop breathing, and nobody names islands after them anymore. Death is just death, numb and endless.

On the twenty-sixth day of September, waves come crashing over the deck. The autumn storms have arrived.

2nd OCTOBER

24 men on the sick list

6th OCTOBER

Reserves of brandy running low

18th OCTOBER

32 men on the sick list

27th OCTOBER

A terrific storm. Not enough healthy men to lower the mainsails. The sailcloth parted in the gale. Hard to keep a steady course.

28th OCTOBER

The *St Peter* sails past a verdant island. However, replenishing the supplies of fresh water proves impossible, as there are now only ten healthy men on board, and they too are so weak that if we lower the anchor, they will not have the strength to raise it again.

30th OCTOBER

40 men sick. Even the healthy are beginning to die of exhaustion and dehydration.

2nd NOVEMBER

Hourly updates in the logbook come to an end. Navigator Kharlam Yushin, hitherto responsible for noting down observations, writes: "I am already exhausted from scurvy, and I stand my watch only because of extreme necessity."

By now, all the men can do is pray that the winds will push them in the right direction, that Kamchatka will appear along the horizon before the last of them succumbs to scurvy and thirst. Eventually, their prayers are answered. On the morning of the fifth day of November, the lookout sounds the alarm. Through the rain, the black strip of a distant shore comes into view, the men see snow-capped mountains, and somewhere someone finds a carefully hidden drop of brandy. They pass the dram around, and the captain momentarily awakes from his slumber, and now there is no shame in weeping for joy.

The others celebrate, but Steller is plagued by a sense of miscalculation. They are not far away, but they cannot have reached their destination either. The officers suggest going ashore at the nearest cove – it is true, this is not Avacha Bay, but nobody knows whether they will be able to travel any further. If they go ashore here, they could send the healthiest men to fetch horses from the nearest village, but Steller insists that they first make sure this really is Kamchatka. They can only lower the anchor once, and if they do so in a bad spot, they won't be able to undo their mistake. The navigator agrees with the naturalist, but by now all the men are at the end of their tether: you curs, you vultures, you blackguards and bastards, and the captain reaches a decision. The terrible weather, the torn sails, the crew at death's door: their final destination, this must be it.

Their crippled ship cuts slowly through the water. They do not make the shore before nightfall, and at midnight a cruel, otherworldly gale whips up across the sea. The sky is bright, but waves rise up as if in a storm, and the sea lashes the anchor cable until it snaps. The crew lowers a second anchor, but that cable snaps too, and panic begins to set in. If the waves knock them into the water, all will be lost. Then one of them thinks of the corpses. Having a body on board is a bad omen, death invites more death, and so they drag their lifeless comrades from the hold and push them overboard. The bodies, which they had spared for a noble burial, are unceremoniously dumped into the sea. Steller looks away. Holy Mary, Mother of God, pray for us sinners, now, and at the hour of our death; he does not want to look but looks nonetheless and watches the sheets wrapped around the bodies unfurl, revealing their contents and floating in the waves for a moment that seems to last an eternity.

Eventually their patron saint has mercy on his stricken ship. The waves push the vessel into shallower waters, the wood splits asunder and the *St Peter* lists but does not topple, takes on water but does not sink. The crew spends the night praying that their sandy anchor will hold, and when daybreak comes, the wind dies down – and they are still alive. They gather their belongings, muster on deck and gaze at the land opening out before them.

Steller paces along the shore looking for any indication of a settlement. There are no signs of ash in the piles of rocks, and they find no huts or paths. This does not necessarily mean anything, people are few and far between in Siberia, and Steller crouches down to examine the plants, but Lepekhin the Cossack taps him on the shoulder. Steller looks up, looks in the direction Lepekhin is pointing and sees a group of dark shapes galloping towards them. Are these bears? No, wolverines, and the Cossack loads his rifle, but then they recognise the animals. Sea otters. The large, stumpy mammals waddle over to them, take stock of them like tame dogs, and Steller's heart feels heavy. The little snout against the leather of his boot – could this creature truly know humans yet fear them so little?

They row the captain commander ashore. Bering is reluctant to leave his berth, but their ship is now a miserable, waterlogged wreck, and combining their strength Steller and Lieutenant Waxell carry him onto dry land. Bering hangs limp between them, and to Steller it feels almost like dragging a cadaver, but he shakes off the thought. The captain may be unable to go ashore on his own two feet, but as he lies on the sand he asks the naturalist for a report on his morning excursion. The pale, agonising wait of a weary man, and Steller drinks his tea, blowing onto the hot liquid. The Lord alone knows whether this is Kamchatka, but the captain seems not to hear. What else could this be? We shall rest here awhile, then send for some horses.

They thrust their oars into the sand, prop the sails between them to provide protection from the wind, and light a fire. Then they roast an otter, its flesh, its liver and kidneys, and the sick men drink tea that Steller has brewed from seagrass. Dusk envelops the landscape, and far up on the hillside a landfowl squawks, caught in a predator's jaws.

They awake to a shout. Lepekhin the Cossack adds some logs to the fire. At first, the flames are reflected in sets of mirror-like eyes, then illuminate the furtive creatures to which they belong. Arctic foxes have sneaked down from the hillside. They have crept up to the camp and gingerly tasted the sick; one man has teeth marks on his fingers, another on his cheek. It is a long night. The foxes are fearless and agile, able to dodge the stones thrown at them, but as the sun rises the crew can take aim properly. They shoot sixty in total; it's almost too easy, the poor things don't even realise that they should flee.

Then come the wind and the rain, a long stretch of sleet, low to the ground, and the sodden sails no longer afford them any protection. They must build a shelter – but how and with what? There are no trees growing on the hillside, but Steller has seen how the Koryaks survive on the steppes without timber, and he orders his assistants to dig a pit. They stretch sailcloth over the opening and crawl to the bottom of the pit where they can rest in the frozen sand as if in a grave of their own making, but at least they are protected from the wind and the snow, and before long the others follow their example. There upon the rocky beach, they create a village of small potholes and light measly fires in the pits to stave off the foxes and the cold.

From among their number, they choose the three men who are the least sick, pack their bags with two weeks' provisions and send them on their way. Their mission is to find the nearest village and bring back horses and equipment. They send off three gaunt, exhausted men, watch as they trudge into the distance, until the sleet obscures them from view, making the panorama soft and empty once again.

No word comes back from the scouts. At first, the crew thinks this a good sign – the journey is taking time because they have found a settlement, they are gathering equipment and steeds, these things take time in Siberia, and their eyes keep returning to the horizon, looking for approaching horses, but the horizon remains empty. Days pass, but no steeds appear.

Steller rows himself out to the shipwreck. It is a lamentable sight. The arsenic has mixed with seawater, and his birds are ruined, weeks of work and nothing but wet, rotten slurry to show for it, but he tries to salvage what he can. He boils up a new solution and asks Lepekhin to shoot some of the seagulls circling over their camp, but the solution is not strong enough. His samples become overrun with maggots, and he curses. On the night of the shipwreck, he should have remembered what was most important: forget about fear and the bodies; he should have saved his birds and chemicals.

For a while, the crew are able to forget their hunger. They eat otters, sea lions and ribbon seals, but their luck does not last for long, and within a few weeks the animals learn to be wary of them. Now they keep their distance from the camp. The crew must travel thirty versts to find a single otter, stumbling over the rocky shores on their rickety legs, weakened from scurvy, and hunger returns like a loyal cur. Food consumes their thoughts, and Steller and Lepekhin come up with a game. If you could eat anything at all, what would it be? Steller dreams of apples and oranges, and the Cossack chortles: a grown man longing for fruit! Steller laughs along with him and concedes that he would not turn down the Cossack's veal calf given half the chance.

Steller has carved himself a pipe from a bird's wing bone. Tobacco makes him feel a little lighter, and Lord knows he needs some cheering up. The weather is abysmal, nothing but a dusky gloom trickling from the sky. The sand, the sky, the sea and their clothes, all the same greyish brown, and for a moment Steller wonders whether he might be suffering from colour-blindness, a symptom of his scant, deficient diet, but then the Cossack shoots an otter, and the rocks are spattered with red.

Today, Steller wakes early and leaves the camp before anyone can put him to work. He plans to evade his responsibilities and observe the seals. He has no desire to listen to the sick bemoaning their suffering, nor hear news of those who died during the night, but walks instead around the end of the cape and arrives at a small cove. His appearance startles the seals lying on the shore back into the waves, and he watches their cumbersome bodies turn light and agile in the water, like an element changing form above a flame. These are a previously unknown species of seal, slender, with long fins, the males twice as large as the females. He names them Bering's seals. There are a great multitude of them on the shores here, but they are unsuitable for consumption. The men know this, for they have already tried; they shot one of them and roasted it on an open fire, but the seal's flesh turned their stomachs. The smell at the camp was indescribable, and they decided to leave the seals in peace: better to die of hunger than to eat this.

Steller tries to estimate the number of the seals, but this proves tricky. They dart here and there in the water, crisscrossing all the while, and he counts the same female several times. As he watches the female swim, he notices something further out to sea, a cluster of large dark shadows beneath the waves, and he stands up to get a better look. Could it be driftwood? Timber would be a valuable find, the hillsides around them produce nothing but scrub and grass, and the crew has been forced to burn wood from their ship to keep warm, but then one of the logs changes direction, turns against the waves and sputters. The sound reminds him of a horse greeting its rider, and a thrill runs through him. Are these whales? Some kind of enormous seal?

But the creatures are too far away, he cannot make them out, and in his enthusiasm he wades out into the sea and is startled by the unpleasant sensation of four-degree water lapping in through the top of his boots.

The assistant surgeon Betge berates him – what were you thinking, getting your feet wet in conditions like this, you'll take ill and succumb – but Steller pays him no heed and instead jumps from one pit to the next, gathering equipment and barking out orders. He has no care for his boot leather, hardened with salt, nor for his toes now numb with the cold; he needs men and a boat, and he needs them now, quickly, before the creatures he spotted disappear out to sea or down into the depths, and he rouses them, waving and shouting, for his breast is filled with the glee that besets any naturalist upon sensing that he might just have encountered the one animal for which he will be remembered in perpetuity.

Steller tells the men to row silently, but his instruction is unnecessary. Only once they are out at sea do they fathom quite how enormous these creatures are. The shadows shimmering beneath the surface are thirty feet in length – what incredible, majestic beasts they are! He counts fifty backs, and the rowers become restless. It would only take one knock to the boat and they would fall into the water's icy embrace, and the rowers refuse to go any closer, but the animals have already noticed them. First they swim further away and group together, gather their young in a great huddle, then one of them leaves the flock and swims towards the boat. The men grip their oars, helpless: should they try to flee and row back to safety? But then the creature raises its head out of the water and their fears turn to confusion at this mermaid greeting their boat with meek, myopic eyes.

Myth and reality come together in the story of the sea cow, and one cannot write about it without writing about mermaids. The connection is so profound that their order is named after mermaids; they are sirenians, Sirens. It has been suggested that the idea of sea cows as the humans of the ocean comes from their habit of observing the world from above the water: they float upright and raise their head above the surface, but unlike fish and whales they can turn their heads from side to side. When sailors saw their heads appear out of the water, they realised that the creature in front of them could be neither a fish nor a whale, nor even a seal with a long snout, and from a distance the sea cow's head does indeed resemble a human head far more than that of any other oceanic being. Sea travellers of the day knew nothing of manatees or sea cows, but they had all heard stories of fish-tailed women who lived in the water, and with that the connection was established.

The first documented sighting of a sirenian is in an entry in Christopher Columbus's log: he recalls that an admiral in his fleet once visited Hispaniola, where he saw three mermaids' heads appear out of the water. Granted, Columbus's admiral notes that the mermaids were not nearly as beautiful as legend would have us believe. It is true that the bald, round-headed manatee does not at all resemble the seductive Sirens of lore. If one were to describe the sirenians in human terms, perhaps a balding, rather chubby old gentleman would be a more apt comparison, but despite this they are always associated with women. In the Malay language, the sea cow is known as "dugong", lady of the sea, and in the mythologies of island peoples, there are many stories of women turning into sea cows to help guide sailors away from danger. Perhaps the reason for this is the sea cow's breasts, which, unlike those of other aquatic mammals, are situated on their upper chest, just under their front limbs. Perhaps this was enough for these sailors, and upon seeing the cows' teats full of milk they could forget all about their bald heads and whiskers.

In the first European contact with manatees and sea cows, the animals are described as mermaids, but soon afterwards naturalists too are able to travel to unknown shores, and the first scientific descriptions of the sirenians begin to appear in the archives. Steller knows the descriptions by those who travelled to the Americas, and Francisco Hernandez's *Nova plantarum, animalium et mineralium Mexicanorum historia* contains two drawings of the *manati gomara*, a gentle sea mammal that grazes in the warm waters along the American coastline. Steller's creature is many times larger than this and lives in the wrong ocean, but he recognises its order, also known by the names *Trichechus, Taurus marinus* and *Vacca marina.* A sturdy, rotund body and a tiny little head – no, there can be no doubt. Floating in front of them is a giant manatee, an unknown sea cow native to these northern waters.

The crew of the *St Peter* has seen many creatures rise up from the depths, each more curious than the last. They have seen glowing fish, transparent fish, flying fish, fish the size of a house, monsters with tentacles long enough to wrap round even the largest warships, but none of them has ever heard of a sea cow the size of a whale. Before the expedition set off, Steller interviewed people in Avacha Bay, asked them to describe all the local animals in exhaustive detail, and once they had told him about all the species they knew, they invented new ones, but this did not concern him. The Academy is interested in ethnographical research too, so he wrote down all their stories, but never before has he heard tales of the giant sea cow. How could such a magnificent creature go without mention on a shore known to man?

Now he knows with absolute certainty that they are lost, but his horror is mixed with a strange sense of elation: it means that the discovery of the sea cow is his alone.

Captain Commander Bering looks at the sky. The wind is driving the clouds together, piling them one on top of the other, and a similar grey blanket has been pulled over his senses. He tries to roll on his side, but he cannot, his body will not obey him but is falling apart in front of his eyes. He catches a sweet smell coming from his flesh but tries to think about it as little as possible. Sleep comes easily, thank God. Through his slumber he hears the naturalist's frantic voice, Steller talking about unprecedented animals, underwater giants, then he drifts deeper into sleep and brushes the voice away as he might an insect.

Captain Commander Vitus Bering never returns to the warm salons of the capital. He never returns to St Petersburg but takes his last breath on this rainswept shore on the morning of the eighth day of December. Even in death, he cannot escape this wretched place. Here, everything bears his name:

the Bering Strait

the Bering Sea

Bering Island.

The men dig a grave. They have to make sure it is good and deep, because the foxes are good at digging too. The ground is in the grip of frost, and the men are tired, but they dig, strike their spades into the sand and slog without a care for their aching limbs. They dig until the pit is deep enough, then gather round and hold a simple funeral. They erect a small wooden cross on top of the grave and mourn their captain and their misery.

Their captain is dead, and there is still no sign of the horses, but today they celebrate Christmas, collect what damp flour they have left and fry pancakes in seal blubber, raise their tea cups as if they were sipping an exquisite wine, give speeches exalting the captain and make a toast to the Tzarina, unaware that during the course of their journey she too has left this world behind. Steller, the cantor's son, sings Christmas carols, and for a brief moment they are somewhere else.

On St Stephen's Day, an exhausted trio appears on the horizon. Their scouts have not died after all, neither have they fled, but worse still, they come bearing bad news: the *St Peter* has been shipwrecked off the shores of an unknown, uninhabited island.

In the beginning, there is a single progenote, compounds gathered within a vesicle. Archaea and bacteria divide in two, again and again, and fill the waters, and there is light, and algae start to suck in the light, and oxygen seeps into the atmosphere, banishing the poisonous gases and creating a layer of protective ozone in the firmament around the earth. The air changes and there is a wave of extinctions, but the cells that remain embrace the oxygen and start to breathe.

At first, this single cell enjoys its solitude. It remains alive by dividing itself in two, until more solitary cells join together; they share responsibilities, and these lifeforms slowly begin to grow in size. The first multicellular organism is the sponge, a soft mass with no limbs, no nervous system or digestive tract, but over time the waters bring forth living creatures abundantly and begin to fill with bilaterians, beings whose bodies are formed of two symmetrical halves, and before long the world's very first set of eyes appear on the face of the flatworm. This is only the first of the worms' innovations. Their descendants devise a digestive tract running through the body with separate orifices for nutrients and waste. The development enables them to eat without pausing, and soon the seas are brimming with life. Molluscs appear beneath the waves, echinoderms, invertebrates and jawless fish. These creatures in turn devise the gamete, and soon afterwards the secluded depths of the primordial seas form the backdrop to the first sex act in history. Lifeforms multiply, filling the waters of the seas, and the plants and sponges begin to seek out less crowded habitats, they creep up and out of the water, and wolf's foot, horsetails and ferns cover the face of all the earth.

Fish living in marshland and shallow waters learn to breathe the air – a useful skill indeed, allowing them to crawl from one pond to another, to move into pools left by the retreating tide and to safety from the great armoured beasts of the sea. In shallower waters, they learn to use their fins, to walk along the seabed in alternate steps, and their limbs become muscular, their wrists and elbows stronger. Their gill covers move to their necks, and eventually they develop lungs, elbows, knees, wrists, fingers, a neck and nostrils – everything they will need for life above the surface – and with that the fish are ready to haul themselves up onto the dry land.

The fish rise up from their ponds. They learn how to drag themselves along the ground, but they never venture far from the sea, as they must still lay their eggs in the water. The shallow pools abound with tadpoles. In fact, this humble larva is the distillation of millions of years of development: first there is the protoplasm, the jelly from which this tiny, spritely aquatic lifeform wriggles forth, then the tadpole grows itself limbs, sheds its tail and swaps its gills for lungs, the water for land, feels the earth beneath its flippers and pushes. The tadpoles develop into snake-like, frog- and salamander-like creatures, and they devise the egg, a watertight, calcium shell, and lo, now they can abandon the seas altogether. They inch their way further inland, disappear into the tangle of ferns, and there the amphibians gradually turn into reptiles and replace their moist skin with scales that can withstand the heat. Animals appear upon the earth, but there is one memory of the sea that remains with us: the hiccough, the reflex that salamander larvae used to change the manner of their breathing, to shift from lungs to gills, from gills to lungs.

In Siberia, a column of lava rises up through the earth. It pushes its way through the crust, setting off a series of volcanic eruptions across the Northern hemisphere. For two million years, the earth belches up carbon and methane; the air is thick with a sulphuric fug, the waters of the seas become warmer, and all living creatures gasp for breath. The populations of the seas and the earth are decimated, but the reptiles stoically struggle on. Now they have enough space to experiment, and thus winged fowl and dinosaurs appear upon the earth, mammals too, small, furry creatures with a four-chambered heart and heightened senses. They scurry between the legs of much larger beasts, until one day it is time for the great lizards to depart the earth forever.

Now it is the mammals who are in experimental mood. The forests and savannahs are filled with new mammalians – monotremes, marsupials and placentalia, the latter being a most curious development whereby the animals gestate their young in a protective membrane inside their body, beneath their very skin. In the boughs of the trees lives the furry, long-tailed progenitor of all placentalia, barely the size of a swallow, munching on insects high up in the canopy. Soon, the placental mammals divide into two separate orders, and it is at this point that the sea cow and humankind bid each other farewell. Sirenians and primates go their separate ways, and Homo sapiens and the sea cow await their respective births on branches pointing in two different directions.

One of these orders are the Boreoeutheria, the northern true beasts, which develop into giraffes, dogs, mice, bats, humans and great whales. One might imagine that the sea cow is related to the whale, but no. Independently of each other, two different clades of mammals hit upon the same idea and return to the ocean: one a small creature, the size of a wolf, that grows into the largest mammal in history, the other a prehistoric proto-elephant whose descendants give rise to the sirenians. The ancient seas are also home to great ground sloths adapted for life in the water, but their sluggish story ends long before ours begins, while the whales and the sea cows remain.

The other clade of placental mammals is given the name Atlantogenata. This group includes the superorders of Xenarthra and Afrotheria, and it is from the latter group that the elephants and sirenians arise. One of them chooses the sea, the other the earth, and forty million years ago, the shores are graced with Prorastomus, the first known ancestor of the sirenians – a clumsy creature the size of a pig and consumed with a lingering yearning for the oceans. New, terrifying predators are creeping and galloping upon the earth, but this creature is drawn to the sea by the aquatic plants and the gently bobbing waves. Prorastomus spends increasing amounts of time in the water, crawling only seldom onto dry land. Its legs become shorter, its toes turn to fins and its narrow tail becomes wider. In the water, its joints no longer need to bear its weight, and it starts to grow and develop a form perfectly suited to life underwater.

And it is at this moment that our protagonist appears, Steller's Sea Cow, though at this point using such a name feels a little out of place. We are still a long way away from the moment when Steller himself emerges from his mother's belly, and indeed, it is another two million years until Homo sapiens appear on the stage at all, but this order of the sirenians is now alive and abundant. In years to come, fossils pushed up from the earth and the seabed will reveal a full twenty-eight genera of portly sea cows. These gentle beings float in the warm coves of ancient seas, but one of their number heads north, gradually moving into cooler latitudes, increasing the thickness of its blubber layer as it makes its way into colder waters. It develops a body that will protect it against the chill, and eventually it is closer in size to an elephant than to other sea cows. Steller's Sea Cow becomes a giant within its own order, an exception after its kind.

In the north, snow starts to gather on the mountaintops. It snows on the rocks, so much so that the already cool summers barely have enough time to reveal the earth at all, and the snow gathers, layer upon layer, and forms ice. Then, very slowly, the ice begins to move, it rolls down the mountainsides, grinding the earth and rock as it goes. Snow continues to fall, ice continues to build up, until eventually it covers the mountains and the valleys, pushing water and mud out of its way, and all around the arrival of the glacier is heralded by decimated forests and the skeletons of dead animals, as far as the eye can see. The land turns from green to grey, then everything is covered in white, the sea fuses with the ice, the shoreline retreats far out to sea, and where once there was water now there is land. Ungulates dig their hooves into the newly revealed seabeds in bewilderment.

This new world order creates the perfect conditions for Steller's Sea Cow. The ocean's once deep trenches become shallow bays that are soon home to thriving forests of kelp. At this point, many of the sea cow's relatives fade into history, and of the twenty-eight genera there are soon only a handful left, because although the sirenians are plump, their blubber layer is all but non-existent. They require warm water and temperate bays, and thus the genera that long for warmer climes perish one after another. But Steller's Sea Cow is unperturbed by the colder winds, undisturbed by the frozen weather and the lowering temperatures, and the species thrives. Herds of Steller's Sea Cows fill the Pacific shores from Japan to the Californian peninsula, and they spread wherever the forests of kelp reach up from the seabed towards the light.

But the ice does not last forever. At first, the changes are small. The sea cow slumbers, turns its belly towards the sky, allowing milder winds to caress its hide. The streams running into the sea become heavier, fuller, the glaciers retreat to reveal the churned earth underneath. In the winter, the edge of the sea ice creeps back a little, but the winter is not long enough to compensate for the destruction wrought by the summer months, and soon the ice retreats more than it returns, and the earth that it reveals starts to turn green. Moss appears on the gravel, the earth brings forth grass, and with the grass come the grass-eaters, and with the grass-eaters the predators. Roots intertwine under the newly formed soil. The tundra turns into plains, bringing forth hay and wild wormwood, then come the trees, the pines, the larches, white spruce and birches, bald cypresses standing two hundred feet tall. Forests push the plains aside, and water runs into the sea, the bays become deeper, the shores steeper, making the tangles of nourishing kelp harder to reach.

In the past, the sea cow was able to roam these shores as it pleased, but now the chain of banks brimming with kelp is broken. The plants reach up towards the light, but the continents keep shrugging off water, and the kelp sinks into the deepening bays. It is replaced by species that prefer the darkness of deeper waters, but the sea cow's body is like a buoy that always bounces back to the surface. It cannot dive more than a few feet, and the undergrowth on the seabed is soon beyond its reach. It lives on kelp that reaches up to the surface, but now the shallow waters have become deep trenches once again, and the herds become separated from one another, left stranded, scrambling for scant ever deeper scraps of seaweed.

Eventually, a new, terrifying predator appears on the shores. In the past, the sea cow has never had to worry about hunters, but wherever humans go, great species soon disappear: the cave bear, the woolly rhinoceros, the dire wolf, the ground sloth, the pouch lion and the moa. A large, bulbous animal with neither eyeteeth nor claws, the sea cow is no match for man's dominion, and today archaeologists dig up their bones from the ashes of ancient campfires.

In the end there is only one herd left, a single group of sea cows at the furthest tip of the archipelago known as the Aleutian Islands. Rising water levels have separated these outcrops from the mainland, leaving the sea cows trapped. Here at least they are safe, for the barren, remotest tip of this chain of islands it too far from civilisation to attract man. And while its brethren slowly disappear elsewhere, the sea cows continue their lazy life by their island, grazing and multiplying, with the foxes, otters and fowls of the air to keep them company, until fate and the winds bring them into contact with humans one final time.

They will be rescued. People on the mainland will become worried and someone will ready a ship! But one after the other, the men realise that no-one can possibly rescue them on an uncharted island. The expedition's other ship returned to Kamchatka in October. The crew of the *St Paul* had found their way to the south-eastern coast of Alaska. Captain Chirikov sent a group of his men to explore the area, but this group never returned. A search party was sent to look for them, but they too disappeared without a trace, and at this point Chirikov abandoned all attempts to go ashore. They added the coast to the map and sailed home, and their accounts did nothing to keep alive the hope that Bering and his crew might one day return. They are declared missing, then dead, and eventually their wives stop waiting for them.

On the map, they name this island after their captain, but for them this place is the blue foxes' island. These Arctic foxes will not leave them in peace. They burrow their way into the crew's pits, then scamper away with belts, boots and tools between their teeth, they snatch seagulls roasting on the fire, and the crew turn their attention to the foxes. It is the foxes' fault that scurvy has claimed half their number, the foxes' fault that their ship is rotting out in the bay, the foxes' fault that their captain is decomposing in the cold sand, and they hunt the foxes, catch them but don't kill them, instead sending them back to their dens half flayed, with no eyes, no tails, their paws singed in the fire. Killing them is insufficient; the men want to hurt them. They need a culprit. But the foxes never learn and return night after night. Their persistence is staggering, senseless, and Steller allows an unscientific thought into his mind: perhaps the foxes are punishing *them*, making the crew pay for the popularity of their skins in St Petersburg.

On the ship, Khitrov was responsible for discipline, forcing even those weakened with scurvy to work, but since Bering's death he has stepped aside. The question of who steered the ship towards this uninhabited shore comes easily to a starving man's lips, and Khitrov has seen the half-skinned foxes. Their captain commander was a good-hearted man, God have mercy on his soul, and alongside an affable man like him, the job of the fleet master was to crack the whip. These simple souls do not understand that he has done everything for the good of the crew. If he had not forced them from their berths, they would still be drifting on the open seas, their sails torn asunder, and their ship would have become a floating grave where, below deck, the rats would feast on their flesh.

Khitrov realises that the tide has turned when he sees Steller digging a pit into the embankment. He demands to be let in and shelter from the wind, but the naturalist just continues his work, striking his spade into the ground as though the fleet master standing next to him were nothing but air, an immaterial spirit, and not his superior with powers bestowed by the Tzarina herself. The crew looks on, but nobody intervenes. Khitrov is not stupid. He steps aside, and the position of commander is assumed by one Lieutenant Sven Waxell, a jovial fellow who is allowed to take the decisions simply because he will not make any decision without asking everybody else's opinion first. Khitrov accepts his lot. If they ever return to the mainland, he will reinstate discipline, but until then he keeps himself to himself, sucks on bird bones in his pit and patiently swallows back any harsh words that come into his mind.

After Bering's death, the foxes' island changes. Now tasks are divided equally. Every man must do his share, and even the officers cover the middens and feed the sick. Steller suggests that he might be allowed to concentrate on his research, but Waxell simply laughs, and the naturalist settles for plucking seagulls, digging pits and disappearing off to watch the sea cows whenever he gets half a chance. This happens less frequently than he would like. There is an endless amount of work, staying alive requires constant, grinding labour, a battle to fend off hunger and misery. The cold has become a garment that they cannot shrug off, they cannot remain still, or their fingers and toes will turn red, then black and begin to smell, and they rub their stiffened limbs to keep warm. Steller bends the surgeon apprentice Konavalov's fingers, and the man implores him to stop, he no longer cares about his fingers and toes, please, I beg you, but Steller looks away and continues. If he gets off the island alive, he will ask the Academy for a new assignment, a new direction. He yearns for air shimmering in the heat, he longs for the desert, the equator, the tropics, anywhere the wind is warm.

After spending more than enough days tending to the sick, Steller becomes restless. Usually good-humoured, he starts snapping at his comrades, and eventually Waxell sends him away to explore the beaches, to find driftwood for their now meagre fires. The task gives Steller the opportunity to examine the animals and the terrain, to choose his direction and spend his days observing the birds and plants, and he learns how to find the sea cows, watches how they swim around the island to shelter from the wind. He was worried that they might leave, abandon the island, but they do not. They never head out to sea but actually avoid the open water, they do not dive but seem to prefer the shallows, they walk along the seabed on their short front limbs, munching on kelp, and if the wind turns, they grip the rocks along the shore and embrace the boulders so as not to be washed out to sea in the waves.

It is true that Steller generally returns from his excursions carrying less firewood than the others, but after days spent wandering the coastline he has the energy to sing again and to tell the others of his observations as they sit round the campfire. The crew has little interest in cormorants and grasses, but he is not the only one excited about the sea cows. The men are all keen to behold this great mammal, the gentle giant of Blue-Fox

Island, and Steller tells them about it like a proud parent. They consider the sea cow, their hungry eyes gaze out at the open waters, imagining what it would be like to sink their teeth into these creatures bobbing beneath the surface – a single specimen would be enough to feed every one of them – and as they speak, the sea cow's flesh seems like manna from heaven. As they chew on seagulls and the flour left from the ship, they imagine the taste of the sea cow, and as they sleep, with a faint moan they dream of swallowing its blubber.

The crew try to hunt them. They load their rifles and shoot, first taking aim from the shore, then from their boats, but this proves difficult. The sea cow is protected by a hide an inch thick, and under that its muscles and vital organs rest behind a wall of dense blubber a further four inches thick. The ammunition rebounds from the sea cows' flanks without causing any damage, and Waxell forbids the men from wasting any more bullets, but they continue to shoot regardless. Occasionally a carefully aimed bullet pierces the animal's pebble-sized eye, and the sea turns red. A cry of joy goes up on the shore, but their elation is short-lived. The herd surrounds their fallen comrade, preventing the men from rowing their boat any closer, and all they can do is lean against the rail of their dinghy and look on as their catch sinks into the depths. But the men do not give up. They shoot again and ram their boats into the animals' sides, they hit and beat them, gash the sea beasts' hide with their axes, but their problem remains unchanged: the sea swallows up their catch. They know how to kill the sea cows but not how to get a carcass weighing several tonnes out of the water and onto the shore, and in the evenings they sit round the campfire drawing up plans and comparing strategies. It is easier to talk about the sea cow than about how they will make their already thin broth last another day.

The sea cows never learn to fear them. They continue grazing, paying no heed to the danger, absorbed in their underwater world, and Steller is able to row the dinghy right up next to them. On one occasion, a young male comes so close that he is able to place his hand on its back. The creature examines their boat, prods its boards with the sensitive whiskers on its snout, and Steller runs his fingers along its hide, its gnarly skin reminds him of the bark of an old oak, and it is warm. He had imagined that a creature swimming in the frigid oceans would be cold to the touch, but beneath his hand he feels the sea cow's calm warmth and strokes it, examining the bumps on its skin, and he becomes restless. He must get closer, see its organs and bones, he must measure it. A naturalist cannot be content with simply stroking a subject. Only by penetrating the surface can he understand the true nature of the sea cow.

A young female is munching a clump of kelp between her rows of teeth, grinding the tough seaweed into a finer and finer mass and fumbling for more. The forest of kelp sways in the waves, and the female's lips grope at its rippled surface, hunting for another strip. Suddenly, pain radiates through its flank, an incandescent light flashes through its nerves, and a warm liquid fills its mouth. Midshipman Johann Sind tugs at the rope to make sure the metal is caught fast. The men have come up with a plan. Sind has seen the way the Greenlanders hunt whales with iron spears, and they have prepared a harpoon, stretched a seal skin between two oars and practised, first on land, then at sea, harpooning seals and improving their aim until the steel tip hits its target, and the men gather together: now they will claim their first sea cow.

Sind gives a sign, and the men assembled on the shore grip the rope and begin to pull. The rope brings the sea cow into the hands of the hungry men, and they do not give in but pull, haul, until the skin is torn from their hands. The sea retreats from around the sea cow. It feels the breeze against its hide and cries out, letting out a sound that startles the rest of the herd into motion. It turns its head, calls its comrades, and Steller listens to its lament. The sound is curiously small; it could be from a child or a bird, and it is hard to conceive that such a sound could come from such a gigantic body. Steller looks on as the sea cow rises out of the sea and becomes wedged against the rocks. They have succeeded. They have hauled a sea monster from its kingdom, and the men behold their catch, raise their eyes and howl like ecstatic dogs.

The sea cow sees something approaching. It distinguishes the shadow from the water but doesn't understand what it sees. With its tiny eyes it can make out the edge of the forest of kelp and identify those of its own kind, and usually it has no need to see any more than this. It has made do with its other senses, the whiskers around its snout that it uses to sense food and other sea cows, to suckle from its mother and to seek out the soft, thick hide of a mate, and with its hearing it perceives the boundaries of its herd, listening to the others' clicks and moans. Now it tries to save itself using all its senses, but nothing it has ever experienced has prepared it for this. The sea cow has spent millennia doing very little besides grazing. It has grown too large to make sensible prey for any of the oceans' many predators, it has had no need for heightened senses, for claws or teeth, but rather it has been able to think of its surroundings with a tranquil curiosity. Now a faint image of jaws and teeth flickers through its mind, but it abandoned fear so long ago that it does not know how to fight or flee. It tries to wrench itself back into the water, but the rocks along the shoreline press into its hide, the rope pulls it out of the waves, and with every yank the harpoon digs deeper into its flesh. It does not know what to do and freezes on the spot, lets out a small, miserable whimper and listens to the sound of approaching footsteps, stares at the black leather boot, pupils wide, until Sind brings down his axe, and the sea cow's basin-sized heart twitches one last time.

Now the men forget all about their weak and aching limbs and rush into the sea, heedless of the icy waves. They climb on the back of their catch, help one another up and cheer as though they have conquered a mountain. They rejoice as they slit the beast's side open, gouge the sea cow as though they had struck gold, and their clothes change colour. Brown and grey become red, and the shore around them turns into an iron-smelling mud. The seagulls smell the blood and call one another to join the banquet, and there on the blood-soaked beach the men laugh and embrace one another.

They drop lumps of lard into the pot, add wood to the fire and look on as the sea cow's blubber melts into a translucent, aromatic liquid. They pour the fat into their cups, raise a toast and drink. Hot fat fills their mouths, and a shiver runs through the whole crew. At first their expression is one of confusion, then of joy, and they drink their fill in silence, swallow, gasp and scoop up some more. If the fat is like this, what will its flesh taste like, and they grab the roasting flesh on the fire, fight over the best cuts of meat, and Waxell is forced to restore order many times. Then the moment is upon them. They sink their teeth into the flesh of the sea cow, the creature they had so longed for, and it melts in their mouths like the finest veal. It is almost overwhelming. Their starved, emaciated bodies, the sudden, unbearable bliss. Tears well in their eyes, and they savour it, swallow it so hungrily that they almost dislocate their jaws, they tear at it, cut and bite it, devour the sea cow with tears running down their cheeks, swallow its loin, its liver, its kidneys, its flank and tongue, they drink its warm, intoxicating blood, they eat so much that it hurts, but they do not complain. Weeks of nothing but thin broth and seaweed, but tonight they shall feast on a sea cow.

For the first time in weeks, Steller does not wake to a nagging hunger. He lies in his berth for a moment, enjoying the sensation. The camp around him is still sleeping off the gluttony of the night before,, and Steller listens to his steady breathing, looks at the Cossack's face, calm from sleep, then sits up, work waits for no man, and he gets up and walks to the cove where they left the remains of the sea cow. He drives the seagulls and the lurking foxes away, and the morning light brings their handiwork into sharp relief. He had hoped to use this specimen for his research, but in their frenzy the men have hacked the creature to pieces, struck it at will, leaving it full of holes, broken its bones, severed its tendons. The cadaver is half submerged in the water. The tide has risen, and inquisitive fish dart here and there in the opened stomach, nibbling the blubber, and it is clear that this individual will be no use for research; for that purpose, he needs a specimen that he can take apart meticulously, one piece at a time.

Swallowing the seal's flesh was a mistake, but the sea cow melts in their stomachs with ease. Its meat is perfectly suited to preservation, and they eat sea cow for breakfast, lunch and dinner, and over time their teeth re-emerge from within their gums. These men, who by rights should have died long ago, stand up and learn to walk again, gingerly at first, waddling like toddlers. They have already lost thirty-two souls, but eventually there comes a day when Waxell no longer asks to be informed of those who died during the night. The mermaids have come to their rescue.

First comes the sea cow, then the spring. The long-tailed ducks, the sandpipers and eiders head down to the water, and the hillsides are filled with the sounds of screeching and mating birds. Steller hears a wren, and for a moment he imagines he is once again in the friendly, verdant woods of his childhood home in Windsheim. Lepekhin looks at him enquiringly: does the naturalist want him to hunt down this bird? It is so small that it cannot easily be shot, but he could put up a net. Steller shakes his head. He knows this bird; there is no need to snare one.

Steller sits down on a rock and watches the sea cows' mating rituals, their playful frolicking. The female allows the male to approach her, then prances further away, and it makes Steller think of the Koryak women. Unlike the officials and soldiers, he did not order them into his bed, but sometimes they appeared all the same, and he tried to talk to them, to write down the curious words they used. They laughed at his desire to talk, laughed at his pronunciation and whispered strange, passionate words into his ears. He thinks of Brigitta-Helena, of the way his wife succumbed to him like a beautiful, noble animal, and he watches as the female sea cow allows the male to mount her, pulls a pencil out of his pocket and writes: penis *ca.* 32 inches.

*

Reading Linnaeus's *Systema Naturae,* Brigitta-Helena learns that animals can be divided into six classes: mammals, birds, amphibians, fish, insects and worms. The amphibians are her favourites, but something interrupts her train of thought and she puts the book down. Someone has left the window ajar. It is a cold, bright day in St Petersburg, and she gets up to close the window, but her mind conjures up an image, and she stops midway. She sees her husband, Georg Wilhelm, standing on a dark shore, gazing out to sea, looking right at her, and it makes her shiver. She would rather not think about Siberia, or Georg Wilhelm, all the cold she declined to experience.

Not that she didn't like Georg Wilhelm. He was a polite, spirited man, a good conversationalist, a sought-after dinner guest, a man who talked with her about the natural sciences, notwithstanding that she was a woman, a weaker vessel and a weaker mind, as her first husband the naturalist Daniel Gottlieb had taken pains to remind her. But Georg Wilhelm deigns to speak with anyone who is interested in grasses, birds and the nervous systems of mammals. Daniel used to say that Steller would have made an excellent doctor had he not been such an excellent naturalist: whenever he set off to fetch some medicine, he was so caught up with classifying all the plants, insects and mushrooms he discovered that he was met with a grieving family and an already cooling cadaver upon his return.

Brigitta-Helena doesn't just listen, she converses too. She knows about plants, knows the pests that nibble at their leaves, she knows to protect her saplings with chalk and ash, and she is fascinated by molluscs too, the golden ratio spiralling from a snail's moist body, its shell spun in a perfect Fibonacci sequence – how can such a simple creature perform such a mathematical feat? Georg Wilhelm listens attentively, and eventually he proposes.

And thus the protégé marries his former benefactor's widow. It is only natural. Brigitta-Helena is used to Steller's presence in her home, so Steller can continue her husband's work, and this younger man will certainly make a change from the learned old man who used to ask her to rub his knobbly joints and fell asleep before his head touched the pillow.

After their wedding, Georg Wilhelm is given an assignment. He is to be sent to Siberia, and Brigitta-Helena too starts to pack her belongings and bids farewell to their garden and arboretum. The white and silk mulberries blossom only in her garden, and she gives her gardener advice far too many times. Eventually Georg Wilhelm has to command her into the sled, and Brigitta-Helena curls up under the furs with tears in her eyes, but as the horses canter off Steller squeezes her hand, and suddenly she feels a faint, wild thrill.

First they travel to Moscow. Once there, they are to confirm their travel arrangements with the Sibirskii Prikaz, but the journey is long and the road in terrible condition. Brigitta-Helena catches a chill, her feet feel numb and her skin becomes so chapped that she barely recognises herself in the mirror, but Georg Wilhelm seems oblivious to the dire conditions, he just talks about birds and clouds as though they were sitting in a grand parlour and not in an uncovered sled in the middle of a forest full of wolves. Brigitta-Helena begins hallucinating about the endless cold, she wakes at night, her sheets damp and dotted with bugs, and upon arrival in Moscow she makes up her mind: she will not go a step further.

Georg Wilhelm rages and weeps, rages and weeps and prays. He had imagined their journey together, imagined them climbing the slopes of uncharted mountains, identifying hitherto unknown species and in the evenings curling up together under warm fleeces, but this was his vision alone. Brigitta-Helena's science is the science of conservatories and greenhouses, she did not choose this journey, nor this brutal, lonely work out on the steppes. Georg Wilhelm rages and weeps but eventually acquiesces, he will not stoop to forcing his wife against her will, and so Brigitta-Helena returns to St Petersburg. Steller continues his journey alone, and in his diary writes the bitter words: "I no longer need my wife, I have the ravens (*Corvus corax*)".

*

Waxell beckons the naturalist and the navigator and spreads out the map. They are not in Kamchatka, but neither can they be very far away, the mainland must be only a few days' journey away. It is hard to imagine that an uncharted island could exist this close to a known settlement – after all, this is no piddling little crag either but a stretch of land ninety versts across and covered in hills – but their calculations cannot be out by much. Khotyaintsov has seen some persistent mist to the south-west, hanging in place even when the weather is clear, and he believes this curtain of fog must be held in place by the Kamchatka peninsula and the mountains lining its coast. Waxell asks the navigator to measure the distance by the stars, to assess the ocean currents; Steller conducts calculations of his own, and the men compare their results. Fleet Master Khitrov watches the men bent over their maps. By rights they ought to ask his opinion, but they do not.

Waxell summons the men together, all forty-six who have survived the voyage, the sickness and the winter. What next? They are alive, they have the easier, lighter days of summer ahead of them, but after the summer comes the autumn, and after autumn, winter. They are the only people on this island, and had a search party been sent to look for them, the mission would have been abandoned long ago. Still, the edge of the mainland cannot be far away. Only a week earlier a piece of driftwood washed ashore, the sea had brought them a white-painted window frame. There must be a settlement somewhere nearby, but their ship is in pieces and they have no wood to mend the damage. One cannot cross the ocean in a dinghy, but they could dismantle the decaying wreck on the sandbank and use the timbers to build a new ship. Two of the *St Peter*'s three carpenters are already rotting in their graves, but in his grace the Lord has spared the third. The crew can either remain on the island, feast on sea cow and protect themselves from the elements until the last man perishes of the cold or old age, or they can build a new ship and cross the sea, and at least attempt to return home.

Thus begins a slow and arduous operation. They row out to the wreck, remove planks from the old ship and pile them on the shore, and the carpenter slowly begins to put them together into a new vessel. As work progresses, a faint inkling of the future starts to creep into their minds, and they begin to look at the foxes and otters with fresh eyes. The helmsman rows a pack of cards back from the wreck, and the men begin to play, to win and lose. During the day they dismantle the old ship and assemble the new one, but as the light fades they take out the playing cards, and animal pelts pass from one man to the next. The following day, they hunt more animals in order to pay their new debts. Summer has arrived, and hunting the foxes and otters is easy. The animals have offspring now, and the female protecting her brood is an easy target. They quickly strip them of their pelts and leave the carcasses to the mercy of the seabirds. Otter meat is no match for that of the sea cow; the only specimens that find their way onto the men's campfire are those expecting young or those that have just whelped, as their flesh is soft and fatty. In the space of two weeks, the men skin nine hundred otters, leaving an endless banquet for the gulls and crabs on the shore.

Some of the men enjoy the taste of the whelps' meat, and Steller observes the behaviour of the females who have lost their young. They weep like small children, and their sorrow dehydrates them so much that their fur loses its lustre until there is no longer any reason to hunt them. The otter is a most caring mother, she plays and frolics with her young such that Steller cannot help but smile, and in the moments when life on the island becomes too much for him, he seeks them out and watches them as they float in the water. As he follows their antics, an amusing thought occurs to him. The otter is as playful as a dog; he could tame a litter, a young otter accustomed to humans from birth would make a loyal companion indeed. He could get a house and build a small pond for his otters, but as he gazes at their skinned bodies abandoned on the shore and draws in the stink of their dying, rotting flesh, he is forced to remind himself of the order of the world, and he shakes off the thought. This is how God intended the matter. He created the world and its creatures under man's dominion, animals best perform their role by benefitting mankind.

Steller does not take part in the games. He has no interest in the cards and their unchanging odds, nor in whose pile of pelts is taller on any given evening. His days have been calm and unhurried, he has spent his time gawking at sea cows, birds and otters like a simpleton, but now the skeleton of their new ship is beginning to take shape in the wash, and he reproaches himself, for his work is yet unfinished. He must classify the birds, the grasses, minerals and mammals, there is still so much to do, and when he is asked to help build the ship, he initially refuses but is put to work against his will. Will this drudgery never end? Why can't he be left in peace to continue his work? He dreams of being able to walk the length and breadth of the island irrespective of his duties and the time of day, able to observe every blade of grass, every bird's egg, to draw up an exhaustive report and fold the island into his satchel like a glove, and whenever the ship builders berate him for how slowly he works, delight flickers in his breast – every setback means more time spent on the island.

Steller asks Johann Sind to gather a group of men and bring him a sea cow. Sind agrees, catching sea cows is a fine distraction, and before long a handsome female is lying on the rocks by the shore. Its offspring follows them to the shallow waters, calling for its mother in shrill bleats, but Steller shakes off all feelings of discomfort. The only way he can bring this creature back to the Academy is by peeling off its skin. A naturalist does not work with ill-defined thoughts and emotions; he needs a sharp knife and a firm, precise incision, an unflinching look into the moist innards.

While he was reading theology at the University of Halle, Steller studied God's Word closely and felt the utterances of every fiery-breasted pietist in his heart most profoundly. He had no time for the Pharisaic life, for vain lip-service or haughty prelates; all he needed was a pure heart and a direct connection to the Lord. He wasn't a bad preacher either, but the rocks, the plants and animals began to allure him, to draw him ever closer. He was closer to God at the botanical garden than in the church, and soon afterwards he found himself at botanical lectures and began spending his evenings at the library where he could pore over reports from far-off expeditions. Are not animals God's creations just like the Word – beautiful creatures that reveal the spirit of their Creator? He cut open a frog and examined the wonders he found inside it, a perfect system where every vein and tendon are in just the right place. Eventually he chose the animals, the plants and rocks, and as he studies the flora and fauna of Siberia, the wild grasses and tiny birds, he thinks of himself as a scribe writing down the Lord's Word. And in front of him now is the greatest and most beautiful of all God's works.

The others strip the *St Peter* of her planks, while Steller strips the sea cow of its hide. The beast is so large that he cannot do this alone. The internal organs need to be removed carefully and intact, and he asks his assistants to help, asks but does not command, because the island has affected the men's behaviour. He bribes them with tobacco. He doesn't ask Toma Lepekhin, and the others agree only begrudgingly, extort more tobacco out of him than he'd been prepared to offer, but needs must, and Steller duly doles out his reserves. They begin with the external measurements. Steller runs the measure along the length of the sea cow's body, tells his assistants to hold it by the animal's snout, then on its fins and tongue, to measure the length from the upper lip to the tip of its tail. He wants to record the sea cow's circumference too, and they try to slide the measure under its body, but this proves impossible. The animal is simply too heavy. They try to dig a trench underneath it, but the ground is rocky and hard to shift, and Steller is unable to take an accurate reading and has to settle for an estimate, and though he is annoyed at this, he realises that he cannot demand the impossible, or certainly not all the time.

He wants to open up the sea cow's skull. The bone is thick, but Piotr Antonov strikes it with his axe, and the skull cracks open. Steller is keen to find out whether the myth is true, whether the sea cow's head contains the famed heavy, bright-white stones known as *lapis manati*. Previous explorers have found these precious stones hidden inside the skulls of manatees, brought them back to Europe and sold them for a considerable price. Worn around the neck, the *lapis manati* is said to prevent blood loss, though Steller doesn't understand how a stone worn around the neck can affect the circulation. Diderot, meanwhile, writes that, ground into a powder and stirred into white wine, the *lapis manati* has very great healing powers indeed, and Steller plans to test the effects that tea made from the stones might have on the men recovering from scurvy, but he is left disappointed. He goes through the skull carefully, but all he finds beneath the bone is soft, warm tissue. Perhaps the stones are only found in the species further to the south, perhaps they need warmer waters and softer light to develop fully.

Steller had dissected frogs, fish, dogs, cats and horses. At the university, there was a constant shortage of human cadavers, so he has much experience when it comes to cutting open animals, but the sheer size of the sea cow presents a whole array of new challenges. How best to remove a liver the size of a large dog from inside the sea cow in one piece, where to make the incision and with which implement – and his assistants lack a proper education in this field. Their tools are not scalpels and surgical knives but blunt axes, and the results are terrible. Steller wants to rebuke them, to show them the correct angle once again, but forces himself to hold his tongue, and they measure the kidney, the liver and the vulva, and slit open the sea cow's stomach. The smell is overwhelming, and now he is relieved that he didn't ask Lepekhin to assist in this task and asks the men to lay out the intestines along the shore. He has to muster all his authority, and eventually the men agree but only once Steller promises that after this they can stop, cut up the animal's flesh and return to the camp. He remains on the shore, alone with his measuring tools, he doesn't even notice the others leaving but measures the beast twice, gushing with excitement. What a terrific, awe-inspiring creature is this, with a full 5,968 inches of bowel in its guts!

Steller's recorded measurements of the sea cow:

Length from the extremity of the upper lip to the extreme right *cornu* of the caudal fork: 296 inches

Circumference of the body at the shoulders: 144 inches

The greatest circumference about the middle of the abdomen: 244 inches

Circumference of the head at the eyes: 48 inches

Height of the nares: 2 inches, 5 tenths

Breadth of the nares: 2 inches, 5 tenths

The diameter of the mouth at the angle (*oris froenum*): 20 inches, 4 tenths

Height of the end of the snout: 8 inches, 4 tenths

From the extremity of the upper lip to the nares: 8 inches

Distance between the eyes at the posterior angles: 22 inches, 2 tenths

From the anterior angle to the posterior angle of the eye: 8 tenths

Length of the tongue: 12 inches

Width of the tongue: 2 inches, 5 tenths

Length of the skull from nares to occiput: 27 inches

Width of the occiput: 10 inches, 5 tenths

Distance between the extreme points of the caudal fin (this is the breadth of the fin): 78 inches

Height of the fin: 8 inches, 8 tenths

Length of the nipples: 4 inches

Length of the vulva: 10 inches, 2 tenths

Length of the ulna: 12 inches, 2 tenths

Width of the humerus: 14 inches, 5 tenths

Width of the heart: 25 inches

Length of the kidneys: 32 inches

Width of the kidneys: 18 inches

Length of the whole intestinal tract, from pharynx to anus: 5,968 inches

It is clear there is no way Steller can preserve the sea cow's hide intact. This would require many barrels of strong preserving solution, and he has neither arsenic nor lye, but he can preserve the skeleton. He gets to work. Now he must make do without his assistants, he has run out of tobacco, and the men decline his requests for help, politely but firmly. The work progresses more slowly by himself, and Waxell berates him. Steller should be helping the crew in their shared endeavours, but instead he spends his days scraping the sea cow's bones clean. No matter: there is no longer any discussion to be had. Khitrov gives Waxell a knowing glance, but the lieutenant lets the naturalist be. Steller helped when they were ill, taught them how to dig pits in the ground to provide shelter, and when all hope seemed lost, he sang for them around the fire. Now that the threat of imminent death has passed, he can be afforded a certain level of eccentricity, and though the men scoff at Steller's work, their taunts are mild, and they chide him the way they would a child or an unruly dog.

Cleaning the sea cow's bones is slow, arduous work, and in an attempt to forget about the impudent seagulls and his aching limbs, Steller starts talking. He begins by explaining the process for preparing arsenic soap. He severs the tendons and recites

Linnaeus's system, scoops out the contents of the skull and cleans it, all the while describing the species he has discovered, and as he cleans the bones of their cartilage with an infuriatingly blunt knife, he tells the sea cow all about the different seaweeds and minerals, the anatomy of seals, the migratory routes of whales, about the seeding of hay and how Arctic cisco swim upstream to lay their eggs. He tells the sea cow about their journey, about the drinking water that turned murky and their comrades decomposing in the hold, about his childhood in Windsheim and his wife, the ravens, and everything he would like to say to Toma Lepekhin. He explains to the sea cow why it had to sacrifice its life and assures it that one day it will be the greatest attraction at the imperial Academy. The sea cow listens, and some days it even answers him.

Steller makes several mistakes. He forgets to number the vertebrae, and now ordering them correctly proves a slow, vexing task. The foxes and seagulls scavenge around the carcass, trying to pinch the smaller bones, and these Steller decides to store at the camp, a decision that is not met with universal approval by the crew. The bones remind them of the men shedding their flesh under makeshift crosses only a few hundred feet from the camp. They would rather not think about the dead, and they are worried about the bodies they threw overboard on the night of the shipwreck too. If such a thing does not bring about restless souls, then surely nothing will, and though Waxell has forbidden all ghost stories, he cannot stop the men whispering around the campfire, cannot stop them making the sign of the cross when the foxes howl in heat further up the hillside. Steller is instructed to keep the bones out of sight, and duly hides them under a tarpaulin, he mutters his objections but obeys all the same, and while the others are asleep, he gropes in the dark for the sea cow's skull and runs his hand along the slanted curvature of its crown.

He falls asleep with the skull in his arms, then snaps wide awake. For a moment, he flails in terror, fumbles through the air until he finds the skull wrapped under his shirt, and his eyes meet Toma Lepekhin's disapproving gaze. Surely Adjunct Steller doesn't want the others to see him caressing the dead? Steller nods, quietly thanks him.

The vertebrae of the neck, the breast, the hip and the tail lie on the beach in a neat line. He has taken the sea cow apart, and by now he has long since forgotten his birds destroyed by the seawater. Now he has this beguiling, miraculous specimen, and when they see it, the learned men of the Academy will surely grant him a bursary for another expedition. Next time, he will do everything correctly, he will be properly prepared and will lead the expedition himself, he will take Toma Lepekhin with him and all the best scientific minds from the Academy.

Lepekhin asks Steller to join him hunting birds, and Steller agrees. On the hillside, he can collect plants and minerals, and the two spend the day wandering across the hills and gathering ptarmigans' eggs. The white-breasted males waddle, honking, in front of them, trying to attract the men's attention, but Lepekhin knows their tactics, knows how to find the females hiding in their nests of moss with the dappled eggs they are protecting.

The two light a fire and eat ptarmigan eggs fried in sea-cow blubber. The grass rustles in the wind, and everything smells of smoke and the sea. At moments like this, they even wonder whether it would be so bad after all if they were to be forgotten here on this shore and never make their way back to the mainland, where responsibilities and the rule of man await them. Neither says this out loud, but it is there in their movements, the way they raise their cups, as if they long for nothing.

They row enough wood back from the shipwreck to build several boats, but their main obstacle is not a lack of materials but of expertise. They piece together their ship by guesswork, one plank at a time, and as they work, the fledglings hatch from their shells, in the coves the sea cows give birth to new, chubby young, and Waxell urges his men to hurry. They snap the old mast of the *St Peter* and shorten it to make it suitable for the new vessel, they burn off the tar from the old ropes and sew new, smaller sails. The prospect of home inches closer, but the lieutenant is afraid they will run out of time. He believes he can smell the approach of autumnal storms in the air, and with worry in his heart he looks on as the fledglings take flight and begin circling the island.

By August, the new ship is ready. A hooker measuring approximately forty-two feet, with no guarantee that it is even seaworthy.

The time has come to give it a name. An unnamed ship is a bad omen, and on this journey they will need all the luck and good fortune they can muster. Someone suggests they name the ship after the Tzarina, then after the captain commander, but eventually it is named the *Hooker St Peter*. As St Peter brought them to this island in the first place, perhaps he can help them leave it too, and the men lower their heads and pray to the guardian of the keys of Heaven to protect their ramshackle vessel.

At first they had envisaged themselves sailing home with all their pelts, rising from the dead as rich men, but they have only forty-two feet to accommodate forty-six men. They can only take absolute essentials with them, and none of them is as shocked to hear this as Steller. He has been pressing flowers, collecting seeds, bones and rocks, he has cleaned the invaluable skeleton of the sea cow; surely, they must make an exception for him! But Waxell asks Steller to look at the vessel, to imagine how it will fit forty-six men, as well as the provisions and water they will need, then to tell him where exactly he thinks they will be able to store a skeleton the length of three men and the width of a rowing boat and which, furthermore, they cannot eat. Steller knows he is in the wrong, but he cannot help complaining, and spends a full day and night sulking on the rocks by the shore, but Waxell's mind is made up. Steller will be allowed to take only his notes and the pipe he fashioned from a bird's bone.

On the morning of the eleventh day of August, the wind is gentle and the sea calm. They cook all the leftover food and prepare for the meagre days at sea by eating their fill. They light a large fire, eat sea cow and ptarmigan, and sing together. Nobody speaks of tomorrow. It is every bit as likely that they will not reach land as it is that they will be saved, but tonight none of that matters. Tonight they will play cards, feast on sea cow and worry only about the here and now.

The others are wolfing down their food and celebrating, but Steller leaves the group. Toma Lepekhin looks at him with quizzical eyes, but the naturalist shakes his head, and the Cossack sits back down and takes another portion of dried peas and sea cow. Steller approaches the skeleton, pulls back the tarpaulin and assesses his handiwork. His most significant discovery, a creature of which no-one has ever seen the like, that even the wildest bestiaries could never have imagined, and all he will have to show for it are the words in his notebook. He stomps off, without even bothering to cover the bones again. What use would it be? Once they have left, the foxes will pull them out, scatter them across the sands and take them back to their dens for their young to gnaw upon, and when he returns to the camp, Steller sits quietly and refuses to sing, though they implore him.

On the morning of the thirteenth day of August, they put their ship out to sea. Only now do they realise quite how cramped it is. They have to sit and lie in shifts, and on top of this, their ship leaks, not enough to sink it but enough to make their conditions miserable. When they see water gathering at the bottom of the ship, some of the men take fright and wish to remain on the shore, ask the rest of the crew to send a rescue party if they survive the journey, but Khitrov bellows at them to hold their tongues. On the island, he took a step back, but at sea the old rules apply once again. The Tzarina's law is in force, and all those who oppose him will be guilty of mutiny.

The ship leaves the shore, and the foxes come down from the hillside. At first they skulk around, cautiously, then more brazenly, as they notice that not a single weapon is fired at them, and the men watch as the foxes occupy their camp. They play with one another, running around with otter skins in their jaws and digging in the ashes of the fire, but the men no longer pay them any attention. Let the foxes have their island back, and they hoist the sails and glide along the edge of the island, and as they gaze upon the now familiar rocks, streams and beaches, they are overcome with a curious melancholy. This was their home for a full eleven months. They leave the foxes' island in good health and bid it farewell sincerely, without bitterness.

On the eastern side of the island, they see a herd of sea cows floating in the grey waters. The adults are grazing and the young, plump from the summer months, are playing in among their parents, suckling milk from their mothers' teats. The men sail past the herd and bid farewell to their mermaids, raise their arms and wave until the tip of the island hides the creatures from view, leaving them surrounded by nothing but open water, whipped by the rain.

On the twenty-seventh day of August, the *Hooker St Peter* sails into the harbour at Avacha Bay, where it is met by a crowd of bewildered onlookers. The crew has been away for sixteen months, but now these men, who had already been declared dead, have returned and are demanding their unpaid wages, causing the utmost administrative chaos. They plan to mend their ship in the harbour, fix the leaks, then sail across the Sea of Okhotsk to the mouth of the Okhota River, and from there they will continue to the capital on horseback. Waxell asks Steller to join him, but the naturalist refuses. He may have left his invaluable samples behind on the island, the foxes may have taken his bones, the rain pummelled his plants and the mud covered his minerals, but he can still make good use of the journey home. He plans to walk back through Siberia, all the way to St Petersburg.

He wishes to visit the delta of the Kolyma River, because there are rumours that explorers there have unearthed the bones of the great northern elephant. He once saw a tusk found in Siberia at the Academy. The older professors believe that it must have come from the body of the Behemoth described in the Book of Job, a creature whose tail is like a cedar, its bones like pipes of brass, yes, this must surely be the first of the ways of God.

Their discovery is not the only evidence of this beast. In Sicily, a group of villagers stumble upon the head of Polyphemus the Cyclops, an enormous skull with a giant hole in the middle of its forehead where once the monster's one and only eye had been, and at Gray's Inn Lane in London workmen strike their spades into the ground and dig up a puzzling, rough-edged tooth.

The tooth is bought by a naturalist by the name of Hans Sloane. His world-famous collections contain 71,000 artefacts, and it is from these that both the British Museum and London's Natural History Museum are born. Sloane is fascinated by these wondrous discoveries and in time acquires more parts of this unknown creature for his collections. As he examines them, he gradually realises that the monstrous skull did not belong to a cyclops but to an enormous elephant: the great hole in the front of the head is not an eye socket but the point at which a nimble, fleshy trunk protruded, though this explanation is no less strange than if the Sicilians had indeed discovered the earthly remains of Poseidon's son.

The bones of this curious elephant present naturalists with an unprecedented conundrum. Namely, the bones are in altogether the wrong places, smoggy London and the cold steppes of Siberia, though the present-day elephant prefers warmer climes. However, of these bones there can be no doubt whatsoever: this is a species of elephant unknown to science, one that can withstand the harsh Arctic conditions. It soon transpires that in Siberia the locals are very familiar with the bones of the giant northern elephant. The Mansi call this creature *mā ān't,* the earth horn, and in the mouths of the Russians this developed into the form *mamant,* mammoth. The peoples living along the banks of the Yenisey River do not believe that the bones are bones at all but that they sprout from the earth like plants or mushrooms, whereas the Mansi know that the creature to which these bones once belonged lives deep within the earth, far beneath the human world, burrowing its way through the peat and soil and never coming to the surface. How else can we explain that far away on the steppes lives a giant animal that no-one wandering the plains has ever seen?

Every now and then, curiosity gets the better of these subterranean elephants, and they plough their way up to the surface. They yearn to sniff the fresh air and see the sun, but their curiosity is their undoing. Their slow, cold bodies cannot withstand the light and the warmth. Not one mammoth ever sees the tundra grasses swaying in the wind, for they die beneath the earth as they strive towards the surface that remains just out of reach, and on occasion the spade of a lucky peasant reveals the bones of an elephant that perished just below the surface. Spring is the best time to find these remains, when meltwaters swell the rivers until they breach their tall embankments. Then the earth may give up the frozen bones of the mammoth, and in one embankment a local merchant even uncovers an entire skeleton. It has been so well preserved that, as it thaws out, the animal starts to ooze blood, and the merchant cuts off the animal's tongue and front leg and takes them with him. He claims that the giant northern elephant was covered in thick reddish fur, but researchers meet this suggestion with scepticism, and the merchant has no proof to back up his claim. His treasure cannot withstand the world above the surface: after coming into contact with the light and the warmth, the *mamant* rots and decomposes.

Siberian folklore has an ethnographic value of its own, but Steller dismisses the idea that an elephant could live underground; only worms live in the earth. However, an elephant might be able to dig a tunnel, to burrow its way into the embankment and make a den, but what would it live on deep inside the earth? No, the elephant is a creature living on the earth's surface, out on the savannahs; there are no herds of subterranean elephants wandering around in tunnels the size of a cathedral. Furthermore, the bones found in different locations across the northern hemisphere prove that the Arctic elephant wandered far and wide across these open plains.

Perhaps Noah forgot about this animal, neglecting to take it on his ark, and its fate was to drown in the waters that covered the earth, or perhaps God undid His own creation and allowed the animal to fade into history, but Steller remains unconvinced by other naturalists' explanations. He cannot believe that God would change His mind and break asunder an order that was supposed to be eternal. The animal world is a perfect, unbroken chain, from an arthropod hiding in the mud by the shore to the crown of all Creation; it is a stable, carefully designed system, and the thought that one of these creatures could simply disappear is unthinkable and godless. Steller knows that the Arctic elephant must still be out there somewhere. Is not his sea cow irrefutable proof that, if one travels far enough, there are still new, unknown beasts waiting to be discovered? That the world remains boundless and open?

On the journey home through Siberia, Steller plans to complete his account of the island and to search for the giant northern elephant. He asks the Cossack to accompany him, but Toma Lepekhin is keen to return to the Bolshaya River, where his wife and child await him. Upon hearing this, Steller is taken aback. He finds it hard to imagine Lepekhin having a past, a time in which their expedition plays no part, but he swallows this disappointment, and the two embrace. And with that, the Cossack is gone. Steller gees his dogs into motion and tries not to think about the ravens.

However, Steller's journey begins slowly for he has run out of money. He must remain where he is and wait for his unpaid wages, so he decides to spend the winter in Kamchatka and settles in the village of Bolsheretsk to organise his notes. While residing there, he becomes embroiled in a curious piece of theatre. The natives have been getting rowdy and many have been imprisoned for treason and resisting Russian officials. But this leaves the officials with a problem: they cannot investigate cases in which they themselves are involved. Luckily for them, Steller, a young adjunct from the Academy of Sciences in St Petersburg, arrives in the village, and the task of interrogating and convicting the Itelmens falls to him.

Steller accepts this duty and interviews the prisoners. He notes that they are honest and good men, and he can feel his blood boiling. If the indigenous people were treated with sense and common decency, the empire would be able to carry out its business in Siberia without shedding a single drop of blood, but the officials' behaviour leaves the natives with no option but to raise up a rebellion. He acquits the Itelmens of all charges.

Steller's wages finally arrive, and he rides off leaving the infuriated officials behind him. He does not find any mammoths, but he does however identify a new tree and a new fish, he puts together a considerable collection of plants and loads his sled with all manner of seeds and saplings which he intends to plant in the soft soils of the botanical garden at the Academy. He spends the following winter in Solikamsk, where one Major Grigorii Demidov, the owner of a salt mine, lives in a manor house surrounded by verdant gardens, a veritable oasis in the middle of Siberia. Lemon trees and palms flourish in the confines of his greenhouses. The garden is Demidov's pride and joy, and he is only too happy to welcome the naturalist to his home, especially as Steller undertakes to train his gardeners. He is given permission to plant his saplings on Demidov's land over the winter, and though this too is a delay, it is one that Steller is prepared to endure. After months on his sled, life at the manor house does not feel like a punishment.

However, the Russian officials have not forgetten the affront he caused them, and a military envoy appears in Solikamsk bringing terrible news: the naturalist Georg Wilhelm Steller is to be charged. An informant sent word all the way to St

Petersburg that Steller was an enemy of the Tzar *slovo i delo,* in word and deed, a traitor of the worst kind, and he is to present himself to the court in Irkutsk without delay.

What a baseless, shameless lie! The informant is anonymous, but Steller does not need a name to find an object for his rage – to hell with these Siberian officials! What madness, to retreat three thousand kilometres back through Siberia to the east! He will need at least two weeks just to prepare for the journey. First he must catalogue all his plants and bird skins, then write to St Petersburg, to the Senate and the Academy, send word that nobody must dig up his plants without his consent. Steller is so furious he bursts into tears. He sobs and curses, leaving the messenger at a loss, not knowing what to do, where to look, as the naturalist pours out his anger: he could have remained in the beautiful cities of Europe, risen to the role of professor and lived a comfortable life, he could have fallen in love, brought children into the world, but he has sacrificed the best years of his life to science. He has tolerated hunger, cold and poverty, risked his life, time and time again, and in return gets nothing but scorn and condescension, charges of treason – a man who has dedicated his life to the Academy! Why do they seek to frustrate his work time after time? He beholds the chaos in his office, the tables and boxes piled high with samples whose names and origins are recorded only in his head. But the messenger has had advance warning of the prisoner's querulous character, and they set off that same evening. Steller is allowed to take his coat and the pages of his manuscript, which he hastily gathers up.

They travel quickly and uncomfortably, stopping only to eat and sleep. At first Steller thought he might be able to make good use of the time, but the humiliation of imprisonment gnaws at his mind. The days pass, his notebook rests in his lap, and he stares out at the passing landscape with unseeing eyes.

In October, they arrive at Tara. Steller travelled through this town eight months ago, and he begins to weep. Why has he been forced back to this ugly place inhabited only by illiterate Tatars and incompetent officials? But it is in Tara that the court awaits him. A postal wagon comes bearing news: Lieutenant Waxell had learned of the charges against Steller, testified to his good character, and now all the charges have been dropped. Upon hearing this, Steller drops to his knees. He clasps his hands together and thanks the Lord and the lieutenant, and rather than staying to tempt fate, he leaves the town that same evening. He must get to St Petersburg, correct these misunderstandings and clear his name, he must deliver his report before another researcher reaches his island. So many lost days, weeks and months – he cannot afford to waste another moment.

He arrives at Tobolsk, and the town's archbishop hosts a banquet in honour of his release. Sophisticated guests are a rarity in Siberia, and the archbishop enjoys conversation with this erudite man who is almost as well read as he. They talk about God and the medicinal qualities of herbs, they raise their glasses, but Steller is restless. He longs to return to his samples, the fossils, skins and seeds still waiting to be put in order, the plants abandoned in the frozen soil, but the archbishop is in no hurry to let his guest go. He hosts Steller for a full three weeks, but by then the naturalist's patience has run out. He packs his belongings and orders his horses to be prepared for the journey, but on the morning he is due to set off he awakes to shivers. A fever ravages his body, sweat breaks out upon his brow and soaks his clothes. The archbishop prays, begs him to stay, but Steller shakes his head. What is a small fever compared to the hardships he experienced on his uninhabited island? He will not hear any argument to the contrary and instead climbs into his sled, his legs trembling.

He travels for three days and nights without stopping. On the morning of the fourth day, he is found freezing on the side of a road leading to Tyumen, his horses worn out with exhaustion.

The town's physician is summoned to the inn. Lying on the gurney in front of him, he finds a febrile, emaciated man calling him strange names and speaking a mixture of Latin, German and Russian. The physician places a cloth on the man's forehead and gives him tea steeped from herbs, but the fever will not drop, and Steller's breath begins to rasp. The physician sends someone to fetch a priest, and a moment before he slips into darkness, Steller smiles. He is sitting by the campfire, the Cossack at his side. They raise mugs of the sea cow's blubber and crack them together.

Steller is buried on the banks of the Tura River that same evening. At night, however, the layer of soil shovelled upon him is brushed away and the shroud wrapped around his body stolen. The thieves did not bother to cover the grave again, and in the summer, dogs can be seen running around the meadows with ribs and shinbones in their jaws.

The physician goes through the belongings that the naturalist left behind. Among them he finds a tightly bound parcel, and inside it pages of notes written in a feverish hand. He does the deceased one last favour and sends these papers to St Petersburg.

News of Steller's death reaches the Academy of Sciences, and the event is noted in the minutes of the academic council as follows:

> *The Council has learned that Adjunct Steller departed this life during his return journey from Irkutsk Province, in the city of Tyumen, on the twelfth day of November.*

They neglect to inform his wife.

List of Steller's Surviving Manuscripts:

- Incomplete list of minerals
- List of minerals found near Irkutsk
- A history of minerals
- *Beasts of the Sea: A Detailed Description of the Sea Cow and Other Inhabitants of Bering Island*
- Description of certain winter animals
- Incomplete description of certain animals
- Incomplete study of land and sea animals
- Study of birds' nests and eggs
- Various observations regarding the description of birds
- Observations regarding birds' nests and eggs
- Descriptions of various birds
- A study of fish
- General observations regarding the reproduction of fish
- Incomplete study of certain fish
- Description of the Arctic cisco
- Incomplete study of certain bird species
- Incomplete study of spiders and other insects
- Study of insects
- Glossaries of several languages
- A study of the Koryak peoples

- *Description of Kamchatka*
- Amendments to the history of the inhabitants of Kamchatka
- Description of the hunting of various animals
- List of insects

and

Second Kamchatka Expedition
undertaken upon His Imperial Majesty's Command
or
Description of the Voyage of the late Captain Commander
Bering
for
The Exploration of Lands North-east of Kamchatka
and of
The Island on which we chanced to land
and on which we wintered in 1742,
what happened to us,
and
the plants, animals, and minerals found there

By
Georg Wilhelm Steller
Adjunct in Natural History of the St Petersburg
Academy of Sciences
1743

All that is left of Steller are his papers and his plants.

The great Linnaeus himself acquires the saplings that Steller left in Siberia, and it is in his garden that they now blossom.

II

Yet, if we wield the sword of extermination as we advance, we have no reason to repine at the havoc committed [...] We have only to reflect, that in thus obtaining possession of the earth by conquest, and defending our acquisitions by force, we exercise no exclusive prerogative. Every species which has spread itself from a small point over a wide area must, in like manner, have marked its progress by the diminution or the entire extirpation of some other, and must maintain its ground by a successful struggle against the encroachments of other plants and animals. [...] The most insignificant and diminutive species, whether in the animal or vegetable kingdom, have each slaughtered their thousands, as they disseminated themselves over the globe, as well as the lion, when first it spread itself over the tropical regions of Africa.

Sir Charles Lyell, *Principles of Geology*, 1833

*

And in every corner of the earth where civilisation has forced its way, the champagne began to flow.

Uno Cygnaeus, in a letter from Sitka, 1840

57°03'11"N, 135°19'51"W

SOUTH-EAST COAST OF ALASKA

1859

Alexander von Nordmann, professor of zoology at the Imperial Alexander University in Finland, raises his glass, and the conversation begins to flow. Speaking Swedish feels homely after all that Russian, French and English, and the professor is delighted with the visit, which is, of course, long overdue. After all, he is a state councillor and an esteemed researcher who has discovered hitherto unseen parasites in the jaws of a bream and presented the new, wondrous science of palaeontology to Finnish academia. And now he has spent four long and uncomfortable months in the northernmost corner of the Americas, so it is only right and proper that the Governor of Alaska should honour him with his presence.

To his relief, von Nordmann sees that Governor Furuhjelm is a progressive man, eager to develop the colony's zoological collections, and the governor promises to send him the second edition of Lamarck's natural history of invertebrates, containing a section dealing with parasites of the gut. They enjoy dinner together, von Nordmann regales the governor with the fascinating life cycle of the sea snail *Tergipes edwardsii,* and time flies by, but when it is time to move to the cognac, Furuhjelm stands up from his chair and makes his apologies: as the professor will surely appreciate, the ins and outs of the shipping company give him no rest.

The two men bid each other farewell in convivial high spirits.

Before taking his leave, Furuhjelm asks whether there is anything he might do to benefit the professor and his university, and at this Alexander von Nordmann does not hesitate: he wishes to find the most precious of all discoveries in the north: he wants the famed *Rhytina stelleri.*

The Governor of Alaska, Johan Hampus Furuhjelm, is returning from the northern regions of the colony, and during the journey his worst fears were realised. The fur-bearing animals have disappeared into the wilderness and the natives and hunters have been getting into scuffles with one another. He makes calculation upon calculation, but whichever way he looks at it he cannot promise that things will get better in the future, even though he has ordered his men to prise glistering, frozen blocks from the lakes. Now the Californians will be able to cool themselves with ice delivered by the Russian-American Company and crunch the pure, northern waters of Redoubt Lake into their whisky glasses, but even this does little to alleviate his problems. Even if every single champagne banquet in the world were to buy ice from their company, this too would be insufficient, because to compensate for even one otter pelt, they would have to harvest an entire shipload of ice. Nonetheless, the governor does not allow his fatigue to show but promises the professor that he will do what he can, though he knows that the last known sighting of the animal von Nordmann has asked about was almost a century ago. And so, he promises to locate it, for what is one more impossible promise on his already lengthy list?

The travelogues from Bering's expedition eventually found

their way to St Petersburg, and since then more ink has appeared on the east of the map. Dark spots mark the positions of the islands, and behind them is an uncharted shoreline, a new, foreign land. And in each report, one exciting word comes up again and again: furs – the smooth skins of the sea otters, the furry pelts of the foxes – and before long the whole world wishes to wrap itself in Alaskan hide.

The riches of Alaska are the stuff of legend, and the Russian-American Company is duly founded to harness those riches. Furs and pelts travel across the globe aboard its ships, to Russian, China, Japan, Chile, Hawaii and California, a total of 51,315 sea-otter skins, 831,396 seal skins, 319,514 beaver skins and 291,655 foxes. Most valuable of all are the otters: clients will pay anything between eight hundred and a thousand dollars for one skin, and each consignment of furs brings the Company around fifty thousand dollars in profit.

The half century that follows is a time of full cargos and full wallets, until suddenly shores that were once crowded with otters exist only in the stories of old men. Walrus tusks keep the books pretty for another decade, but eventually the supply of northern ivory runs dry too, and in St Petersburg tongues begin to wag. The Company needs a new leader, a governor who will get profits soaring again, and officials in the capital believe they have found just the man for the job.

*

Johan Hampus Furuhjelm has already overseen Russian military operations in eastern Siberia. As commander of the harbour at Ayan, he kept the soldiers and the town in good order and, more importantly, managed to negotiate a lucrative trade deal with the intractable Japanese. Now he has been recalled to St Petersburg. There follows a slew of negotiations, tentative dinner invitations, and on Christmas Day the news is finally announced: Furuhjelm has been named the new Governor of Russian Alaska. His new residence will be at Novo-Arkhangelsk, and he is to assume his position without delay.

Before taking control of the north, however, there is one more feat that Furuhjelm must undertake. At thirty-seven years of age, he is still a bachelor, and the Company has had bad experiences of unmarried governors. Blue-eyed children among the natives bring dishonour upon the colony, and besides, the governor ought to be an example to his subordinates: he must arrive in the north a married man.

Furuhjelm needs a wife in her prime, a woman who can withstand the irksome, uncomfortable journey and the Alaskan winter, but he has not set foot in Europe in eight years, and one does not meet women of good reputation in a military harbour. He is told not to worry; they have found him a splendid wife in Helsinki, one Anna Elisabet von Schoultz, a 23-year-old lady of excellent Scots-Swedish extraction who speaks many languages and will not fall ill at the drop of a hat. The only stain against Miss von Schoultz's character is her father, a man of little honour who abandoned his family and disappeared without a trace – rumour has it he was hanged during the Canadian Rebellions – but with any luck the governor will not hold the sins of the father against the daughter. Furuhjelm shakes his head, as in fact the knowledge of her background makes him gaze at Anna's photograph all the more wistfully: they could be made for each other, the honourable children of dishonourable fathers.

Anna and Hampus first meet at a New Year's ball held near Senate Square. The Langenskiöld house is small, but the ballroom is festooned with shields and lanterns, and the two dance together. Hampus is quiet and serious, he looks older than his thirty-seven years, but he dances well, and the following day he stops in for lunch. After this, everything happens rather quickly. The wedding is held in February. The cream of Helsinki society is invited to the reception, and after the celebrations the newly-weds travel to the countryside to visit their respective families, but their honeymoon is short-lived. Four days of tea and champagne, then they must begin their journey to Alaska.

A governor's wife. Anna can hardly believe her luck. In her eyes, Hampus is the perfect husband, polite and respectable; no wife could possibly want for more. Anna's mother gives her some marriage guides, and she reads the books carefully and takes notes. A good wife should be placid and calm, she should earn her husband's respect with impeccable behaviour and meticulous housekeeping – but what does Anna know of running a large household? She is more acquainted with the carefree urban life, her comfortable house on Mikonkatu where she never has to bother herself with menus or the price of foodstuffs. She writes to her mother: *I have but one wish, one desire, that he may never, never find himself disappointed in me.*

First they travel to St Petersburg. Hampus signs agreements and contracts, pores over ledgers, while Anna accustoms herself to her new role. She is the governor's wife, a colonial queen, but to her frustration she must introduce herself to high society without her husband, for Hampus has no time to partake in the festivities. Luckily, as the governor's wife she is warmly received in all quarters, there is no end to the balls and engagements, and she must have new clothes tailored for herself. After her father disappeared, the family had a chronic lack of money, but now she can buy hats and fabrics, acquire pink silk and dark-green damask and tell her mother about all the items she has bought and how much everything cost. *My own most precious darling Mother, these have been such happy days! Hampus sends you his dear love but cannot write this time, though I am sure you are never far from his thoughts.*

The governor's workload is endless. Hampus intends to show his superiors that he is worthy of their trust. The officers must not think he is more interested in social engagements and the perks of his new position, and he heads to London. He wishes to travel quickly and easily. Such an excursion is unsuitable for women, so Anna follows him later and makes her way through Europe by herself. She sits in the carriage, wistfully writing Hampus one letter after another. On the outskirts of Warsaw, the road leads through a great forest, and through the carriage window Anna sees a wolf. Its wily figure is hunched at the edge of a clearing, and as it notices them it scarpers back into the woods. Anna has seen wolves at the zoos in London and Stockholm, but standing between the trees, the creature looked different; *oh Hampus, it was like looking at another creature altogether!* She writes to her love daily, sharing her thoughts and opening her heart, but Hampus is a busy man, and only rarely does she receive a reply.

It seems it is hard to find skilled people in Alaska, and fine fabrics are always in short supply, so Anna stops at Dresden, buys a collection of bedlinen and hires a housekeeper. Ida Höerle is an industrious, forty-year-old woman who has been looking after her own sister's household and children, but now she has begun to think of the future, of an income that she can save for her old age, and to her sister's disappointment she takes up the offer of a position with the governor's family. Anna could not be happier. What a stroke of luck to find a housekeeper who knows her way around the pantry and the children's rooms, for Anna senses that it will not be long before she is blessed with a child. They may not have had time to be together during the daytime, but in St Petersburg Hampus visited her chamber every night.

Her inkling is correct. Unbeknownst to her, their gametes fuse together inside her, the cells divide and begin to replicate themselves once every twenty hours. As Anna crosses Europe, a process first developed by her insect-eating ancestors begins to play out in her womb. The placenta takes shape, the spiral arteries open, and a fine filament reaches out from the tissue, binding Anna and the embryo together, and the life inside her starts to grow.

Anna arrives in England. Dear old London! She has family and friends in the city, and she's keen to introduce her fine new husband, the great ruler of the colony of Alaska. She has missed him terribly, written to him three times a day, but she will save the most important news until they meet again. Her bleeding has stopped, and she recognises all the signs she read about in the books her mother gave her. But by the time she arrives in London, Hampus has already left. He is touring harbours and manor houses, meeting all the right people.

Anna has to call a doctor. Her heart lurches in her chest, beats so frantically that she cannot sleep, but the doctor can find nothing wrong with her and assures her it must be her nerves, apparently such a thing is not uncommon in newly-weds, and he orders her to rest and to find pleasant things with which to amuse herself.

There is certainly no shortage of amusements in London, and Anna does as she is told. She meets her friends, who are all terribly envious of her. How frightfully lucky to be able to tour the known world, to travel in the finest cabins and visit the great cities of America! Anna sips champagne and distracts herself with some shopping, buying only the bare essentials and a grand piano. The merchant packs the instrument in a tin coffer and sends it to Plymouth, where it will travel to Alaska on board a cargo ship. Now she will be able to hold musical soirées in Novo-Arkhangelsk, and she can barely remember where her woes came from. Her life is a perfect fairy tale.

The new attractions in London include an exhibition of ferocious lizards – surely Anna has already seen the knobbly skull of the Triceratops? Prince Albert himself is fanatical about these ancient bones dug up from the earth, and people throng to the

Natural History Museum to see them. Distant islands, shores and mountains have revealed very curious creatures indeed, and explorers are keen to present these strange new discoveries to the public: the newspapers abound with stories of long-tailed birds of paradise and sea cows the size of a whale, but the wonders do not stop there. Now scientists have decided to turn their attention to the depths of the earth, to dig their way back through history, and from deep within the crust of the earth, layers of rock reveal a world billions of years old, a world of strange plants, cartilaginous fish, and monsters whose size and ferocity defy even the wildest imagination.

*

In America, the bones of strange elephants are uncovered, and a young congressman by the name of Thomas Jefferson resolves to disprove an especially pernicious claim: Georges-Louis Leclerc, the greatest naturalist of his generation, has had the gall to suggest that the climate in the Americas has made both people and animals alike small and weak. But America is a land full of beautiful and impressive creatures, and what could better prove this than the discovery of a living, breathing mammoth? To that end, Jefferson funds an expedition, hires a group of fearless men and sends them westwards to seek out the habitat of these hairy elephants, for they must be lurking somewhere, and what better hiding place than America's vast, unexplored plains?

Jefferson arranges for the tooth of an American mammoth to be sent across the Atlantic. The specimen is received by one Prof. Georges Cuvier, founder of La Galerie de Paléontologie et d'Anatomie Comparée in Paris. He compares it to the teeth of the European and Siberian mammoths, and as he places the rostral pads alongside one another, he understands that Jefferson's animal is not a mammoth at all, and that what lies on the table in front of him must belong to a new species of elephant, one hitherto unknown to science.

Cuvier sits at his desk, the ossified tooth in his hands, and thinks of names. The discoverer always has the right to name his discovery, and he considers various options, savours different phrases from the languages of Antiquity. Evening is drawing in, he has already enjoyed a glass or two of fine wine and runs his fingers across the rippled surface of the tooth. Its curves conjure up a lewd image, and suddenly the name comes to him: this animal shall be called mastodon, "the nipple tooth".

Cuvier chuckles to himself, stands up and stretches his shoulders, stiff from his chair. He wants to share the joke with his friends and decides to go to the restaurant where all the scientists in Paris convene for dinner, but before leaving he walks down into the museum to admire the collections filling his gallery.

The exhibition begins with a man on a plinth, staring into the distance, his arm raised into the air. His posture makes him look like some sort of commander rousing his troops for a battle unknown to us, but instead of a uniform, he stands in front of his regiment without clothes and leathers, the tendons criss-crossing between his bare muscles. Following behind him is a legion of the flayed. The man has lost his skin, but the animals behind him have been stripped of their flesh too. The bony animals follow mankind in order of size: first the small mammals, the apes and dogs, then the horses and other ungulates, and after them the camels, rhinoceroses, elephants and giraffes, and right at the back, arching above the rest, are the greatest, most majestic creatures of them all, the whales and their calves.

Cuvier beholds this parade of the dead, this solemn march of Creation's plenitude through the great hall, and he considers the mastodon, an animal that no-one has ever seen in the flesh. The thought takes form quite innocently. How curious that such an animal could go unnoticed. The greatest scientific minds of our age have travelled to far-off atolls and to the furthest reaches of the oceans, but not one of these explorers has encountered the Stegosaurus or the cave lion. As it retreats, the permafrost does not reveal a subterranean city of mammoths, nor are vast plains inhabited by dinosaurs discovered in the heart of the jungle, and suddenly the realisation hits him like a bullet: *these creatures no longer exist*. It must be so. There is no longer any remote location where the Irish elk wanders proudly with a crown of antlers more than ten feet across, no cave where the sabre-toothed tiger lies waiting to be discovered.

That evening, Cuvier does not head to the bistro after all but hurries instead to the room in the museum housing all the bones dug up from the ground, the strange and magnificent creatures, the great sloths, the cave bears and dinosaurs, the skeleton of a pterodactyl that the Germans pulled out of a chalk quarry and that local researchers initially thought to be a fish, before Cuvier recognised the bones as characteristic of a reptile. Now he examines these ancient remains again, wandering from one fantastical creature to the next, and a bleak certainty fills his mind: Jefferson will never find his mastodon.

Cuvier catalogues twenty-three species that he believes may be lost, gathers the learned men of science together, and with this his theory becomes a reality.

A new, terrifying word enters the lexicon: *extinction*. The irreparable destruction of a species. What a remarkable, godless notion, and at first scientists try to avoid it at all costs. Perhaps these weird and wonderful bones belong to the ancestors of existing creatures, animals that changed as their climate and diet shaped them into new, sleeker forms. But the naturalists shake their heads. The chalk beds do not reveal a complete lineage like this, palaeontologists have been unable to find a chain of evidence from one creature to the next, and besides, what living creature could possibly be a descendant of the tyrannosaurus or the glyptodon? No, surely the earth cannot be home to such a beast.

Cuvier spends terrified nights considering the theological implications of his assertion, searching for a way to reconcile the truth of the Bible with what he can see in front of his very eyes. Eventually, he comes up with an answer. The flood depicted in Genesis – this must be the catastrophe that submerged even the tallest mountains, drowning the dinosaurs and mammoths, all the creatures that the Lord did not deem it necessary to save.

But his explanation is imperfect, for the new science of

geology is constantly revealing lost animals separated by millions of years. The same flood cannot have swept away both the trilobite and the sabre-toothed tiger. This means that the world must have experienced multiple catastrophes, one after the other. The implications of this conclusion are immense, hard to fathom. A stable, unchanging system becomes a world in which destruction follows destruction, waters flood the land, an asteroid can darken the sky, time and time again, and where all that is left of many species is bone and dust.

The idea of extinction is both thrilling and horrifying, and visitors cannot get enough of these beasts of the past. They throng around the skeletons, hungry for more, they read everything they can about the dinosaurs and the mammoths and fill the benches of lecture halls as palaeontologists present their latest discoveries. Extinct species become almost fashionable, and eventually the sculptor Benjamin Waterhouse Hawkins is given the task of bringing these lost creatures to life. His assistant is one Richard Owens, a keen young researcher who was the first to understand that the bones found within the earth form a distinct taxonomical class of their own. He coins the word "dinosaur" and divides these ferocious reptiles into three genera: the carnivorous, the herbivorous and the armoured. Hawkins and Owens examine the bones, imagine them covered with flesh and skin, and using clay and concrete Hawkins gradually restores these lost animals to their natural size.

The sculptures become a sensation long before the exhibition even opens. On New Year's Eve 1853, Hawkins and Owens hold a dinner to which they invite all the leading palaeontologists in the United Kingdom, journalists and the board of the Crystal Palace, and set out a dining table inside the iguanodon. The occasion is unforgettable. The guests enjoy an eight-course meal inside a dinosaur – oysters, pigeon, lamb shanks, pheasant, pastries and the finest wines – and make merry long into the night. The story of a banquet inside the body of an extinct animal quickly travels round the world. *Punch* congratulates the men for the age in which they live, for "if it had been an earlier geological period, they might perhaps have occupied the Iguanodon's inside without having any dinner there", and the *London Quarterly Review* lauds the miracle that is humanity: "Saurians, Pterodactyls all! Dreamed ye ever of a race to come dwelling above your tombs and dining on your ghosts?", and soon everybody is on tenterhooks, waiting for these beasts to be brought to life.

Hawkins and Owens do not offer the public mere statues; they create an entire world. The gardens at the Crystal Palace become an archipelago of the extinct, a place where visitors can wander through the past, experience the marvels of palaeontology and see living history with their own eyes. The Crystal Palace becomes the world's first dinosaur theme park, a zoo whose enclosures are populated not by lions but by animals that have long since disappeared. Before this, the dinosaurs were nothing but bones and sketches, but now these large, heavy beings are finally made flesh again. A lake is dug for them, complete with three islands. Hawkins's sculptures are not displayed in a museum or gallery but are released into the wild. Now these terrific reptiles can dig their claws into the mud, and Hawkins tries to imagine the moment at which they became trapped in the clay once and for all. The silent cry of a flying lizard carries across the islands, and visitors see the world as it was long ago.

*

Anna's second cousin takes her to the gardens at the Crystal Palace, and she finally has the chance to see the famed statues for herself. Henry is considerate and borrows a wheelchair so she doesn't have to exert herself, and the Palace's very own curator gives them a private tour. Anna gives her sunniest smile and Henry pushes her along the neatly raked pathways. The winding walkways, the sparkling waters of the reservoir and the willows, pretty and pleasant, leaning over the water. Then they see the statues, the ichthyosaurs and Teleosaurus lurking in the shallow waters, the rough-hewn monsters on the islands, the Megalosaurus and the warty-backed Labyrinthodon. Hawkins has fashioned every scale and claw, chiselled lips that curve to give each of his creations a malevolent smile, and when the wind shakes the branches of the trees, their shadows shimmer above the statues, as though the dinosaurs are merely biding their time, their chests puffed out, ready to break into a gallop. But then a squirrel climbs along the Iguanodon's tail, starts nibbling a pinecone, and the vivacity of a living creature, the movement of its little paws, makes the statue look like a statue once again. It is a curious frieze, two ages, two worlds, superimposed: the squirrels, the coots swimming lazily by, and the geese waddling in amongst the dinosaurs; the lost and the living side by side, one on top of the other.

Anna looks at the dinosaurs, at the squirrels and titmice resting on their scales, and is strangely moved. How brutal and wild the world has been, how in flux. Groves, the curator, interrupts his presentation and smiles. That is true, he says, but no need for Madam Furuhjelm to worry, we are not at the mercy of nature like the poor dinosaurs. The best scientific minds are at work charting the laws of nature, and before long the world will open up to us like a book. Then we will be able to gauge the future and stave off catastrophes, to predict and prevent earthquakes, hurricanes, volcanic eruptions, to turn hostile forests and bogland into towns and beautiful, controllable systems, and the world will be like one enormous garden, a new Eden born of man's needs and desires. Wild nature is hideous and dying, and only man can make it agreeable and living, as the great naturalist de Buffon has written. As she listens to the curator, Anna realises that this is their mission in the north too: they are to bring the colony into the realm of the laws of man, to bring culture and education and make Alaska a prim and proper place.

They leave the statues behind. Henry pushes Anna along the meandering pathways, and in the Palace's little boutique they buy a small ceramic dinosaur as a souvenir. The jaws of the plesiosaur are decorated with rows of sharp teeth, but its eyes seem to peer at them in a way that gives the toy a quirky appearance, and Anna smiles as she thinks of the child that will soon hold it in its hands.

*

The sailors ring the bells, and Anna grips her husband's hand. These are their final moments on the old continent. Soon the ropes will be untied, the ship will carry them to a recently discovered corner of the new world, and a long silence will descend between Anna and her family. Until now, she has been able to write to her mother and sister daily and has received post from them twice a day, but now this contact will be severed. She has calculated that it might take up to two months for letters to reach Novo-Arkhangelsk. Soon, their thoughts will be separated by an ocean and sixty long days, and Anna is reluctant to step aboard the ship and writes her mother one final letter, scratching her pen across the paper and trying not to let her breathing become too shallow.

The SS *Magdalena* begins her voyage across the Atlantic. Crossing the ocean is an endless ordeal. Anna lies in her cabin, unable to eat or sleep, she becomes weak with nausea and hunger, and Ida Höerle is unable to console her, as she is every bit as poorly as her lady. Anna starts to fear that she might lose the child – how can it possibly survive if she can barely swallow a single morsel? Worry makes her as restless as the churning sea. Weeks of agony and misery, for Anna must not let her husband see her in such a state, but eventually the ship arrives in the archipelago of the West Indies, and the winds die down.

Now she can finally join her husband. Fear is replaced with a weary happiness: she can see Hampus again and she has not lost the child. They dine at the captain's table, and Anna is pleasantly surprised at the quality of life in high society: for their entourage alone, the ship's kitchen slaughters three cows, three lambs and three dozen chickens every day, and the passengers in first class are young and bright. After luncheon, they perform plays and recite poetry, and an officer strikes up an especially warm friendship with one of the young ladies, which gives the older women plenty to talk about. Here in the tropics the air is humid, but they are brought buckets of ice with which to cool their drinks and themselves. Everything is most agreeable, though jolly expensive, and they take to throwing their dirty clothes overboard, as it is cheaper to buy new ones than to have the old ones laundered. Every evening, they gather on deck, cast their clothes into the sea and raise a merry toast to their socks.

Anna had hoped that the journey would give them a chance to open their hearts to each other, but Hampus spends all day in his cabin reading through the colony's affairs. He has no time for parlour games, nor for walks on the moonlit deck, and Anna has the idea of asking him to read these reports aloud to her. That way, she can keep her husband company without disturbing his work, and at the same time she can learn about her new home, and so Hampus reads to her about Juvenaly of Alaska, a monk who was sent to convert the natives. Soon after his arrival, however, Juvenaly disappears, and sailors begin telling stories of the man who tried to make the Aleutians relinquish their old gods. The savages were unimpressed by the monk's sermon and killed him. Then, a miracle happened. Having been bludgeoned to death, Juvenaly stands up again and proclaims the greatness of his god and does not fall silent until the natives hack him to pieces and swallow his flesh, and this is how Juvenaly became patron saint of their new colony. Anna makes the sign of the cross, but Hampus just scoffs. The church has its own motivations to portray the natives as cruel barbarians, though the main reason that their true and righteous faith has not spread is that, instead of sending its best, most gifted clergymen, the church sends those it wishes to get rid of. He suddenly remembers his wife's disposition – surely this story is too much for her? But Anna shakes her head: by her beloved's side, she is ready to encounter even the infamous cannibals.

In April they reach the coast of South America. They go ashore at Cartagena, and never in her life has Anna seen a place more disagreeable than this. Dusty streets, filthy women with cigars wedged between their teeth, and fruit bats fluttering over the roofs. Their leather wings make her hands sweaty, and though the hills surrounding the city are beautiful, even they are a source of disappointment. With careful planning, these hills could be turned into profitable farmland, and the location of the city could not be better, from here fruit could be transported easily and efficiently to the great cities of America, but the locals seem uninterested in turning their natural bounty into money. It pains her to look on as the possibility of progress goes to waste.

To Anna's relief, they soon leave Cartagena behind them and take a train to Panama. Legend has it that every mile of track cost the life of one labourer. Of the three hundred Jamaicans sent to construct the railway, only twenty-five returned to their island alive. Anna shudders. She imagines the men's bones hidden beneath the tracks but decides to turn her thoughts to the future instead. The isthmus connecting the Americas will soon be cut in two, the continents will release their grip on each other and allow two oceans to join together, and the wrongs of history can finally be left behind. Anna leans her elbows against the windowsill and inspects the landscape. The train passes through a jungle, and the trees grow so close to the track that she could reach out a hand and pluck a fragrant flower if she so desired. *My own beloved Mother,* she writes, *were everything not growing in such wild confusion, one could well imagine oneself driving through a most choice greenhouse.*

They arrive at San Francisco. The city is a pleasant surprise, its population has grown ten-fold in as many years, and its boutiques are every bit as good as those in London and Paris. Their arrival has been long anticipated, and local officials and politicians clamour round them like hungry gnats. Hampus spends the daytime in meetings, and when he returns home in the evenings he is too tired to socialise, and the knotted feeling returns to Anna's breast.

Inside her, a life continues to grow. Axons sprout from the brain stem, bringing nerves to the organs, the eyes, the ears and nose, and the foetus inside her begins to sense the world around it. But to Anna the changes taking place under her skin remain secret. Her waist expands, but though she presses a hand against her stomach, she still cannot feel the child inside her. She takes drops to calm her nerves, listens to the beating of her heart and the child's absent movements and dreams of the moment when they finally reach their home.

Before long, the moment is at hand: Anna feels the Alaskan soil under her feet. She has chosen her attire carefully – a black, tastefully cut silk skirt, a cloak with fur trim, and a pink bonnet, the kind of attire that would not be out of place on the boulevards of Paris. Her stomach is now clearly visible under her skirt, and knowing whispers spread through the crowds gathered on the quayside. She will have her firstborn in this unknown town, on this strange continent, and she might well have been afraid, but she is not, for that morning she saw a whale. She was standing on deck, and the creature's gnarled back rose up from the sea. Just then, Baranof Island appeared through the mists, and Anna saw the lighthouse crowning their new home. This is surely a good omen; she decides that it must be and fills her lungs with the damp air of the Alaskan July.

The departing governor hosts them for three days. Voevodskii has difficulty containing his excitement at returning to St Petersburg, but he does at least try to conceal his enthusiasm, and his wife welcomes Anna most warmly. Anna Vasilevna's friendship is overwhelming. She kisses Anna as though they were long lost sisters, speaks empathetically about the difficulties that lie ahead, the servants' laziness and the stubborn rector of the local girls' school. She gives Anna a hat made of sea-otter fur as a gift and speaks so much that Anna cannot get a word in. Anna Vasilevna talks for three days, then the Voevodskiis set off on their journey back to the civilised world. Anna and Hampus stand on the quayside and wave until they can no longer make out the governor and his wife on deck, then they turn to face the town that is now theirs.

Before them stands Novo-Arkhangelsk, the archangels' new abode created on this rugged shoreline barely five decades ago. The town was founded by the first governor of the Russian-American Company, Aleksandr Baranov, but to his misfortune he did not arrive in a pristine, uninhabited paradise. Baranov began construction work on the town, but the Tlingit destroyed the fortress he built. The Company was forced to pay an exorbitant ransom for those taken alive, and the Russians decided to abandon the town, but three years later Baranov returned. Now he knew what to expect. He brought a troop of soldiers with him, expelled the natives and built a new fortress, surrounding it with a moat and manning its walls with guards and cannons. Thus protected, a small village of low houses slowly built up around the stronghold, and this settlement became the capital of Russian Alaska.

Anna and Hampus have spent three days in Novo-Arkhangelsk, but it is already clear that the term "capital" makes it sound far grander than is the case. They stroll along the main street, trying not to let their disappointment show: algae creeping its way up the walls, houses leaning against one another like drunkards. Their brave northern colony is falling apart before their very eyes.

The city is rotten, but the governor's fortress is worthy of its name. Kekoor Castle is built on a hilltop and named after that hill. There is a set of white steps leading to the summit, the yard smells of the sea and freshly painted wood, and on top of the governor's house is a charming light that guides ships through fog and darkness to safety. An elderly Yupik guards the lighthouse tower. Anna and Hampus greet him politely. Luckily the house itself is equipped with modern conveniences, including a reception area on the first floor, a dancing and billiard hall, a smoking room and offices, while the ground floor is home to the bedrooms, the kitchen, the servants' quarters and the governate's natural history collections, stuffed birds and animals, the natives' curious attire.

They have spent three days at Kekoor Castle, but it is one thing to stay in a house as a guest and quite another to live there and consider it one's own, they think to themselves as they wander through its many rooms. In the ballroom they find a life-size portrait of the Tzar, furniture of exquisite St Petersburg quality, but most beautiful of all is the panorama from the windows: behind the house, the mountains, in front of it the ocean, and bobbing in the ocean the tree-covered islands. The windowpanes have been blown from fine, thin glass, allowing them to take in the view as though the panes didn't exist at all, and to the west on a clear day they can make out the rounded summit of Mount Edgecumbe, the place that the Tlingit call *L'úx,* the flashing one. Anna is pleased to discover that the house has an excellent library too. One thousand two hundred books have been sent to the colony from St Petersburg, books in all the languages of the civilised world, though Baranov is claimed to have said that, given the choice, he would have brought a doctor instead of books, for in the colony there are very few who can read Latin or Greek. But nobody asked his opinion.

Kekoor Castle is more splendid than any house Anna has lived in before. If it were anywhere else, calling it a castle might seem something of an exaggeration, but here the name is warranted. The structure towers high above the crumbling town, like something from another world, a realm of mirrors and lighting fixtures where they can afford to keep the lights on in every lamp. The governor's wage includes limitless supplies of candles, paraffin, meat and fish. Additionally, the Company gives them a substantial discount on tea, coffee and sugar. My, what a pleasant life they have!

There is only one thing that disturbs Anna. She tries to open her bedroom window, just a fraction, but it has been been bolted shut. And while Anna Vasilevna was a sweet lady, her housekeeping left much to be desired. The house is dark and dusty, sealed up as though they had arrived in the Arctic and not a place where there is barely any winter to speak of. The only thing that might fly out of those windows is her health, and Anna asks the servants to remove the bolts. There will be a breeze in this house; everybody knows that fresh air keeps diseases at bay. The servants try to dissuade her, but Anna pays no heed to their objections; she pushes the windows wide open, and a summery sea breeze blows through the house.

She had imagined the north would be covered in nothing but desiccated lichen and stunted trees, but the garden at Kekoor Castle is lush. Herbs and berry bushes push up through the rich soil, few-flowered shooting stars and harebells too, and their scent attracts rufous hummingbirds. Anna has never seen anything like them, these tiny, translucent winged creatures. She sits in the summerhouse, eating blackberries and listening to the hum of the birds, and suddenly she feels the child move inside her.

She has a handsome home and a fine, attentive husband. On her birthday, Hampus arranges a party and gives her a gift of two canaries. They sing to her like obedient toys, and the guests are enchanted – what an expensive and special gift – and Anna is thrilled. The English royal family keep canaries in their rooms too, and after all she is related to them, albeit distantly, and she looks on as local officials flock to the cage. How did the governor manage to bring the birds all the way out here, alive, these light, bright creatures made for palm leaves and softer winds?

One of the duties of the governor's wife is to invite the ladies of the colony to the castle. Being an excellent housekeeper and a loving wife who looks after her husband and the manor is not enough; as the governor's wife, her duties include the *mission civilisatrice*. She must educate the women and children of the colony, steer them towards a life of virtue and set a good example in both deed and demeanour, and to that end she finds herself sitting in the blue salon surrounded by the other wives, and she is taken aback at her guests' attire. The women are shabbily dressed, wearing badly cut skirts in garish colours, and what's more they do not hesitate to tell Anna how much they miss her predecessor, Anna Vasilevna. The dear lady was always so happy, her laughter knew no end, and she never forgot to send the women gifts on their name days. And they sing the praises of Margaretha Etholén too, the wife of the previous Finnish governor, what a wonderful woman she was, and they forget themselves and start speaking Russian, but Anna doesn't speak the language well enough to take part in their conversation. She sits in her chair, dumbfounded, and realises that of all the residents of Novo-Arkhangelsk, the governor's wife is surely the loneliest, for in all the colony there is no-one quite her equal.

Their colony is home to two thousand four hundred souls, four hundred settlers and two thousand Indians. Five natives for every Christian – a ratio that it doesn't do to dwell upon. In the mornings, the natives are allowed to approach the gates of the town, and the Tlingit, the Aleuts and the Yupik can sell their wares to the settlers – fish, meat and handicrafts, spoons and handles carved from the horns of mountain goats – but otherwise they have no business in the town. Only a year ago, there was a terrible incident in which the Tlingit killed two merchants. The motives for the attack were unclear, though Hampus suspects they are in fact very well known, but that they are the kind of motives that the Company is better off not knowing about. Be that as it may, in response the Company's soldiers shot seventy Indians, and tensions have been high ever since. Now it is Hampus's task to make sure such a thing never happens again. Everybody knows that a warring colony reaps only poor dividends.

The officials and the workers lower their heads and doff their caps as the governor passes, but when they visit the morning market afterwards, Anna notices that the natives do not bow their heads out of respect but stare at them with harsh eyes, muttering words she does not understand but in a tone that is unmistakable. Hampus does not seem to notice this insolence, but buys a raven carved from a walrus's tusk. This is Kah-shu-gooh-yah, the first bird who created the world and its ways. Despite Anna's protestations, Hampus invites the tribal elders to Kekoor Castle and decides not to put the soldiers on guard to protect them. Anna does not attend the dinner but watches through the window as the chieftains process through their door. The Tlingit have axes on their belts, and their clothes are embroidered with strange, grimacing creatures, the insignia of their respective tribes, with names like *Auke, Hoonah, Chilkat, Stikine, Tuxekan* and *Sitka,* or the tribes of the small lake, the lee of the north wind, the salmon cache, the bitter water, the coast town, and the edge of the branch. The curious names feel like stones turning in her mouth.

In August, a ship docks in the harbour at Novo-Arkhangelsk, carrying post from Europe. Anna wakes up early, quickly dresses, then settles herself in the garden. The sun rises and Anna takes her breakfast of scones and honey, and at half past seven she makes out the sails of the *Sophie Adelaide.* From her summerhouse, she watches the bark slowly make its approach until shortly after noon it lowers anchor, and she sends one of Hampus's manservants down to the harbour. She would dearly like to go to the quayside herself, to get her hands on her mother's words the very moment they arrive in Alaska, but Hampus has no time to go down into the town and Anna doesn't dare walk around outdoors without her husband to escort her, so she sends Wickström in her place, tells him to hurry, and bedamns him when he stops on the steps to catch his breath.

Finally, the moment has arrived. There are a great many letters, and Anna hurries back to the summerhouse with the bundle of post in her arms. She places the letters on the table then savours the excitement a moment longer before beginning to look among the names on the envelopes for her mother's familiar hand. She goes through the letters once, then again, but not one of the envelopes bears her name.

How is this possible? She has written to her mother every day, sent a thick bundle of letters with every departing ship, all tied together with pretty ribbons. She has sent her correct address many times, but the *Sophie Adelaide* does not bring a single line from her mother or Florence, and the next ship is not due until October. Will she have to suffer a full six months without news, half a year of unbearable silence? Has something happened, has her mother forgotten that she has another daughter too, one that has been sent to the ends of the earth all alone? At luncheon that day, she watches as the officials read their post, each with a letter in his hand, and she is unable to swallow a single morsel of food.

But the greatest tribulation of all is yet to come, as soon after this Hampus leaves too. He is due to travel out into the territories and does not take Anna with him; he refuses flat out no matter how much she begs and pleads. She is too close, Hampus will not be back in time for the birth of the child, and Anna cannot bear the thought that it might take weeks before he learns that he has become a father. She cries and complains so much that her usually calm husband loses his temper. Imagine wishing to travel out into a wilderness populated with wolves and bears with a little one in your belly – what an ungodly idea! Anna should think of the child and of her husband, she should control her emotions and help Hampus to overcome the anguish of their separation – surely she understands that the governor cannot put himself and his family before the needs of the Company? Anna does understand. Hampus sets off and she remains at home, an obedient wife, she bids her husband farewell on the quayside as the others stare at them, she kisses him on the cheek and wishes him Godspeed on his journey, though she feels the urge to scream.

For three days, Anna lies in bed bemoaning her fate, until eventually forcing herself onto her feet. She decides to drown her sorrows in work. This should be easy, as there's endless amounts to do, and she is keenly aware that she is constantly being compared to the wife of the Finnish governor who preceded the Voevodskiis. Margaretha Etholén held dances, masked balls and musical soirées, and all those who visited Novo-Arkhangelsk marvelled to find such a refined cultural life in the colonies. Margaretha seemed indefatigable: she founded a school for the local girls where she taught them Russian, history, geography and housekeeping; she invited them for dinner at Kekoor Castle, where they practised dances and learned the art of sophisticated conversation. Some of them even learned French, and these girls made excellent wives for the Company's officials. For this, Margaretha received plaudits all the way from St Petersburg, as there was a constant dearth of suitable wives out in the territories. In Anna's imagination, Margaretha was as perfect as a statue.

Anna visits the girls' school. She decides to give the children some Bibles and to read the Word for them, but the Orthodox monks forbid her from sticking her nose into the children's religious education. What else could she teach the children, what can she talk to them about? The girls sit at their desks, stony-faced, and Anna is at a loss as to how best to win their affection. The native children do not understand what is best for them, many of them try to flee the school and run back to their families, to a life of poverty and misery. Anna has heard the servants saying that the girls even sell their services to visiting sailors, and the thought makes her feel sick. The child inside her slumps like a slippery fish, and the teacher complains about the children's laziness and the school's leaking ceiling. The classrooms smell of fungus and algae, and Anna escapes the building at the first opportunity.

On the Tzarina's name day, Anna hosts a dinner party, but nothing goes the way she plans. The cook drinks the port wine intended for the jelly, and in a drunken stupor he neglects to prepare some of the dishes. There isn't enough soup to go round, and in an attempt to rectify matters the cook offers the remaining guests bowls of coloured water. Anna has never felt so mortified, and she cannot even sack him as there is no-one else capable of making pastries in this ghastly town. But she stops visiting the kitchen and instead passes on her wishes via the housekeeper, though she knows that the servants laugh at her, at her weakness, and she is sure she hears giggling each time a door closes behind her.

When she was in London, Anna picked up a copy of Dr Bull's *Hints to mothers for the management of health during the period of pregnancy and in the lying-in room, with an exposure of popular errors in connexion with those subjects, and hints upon nursing*. She follows these guidelines most diligently, wakes up early in the morning, does some physical exercise and washes her nipples with a tincture made from green tea and birch bark, she bathes in cool water and dries her body with a rough linen sheet, tries to remain calm and happy, to avoid vexation and palpitations. But everybody knows someone who has died in childbirth. She is to have her firstborn in this unknown town, on this strange continent, and she will do so alone, without the support of her husband, her mother or friends, and she does not trust the colony's doctor, a young man with a penchant for drink and who cannot answer even the most rudimentary questions without first consulting his books. Anna writes letters one after the other, imploring her mother for guidance and advice, though she knows that her letters will not reach Europe before her time has come.

Summer comes to an end. The hummingbirds leave the garden, wind presses the clouds against the mountains and water runs down into the town. The duckboards placed along the streets sink squelching into the mud, and one cannot step outside without dirtying one's shoes. Dampness creeps into the walls of Kekoor Castle too, but Anna pulls a shawl around her shoulders and opens the windows to allow fresh air inside. She airs the room until she wakes up, her fingers blue with the cold, and she flinches, frightened that she might have hurt the child, and eventually swallows her pride and asks the housekeeper to seal the windows shut once again.

Their town is only called Novo-Arkhangelsk on maps and in St Petersburg. To the locals, it is Sitka, and this old world continues to seep through their lives. The church has clearly neglected its responsibilities, for in a hundred years only a handful of the natives have accepted the true and righteous faith, and the colonists are no better than them – they know what is right, but they have chosen differently. In Sitka, Anna witnesses sins she cannot even name, and by the shores she sees the totem poles: the raven–bear, the bear–frog, the frog on a man's shoulders. She sees their wooden, grimacing mouths and wakes from her dream, covered in sweat. The cat has jumped onto her bed, a primitive, distasteful beast that brings voles and rats indoors and crunches their bones under her bed. Everything around her is brutal, foreign and ugly. She has had enough of her *mission civilisatrice,* and she gets up and writes another letter to her mother in which she says she has decided henceforth to concentrate only on the upbringing of her own children for she believes a mother's responsibility is always first and foremost to *her* family.

In December, Anna gives birth to a daughter. The birth is difficult, the midwife is sweating and Anna is screaming, panting and praying as blood, mucus and faeces pour out of her, things she wishes neither to see nor name, but eventually she is able to hold the newborn baby in her arms. She lifts the girl up to her breast: she is a modern woman who will nurse her baby herself, allow nutrients to flow from her body and spend sweet, precious days alone with her in the nursery. But try as she might, she produces no milk, though she does exactly as the books instructed her: swallows tinctures, wraps herself first in warm, then cold towels and allows the confused doctor to examine her breasts. Nothing seems to help. She cannot express any milk, then to compound matters further she comes down with a fever. Through her slumber she can hear the child crying with hunger; at first she sounds angry, then gradually weaker, until she no longer has the strength to demand food but simply lies in her crib, limp and pale, and Anna cannot understand what she has done wrong. Why can't she do something that even the simplest beast can do?

Eventually, she is left with no option. The doctor goes looking for a wetnurse, but in this godforsaken place there are no women of sufficient standing currently nursing a child of their own. They will have to find an Indian woman from one of the local villages, where there is no shortage of children, but at this Anna draws the line. No heathen will suckle a child of hers; let the girl drink cow's milk. But here, even that is hard to come by. There are very few cows, for keeping them is so impractical; the bears are all too keen to help themselves to some easy prey, and they pluck the livestock from their enclosures like berries. Despite their numerous attempts, the Alaskan soil resolutely refuses to be turned into fertile farming land, and animal feed must be imported from elsewhere, but then the humid air rots the hay, meaning that during the winter the cattle have nothing but mouldy fodder, and after eating this they become thin and sickly and produce no milk. Anna does not care. Let them fetch milk from California if necessary; she will pay whatever it costs.

Anna Elisabeth Furuhjelm, the doyenne of Novo-Arkhangelsk high society, the nubile young wife of the Governor of Alaska, lies in bed chewing the drawstrings on her nightgown. It is already midday, but she has not yet risen, has not asked the housekeeper whether she has fetched everything they will need for dinner. She does not meet the pastor to discuss the morals of the girls at the school but sits in bed feeling the patterns of her lace gown between her teeth and imagines she is somewhere else, someone else, someone who knows not what it feels like when a husband abandons his newly wed wife at the edge of the known world. She doesn't get out of bed for six weeks. This she does not mention in letters to her mother.

*

Constance Furuhjelm has imagined the meeting in advance, gone over it in her mind so many times that it's almost as though they have already met. She has decided to stand with her back straight, her face relaxed, to look her brother's wife firmly in the eye, but now that she is finally standing on the quayside, a headache is making her eyes water. She has to lower her gaze and look at the ground so as not to be dazzled by the light. When she stepped off the boat, she very nearly stumbled and fell into the sea. Only the quick reactions of the rower stopped her from tumbling into the waves, but the fear of drowning remains, and she cannot stop herself trembling. She is so tired that, if she were to close her eyes, she would fall asleep on the spot, sink into a deep sleep there on the crowded quayside, but Anna seems not to notice her misery; she simply opens her arms and clasps Constance against her.

Anna tries to look like the considerate, warm-hearted hostess that she is supposed to be, but she is terrified. Her back is damp with sweat and her heartbeat is erratic. She has not left her chamber for weeks, but today she has taken the steps down from the house and walked through the town, with servants and guards to protect her, to receive her husband's beloved, long-awaited sister. The two women have never met before. Constance was too sickly to attend her brother's wedding, but now she has been sent across the world to their residence, and Hampus has told Anna nothing about his sister except that she suffers from falling fits, and this is why she has never married. He has told her nothing else because he barely remembers his sister and cannot imagine a grown woman where only recently there was a child skulking in the doorway, but in Anna's imagination Constance is an eerie, cunning creature that will make Hampus see all of his wife's flaws. She too has pictured their meeting, she has worried and fretted about it, yet now there is nothing but this gaunt, scrawny thing in her arms, and she releases her grip and looks at the woman standing before her. Anna smiles, but Constance can tell that her sister-in-law is unhappy, she knows she ought to say something, but the words will not come, and the two women stare at each other, silent as rabbits.

Constance waits for the door to close behind her, then slumps into a chair. Pain swirls in her head, and she presses her forehead against the window. The moisture of her breath condenses on the glass and turns to frost. She looks at her new home: the water, the rocks and the decaying town in between, but she is concerned neither by rotting wood nor dwindling morality. No – she likes the sound of this town of whores and drunks. The ebb and flow of the ocean helps her withstand the throbbing pain in her temples, and she breathes in time with it. The waves are like the ticking of a clock, you cannot hear it without concentrating, but it is there all the same, always in the background, an even, reassuring hum, and she closes her eyes and drifts into sleep, and in the morning she hears Anna complaining to the housekeeper: Constance leaves greasy marks on the windows.

Of course, there is nothing Constance can do about her condition. They say that those with falling fits enjoy God's special protection, that it is a sacred disease, but Anna thinks this is probably nothing but Catholic heresy and she is anxious about having to witness all that thrashing and moaning. Her sister-in-law is timid and taciturn. Anna finds it hard to believe that this young woman is related to her husband, until one day she sees Hampus's expression in Constance's face, as if imitated by a bad actor. She watches her sister-in-law with a mixture of fear and curiosity, looking for clues as to when she might start having a seizure. Constance asks if she can hold the baby – what a mad thought; she might start having a fit and drop the girl – and Anna gives the servants strict instructions: her sister-in-law must never be left alone with the child, and she may only appear in public when accompanied by a member of staff, who must be ready to whisk her away again at the slightest sign of an attack.

The governor's sister arouses great curiosity among the residents of Sitka. The officers and officials try to catch a glimpse of Constance as she arrives for luncheon, and their wives invite the two ladies for tea, but Anna declines these offers and sends Constance to her room whenever someone is visiting the house. Her sister-in-law is not suited for polite society. Her mind and memory are weak. For the most part, Constance is silent, and when she does open her mouth she babbles like a child, twitches restlessly and gracelessly, and Anna resolves that Constance should not attend Mass. Pastor Winter can provide her with communion at their home, and Anna can keep her company, so Hampus's dear sister will not have to strain herself by leaving the house.

Anna greets her husband at the gates of Kekoor Castle. She tries to remember to breathe, but it is hard. She knows that men wish to have sons, but she has given him a small, burbling daughter instead. One of the servants carries the child to the governor for inspection, thank God the girl doesn't start wailing but stares at her father calmly and seriously. Hampus lets the child grip his fingers. Anna says she would like to call the girl Annie after her grandmother. Hampus nods, presents Anna with a pearl necklace and some European novels and wants to hear all about the child, what she can do, what she likes, her disposition, and Anna tries to think of something, but such a young baby cannot do very much, she sleeps and cries and sleeps again, and Anna does not know quite what to say.

The ship that brought Hampus home also brings Anna's long-awaited piano. Finally, she can play for the family. Her hands fumble across the keys, Beethoven, Mozart, Mendelssohn and Chopin, and Hampus appears not to notice the stiffness in her fingers but closes his eyes and listens, his face relaxed. Constance takes the hint, complains of a headache and retires to her room early; this evening, the couple can dine alone. Once Constance has gone, Hampus admits that had he bumped into his sister in the street he would not have recognised her, and Anna finds herself smiling for the first time in weeks. They eat, dusk descends outside, and after dinner they gaze out of the dining-room windows at Sitka sprawling at the base of the manor. Here there are no street lamps, the evening outside is dark, and people walk along the streets carrying small lanterns. They watch these dots of light bobbing in the darkness, and for a moment their town looks beautiful.

In the morning, Anna wakes happy, but as she sits down to breakfast and sees her husband's expression, her happiness fades. Hampus has examined his daughter. She ought to be rosy-cheeked and sprightly, but Annie is pale and limp – surely she is not ill? When he hears that the girl is being fed cow's milk, he becomes upset. What on earth has his beloved wife been thinking? They must find Annie a wetnurse without delay, and with that the doctor drags a scrawny, dirty woman to their door, a Yupik who lost her child only seven days ago but who is still expressing milk. The servants heat up the sauna, wash the woman and burn her clothes, cut her hair and tie it in neat plaits. The woman does not speak any known language but neither does she resist their treatment, and when the doctor shows her the child, she takes Annie in her arms and begins singing her a soft, gentle lullaby. Anna looks on as the heathen lifts her baby to her breast, her daughter's lips pucker, she takes the nipple and drinks.

Anna orders the housekeeper to sleep with the wetnurse. Ida Höerle is to ensure that the wetnurse does not mistreat Annie, does not touch her unnecessarily or speak her own language, but the housekeeper shakes her head: this job should fall to a maid. But Anna is resolute. Nobody else has experience of rearing a child properly; dear, sweet Ida is the only one Anna can trust in this matter. She has her way, but she is saddened to note that Ida Höerle no longer seeks out her company, she does not sit down and tell her about the day's events, the village gossip or her family in Dresden, but listens to Anna, her lips clenched in a taut line, and leaves immediately upon receiving her instructions. It seems Montaigne was right: *plus de valets, plus d'ennemis.*

Finally, the long-awaited day arrives, and a ship comes bearing a letter from Anna's mother. Anna retires to her room to read her mother's words. Now all will be explained! But her mother writes as though their communication had never been interrupted, she does not explain her lengthy silence but gives advice for the birth and for nursing a child – too late, all of it. Little Annie has already learned to crawl, she is wary of her mother and holds her wetnurse tight whenever Anna comes too close. Anna has been waiting for a letter, for her mother's warm words of encouragement, but her mother does not appear thrilled at the news of another grandchild, she offers perfunctory congratulations and tells Anna about her sister Florence and her sons, how affectionate they are to their grandmother, what splendid times they have together.

Anna's mother asks her to describe the landscape around their new home, and Anna looks out at the mountains, the sea and the forests, the rain driving in across the ocean, and cannot think how to turn this panorama into words. To her, the steep shoreline means simply that she is far away from everything she knows, from towns and civilisation, thousands of miles from decent roads, theatres and museums. To her, the sea and the mountains are a dull façade, their drab town nestling right in the middle. She apologises that she cannot describe the view and instead lists the rooms at Kekoor Castle, depicts the furniture and silverware and attaches a sketch to her letter. In the sketch, Kekoor Castle seems separated from its surroundings; it is a house on a white sheet of paper, devoid of any backdrop. *My own dearest mother, everything here is going marvellously, the sea air is so terribly good for one. We are so proud of Little Annie, and I have a friend here now, Hampus's sister has been sent to keep me company, never was any woman as happy as I.*

The governor's family spends the evening in the salon, but the atmosphere is flat. Constance is sitting in the corner reading and takes no part in the conversation, and her sister-in-law's withdrawal irritates Anna. Has she not treated her well, tolerated her eccentricities? Yet Constance behaves like a thrashed dog and makes Anna look like a bad hostess. Constance – the name truly is an omen: her constant, agonising presence, her twitching at dinner and in the salon, and Anna and Hampus never have a moment to themselves. Anna tries to be patient, but Constance makes it so difficult, she tries to help but forgets her instructions, and she is so timid around the servants that she will not ask for advice, she tries to polish the silverware, but her hands tremble so much that she spills the lye, leaving a misshapen blotch on the tabletop. Now it looks as though the table has some kind of frightful, exotic disease too. It will have to be sanded and lacquered again, and for this they will have to send it to California, as Anna does not trust the local carpenters. An expensive and troublesome endeavour; anyone would have lost their temper.

Anna invites Constance to take part in a game. Constance obediently sits down at the table, but she cannot remember the rules and plays the wrong card time after time. Anna takes a deep breath. She has decided this will be a sweet, pleasant evening. The home should be a place where Hampus can unwind and take a break from the woes of the world, for there are certainly plenty of them. He has returned from his travels tired and worried, he works more than before, locks himself away in his study and sighs over his papers late into the evening. Now he has put the reports aside and come down to the salon to spend time with his family, and Anna wishes to give him a moment's respite from his concerns. This always sounds so easy in books, but Constance keeps dropping her cards and Annie is fretful in her playpen, throwing her head from side to side and grizzling. The wetnurse takes the girl away, and Anna watches as the girl rests her head against the Yupik woman's shoulder. She cannot even play the piano – the humidity has loosened the strings so much that her sonatas sound like a terrible dirge – so they continue with their parlour game, but Constance cannot seem to get her cards in order.

Hampus was not especially elated at the news of his sister's imminent arrival. Why would he be? His father had sent Constance to the ends of the earth as revenge, to plague his son. After hearing of Hampus's appointment, his father celebrated his success, offered drinks all round and bought gifts on credit by telling moneylenders of his son's good fortune, and now he writes to Hampus asking for money but has not yet received a reply. Only an ingrate would leave his own flesh and blood in such trouble, but Hampus's father has plenty of imagination, and if his son will not send him money, he will send his son an extra expense: Constance, pack your belongings, you are going to Alaska.

And, likewise, Hampus is far from elated by his sister's arrival, but he accepts his lot. It would be cruel to send a sick woman back to the other side of the world, and perhaps his sister will be good company for Anna, but nothing works out as he had hoped. Now he must listen to Anna's complaints about how Constance blows her nose into her sleeve cuffs, laughs at inappropriate moments and drools. He must listen to tittle-tattle about the housekeeping, though the fate of the colony rests upon his shoulders. But the more he learns about the situation in Alaska, the further away any solution seems to be: the otters are few and far between, and now they are running out of hunters too.

When otter numbers began to drop, the Company concluded that noisy, unregulated hunting must have driven the animals away, forcing them to flee to quieter shores. As a result, the hunters were given strict orders: otters can no longer be hunted with firearms, so that the shots and the smell of gunpowder do not scare off the remaining animals. From this point onwards, hunting the otters has been the job of the Aleuts, skilled coastal warriors who work with spears and arrows.

The villages are suddenly emptied of men, who are now transported from one hunting ground to the next. This is an excellent solution. The Aleuts are cheap and competent, and they do not seem to suffer unduly from poor provisions, but over time it transpires that they are particularly susceptible to disease and can even succumb to the common cold. Thus, their hunters dwindle in number, and the remaining natives start to complain about their conditions: the Company sends the men on long hunting expeditions, leaving their women and children behind. They support themselves by fishing and collecting cockles, but despite the otters' disappearance, fish and mollusc stocks have diminished too. Food is in short supply, and on top of this they must contend with the cold, for every pelt upon every animal in Alaska is now the Company's property, and the price has risen so high that the Aleuts' hunting wages are not enough to buy furs. Now they are forced to darn their old clothes, to patch their dwellings with hay and grass, and before long it is not only the otters and walruses that have disappeared from the coastline but humans too. Islands become uninhabited one after the other, and Hampus is left scratching his head: with neither prey nor hunters, how can they continue to hunt?

There seems no end to his problems. He must rescue the

colony's economy, and he must do it soon. He can no longer waste a single evening listening to the women's bickering, but neither can he send his infirm sister away – how dreadful that would look – so he must find a way of getting rid of Constance without sending her into exile. A thud wakes him from his thoughts. A bird has flown against the windowpane, leaving blood and feathers smeared across the glass as it falls to the ground. Hampus stands up from his desk and looks down at the winged creature lying in the flowerbed below the window. This is not a species he recognises, but it is beautiful and yellow, its wings twitch for a moment, then it lies still. Now he knows what to do; the answer flew right at him.

Hampus places his cards on the table. He apologises for interrupting such an agreeable game but says he has a suggestion. He understands that housekeeping is a hard job that requires all possible help, but could Anna imagine letting Constance go, as he has a job for his sister. Anna lowers her head and considers this. The housekeeping certainly is hard work, but if her dear Hampus needs his sister, she will make sure she can survive with a little less help, and they smile at each other like accomplices. Constance is not asked: she will now take responsibility for the governate's zoological collections.

Constance is rather afraid of animals, and they are afraid of her. Dogs, cats and horses can smell her nervousness, and they become unpredictable in her presence, and at first the thought of the zoological collections fills her with dread. But she knows not how to refuse, so she dutifully follows her brother to the room downstairs.

Two corridors run through the lobby: one leading to the family's bedrooms, the other to the kitchen and the servants' quarters. However, Hampus and Constance do not step into either one but open a door right at the back of the lobby. Behind the door is a room containing the colony's natural world in all its awe-inspiring glory. The room is large, but it is so full that Constance feels almost as though she will not fit inside. The shelves running along the walls are stacked with stuffed birds and mammals. Rows of shelves run across all four walls, displaying animals' heads and antlers alongside the natives' handicrafts, headdresses carved from wood, embroidered shawls, baskets woven from seagrass, harpoons, and a translucent garment sewn from otter gut. Hanging from the ceiling are stuffed fish and kayaks, the Aleuts' one-seater *baidarka,* a Tlingit canoe decorated with images of whales, and a Yupik *umiak* built from whale bones and skin, and in the corner of the room, standing ten feet tall, is the imposing figure of a grizzly bear.

Hampus presents the room to his sister, but Constance does not listen and instead concentrates on the odour of the collection. Dust, arsenic and the smell of animals, the stench of furs, feathers and the grease protecting them, and she begins to understand: these animals' fear ended with a snare and a bullet long before she arrived. She can take a puffin from the shelf without worrying that it might squawk and flap its wings, and she runs her fingers across its leathery feet. What a silly, clumsy creature this is, and all of a sudden she giggles – what suitable company for her!

Constance's job is to keep the materials in order and to make sure the labels and the animals match up. The collection has been maintained quite carelessly, the shelves contain birds that have not been properly labelled and the lists feature animals that the collection does not hold, and she knows nothing about these creatures. She understands that her brother did not give her this task because of her skills but because of her very lack of skills, but she is not upset, because the job gives her an excuse to spend her days in a darkened room with nobody to disturb her. She cannot imagine anything better. In the presence of these dead animals, she does not have to behave herself or control her body when it starts to twitch, flap and ache, and she touches, strokes and caresses the skulls and feathers, takes the birds and mammals from the shelves, gently blows on them and breathes in the dust.

She goes through the collection, one animal at a time, always in the same order. First the water birds, the seagulls, the swans and geese, and on mornings when she cannot get up but lies in bed, her body awash with strange sensations, she goes through the collection in her head. The water birds, the seagulls, the swans and geese, the surf scoter and the blue-winged teal, then the birds of prey, the hawks and eagles, and after them the smaller birds, the scissor-tailed flycatcher and the blue feathers of Steller's jay. Then the mammals. The seals, the deer and pine martens, the lithe body of the sea otter, and finally the grizzly bear standing on its hind legs. If she gets to the bear, it has been a good day, and she gratefully wipes its paws and polishes its glass eyes.

In the company of dead animals, Constance notices that her father was wrong. He believed there was no point educating a half-wit, that knowledge would run off the girl like water off a sea bird's feathers without so much as dampening the skin, and Constance was never afforded any learning beyond her sister teaching her to read and write. But now she has a silent school all of her own, and she goes through the catalogues of animals, deciphers the names one letter at a time and learns to associate them with the creature waiting on the shelf. She reads about the animals and Alaskan nature. Reading is hard work for her, the lines jump up and down before her eyes, and some days she believes her father might have been right, but her animals are patient.

She reads slowly but diligently, uses the excuse of a headache to decline dinner, and instead reads the second edition of Lamarck's natural history of invertebrates. She reads about the parasites of the gut and smiles – if only Anna knew everything that humans and nature can hold inside them. She reads and gradually becomes familiar with these animals, she goes through the descriptions beneath their names and tries to find a unique sound for each animal, the *pwit pwit pwit pit pittrrrrr* of the wren tit, but her song does not sound like a bird's. Anna listens to these noises through the door but dares not step inside. She would rather not know anything about it.

Constance compiles a list of birds missing from the collections.

This is an easy task, for John Cassin, curator of the Philadelphia Academy of Natural Sciences, had taken it upon himself to describe every bird known in North America. He discovered almost two hundred species previously unknown to science, classified the green hylia and Hartlaub's duck and put all his discoveries together in a book, and all Constance has to do is compare his list to the collection catalogue. *Illustrations of the Birds of California, Texas, Oregon, British and Russian America* is an impressive work. Cassin has painted each bird by hand and situated them in their own habitats, the shearwaters on cliffs covered with lichen, the Gambel's quail in the sands of Arizona, though in fact he has only imagined these habitats; he paints the birds from stuffed models in his cramped study and eventually dies of arsenic poisoning from touching the birds with his bare hands.

*

Hampus has not forgotten the promise he made to the professor and allows word to spread: anyone who brings him the skeleton of a Steller's Sea Cow will be generously rewarded. He is not hopeful, but enthusiastic sailors and merchants note his request, and before long a pile of discoloured remains begins to accumulate on the desk of the governate's taxidermist – whale, porpoise and walrus bones and a mammoth's tooth, which the governor buys for a handsome price. But the taxidermist Martin Wolff shakes his head: none of the items brought before him belongs to the famed *morskaya korova*.

A table presents an estimate of the number of sea cows hunted on Bering Island and describes how their bodies were used.

There are four categories:

Killed and consumed immediately.

Killed for immediate consumption but wasted.

Killed and carried on board as provisions.

Killed for provisions but wasted.

The column for the year 1742 tells a familiar story. Bering's expedition kills around forty sea cows. Of the animals they slaughtered, they eat only about a fifth, between five and eight animals, and the rest sink into the depths, but even five animals is plenty for them. Then humans leave the island. The St Peter *sails off, and for a while the sea cow can return to its gentle rhythm, regulated by the weather, its mating cycles, and the changing of the seasons. It takes time for word to spread, and in 1743 not a single ship comes ashore on the sea cows' island.*

Then fur hunters set off. They come for the otters and the foxes, hungry for Alaska's soft gold; however, it is not its hide that seals the sea cow's fate but what lies beneath its rough skin. Contemporary accounts suggest that reports of the tastiness of the sea cow's flesh reach almost mythical proportions. Sailors often claim that the giant tortoise is the most delicious creature on earth. In fact, it is so tasty that its scientific classification took three hundred years, for in all that time not a single specimen survived the journey from its native island back to the academies of Europe without being eaten, including those loaded aboard Darwin's ship, HMS Beagle. *Furthermore, the tortoises' flavour is said to have played a part in one of the most famous of all extinctions. You will have heard of the dodo, that fabled, stumpy bird that was not afraid of humans, but which had a habit of gathering around the bodies of fallen conspecifics, meaning that a hunter simply had to fire his weapon and wait. But the hunters were in for a disappointment. The dodo's flesh tasted terrible. It was tough and bitter. Then a clever seaman came up with a solution: when the dodo's meat is spread with fat from the giant tortoise it becomes soft and tender, and in this way one creature helps us to swallow another. One lucky apprentice claimed to have tasted both these famous giants and swore that the sea cow was the tastier. Its flesh was like butter and manna, and its fat burned in blubber lamps without smoking, letting a sweet, delicate aroma fill the room.*

In their first year on the island, fur hunters kill two hundred sea cows. Their technique is not very refined, and of the animals they kill they eat only a few dozen. After this, a steady stream of ships begins to arrive. A determined hunter can quickly clear an island of its furs, but there is always the next island, and beyond that a whole continent brimming with otters and foxes. Merchants leaving Kamchatka take to stopping at Bering Island, where they fill their barrels with the flesh of the sea cow, though they are less interested in learning the art of harpooning. They are happy to shoot into the water at random, in the hope that the waves will wash at least one of the dead animals ashore. They are only interested in preserving the otters and the foxes; for them, the sea cow is merely a sumptuous sport.

The columns begin to grow in size. The year 1754 shows an ominous statistical spike. That year, the fur hunters claim around five hundred sea cows, five hundred marine mammals each weighing several tonnes, of which only a fifth are used for food. This means that four hundred sea cows, four hundred corpses, are left to rot in the island's shallow coastal waters, four thousand four hundred tonnes of meat, fourteen thousand ribs, nineteen thousand vertebrae slowly buried under layers of sediment, generations of well-nourished crabs and sea urchins climbing through an ever expanding bone garden at the bottom of the sea.

Ships set sail from Bering Island, their holds full of pelts, and when one predator removes another, at the bottom of the food chain the banquet can begin. The mouth of the sea urchin is a bizarre contraption. Also known as Aristotle's lantern, this creature has five jaws and a fleshy, tongue-like lump, and it sucks up algae, tonnes of algae. By now the otters have been hunted to the brink of extinction, meaning that the sea urchins are no longer caught in their nimble paws and cracked open, and the echinoderms can now stand up on their suctioned legs and eat their fill. The sea urchins reproduce unimpeded, and before long the clusters of kelp that were once almost impenetrable now let in the light.

Now, to add to their other woes, the sea cows have to cope with hunger too. The stricken mammals are beset with disease, and the sailors look on as the young suckle at their mothers' already empty teats. The herds grow smaller and thinner, and merely twenty-seven years after Steller first made out a dark shape moving under the water's surface, the fur hunters find only a single sea cow in the shallow waters along the island's coast.

In English and French, a species is extinguished, life dwindles, smoulders and is eventually snuffed out, while in Swedish a species is pulled up by the roots, eradicated from the earth like weeds from a garden, but the Finnish "sukupuutto" does not mean the death of all individuals. In Finnish, even the last sea cow floating in the water has experienced "sukupuutto", the lack of a mate. Blood still flows through its veins, its nerves still send neurological impulses to its limbs, but as it swims from one cove to the next looking for one of its own kind, it has already encountered the greatest, most profound loneliness of all, the lack of its kin, and its species reaches an end long before a bullet pierces its eye.

The fur hunters load their rifles. The final mammal, the final column, after this there is nothing left to hunt. Steller died in the belief that the species he had discovered would feed the whole of Siberia, but he had underestimated human greed and hunger.

Its flesh and blubber are now a thing of the past, but scientists and the academies have renewed interest in the sea cow's remains. Hunters scavenge the shorelines for pieces of the animal and sell them for a hefty price. On his expedition through the North-east Passage, Adolf Erik Nordenskiöld collects many sea-cow bones and presents his findings in a composite skeleton put on display at the Royal Palace in Stockholm. For a while, the sea cow is Stockholm's foremost attraction, but after this the shores are cleared, the bones gone, and the sea cow lost. Nobody has seen one for around a century, and some scientists claim that it is a mythical creature, the ravings of starving seamen, that Steller lost his mind and concocted the creature in order to bolster his reputation. Some researchers claim that the sea cow has been hunted to extinction, but such claims are met with scorn and derision. Extinction is something that affects dinosaurs and mammoths, the great, terrifying beasts of the past, but a similar catastrophe has not befallen the Bering Sea. The sea cow has not experienced a flood or an earthquake, and the world around the island is the same as it always was. This means that the sea cow must still be out there, that somewhere there is a cold and quiet place that humans have not discovered, and in that place the sea cow's calf can turn its stomach towards the sky and drift into sleep without fear.

Constance spends her days with the collections, and in the evenings she is too tired to join the others. She is barely seen at all, and Anna and Hampus finally have the chance to be alone. Anna gets her husband back, but Alaska has left its mark on him. He has lost weight and has started to see danger and adversity everywhere; he is afraid of shipwrecks and running out of money. Anna is not wasting their allowance, is she? She hands over the account books for her husband to inspect, shows him how frugally she has been using their funds, and even makes Ida Höerle haggle over the price of eggs. She only ever buys the most modest fabrics. Why dress up smartly in a place where there is nobody to see it? She sees her bonnet on the dresser and smiles – Sitka truly is no Paris. If they wish to save money, Hampus should turn his attention to his sisters. Ludmila is constantly writing to him, demanding money for dresses and tours, and Constance eats like a horse.

They do not know how Constance spends her time, but it doesn't matter, for Hampus employs a real curator too, a man whose job it is to acquire new species for the collection and to exchange the worn old samples for new ones, for skins preserved using the newest methods. Anna doubts the need for a new employee, but Hampus puts her right: a taxidermist is essential. The governate's collection must be brought up to date, so that he can present the Company's scientific achievements to those visiting the colony. The English and the French have chastised Russia for its brutality and its expansionist policies, so now it is all the more important to demonstrate that, alongside the trade in furs, the empire has higher objectives too.

Martin Wolff was on his way to South America. He was planning to compile a study of the birds of the Tierra del Fuego, but crossing the Atlantic ate into his savings more quickly than he had calculated, and his father no longer wished to support his proposed project. He had hoped his son would become a soldier; but Wolff is uninterested in species classification and frontier lands, and now he is on his own. However, in Panama he meets an official from the Russian-American Company who tells him that the governor of Alaska is looking for a taxidermist. Back in Hesse, Wolff has been supporting himself by stuffing hunting trophies, the heads of elks, deer and wild boar, along with hazel hens and other grouse to be displayed on shelves and mantelpieces, and now he follows his instinct and heads north. He arrives in Sitka and loathes every minute of it, the endless rain, the algae growing up the walls of his dorm, but to his relief the official was not lying: the governor pays well, and though every evening Wolff resolves to leave, every morning he decides to stay until the next payday.

Hampus imagined his sister would be thrilled at the new taxidermist, but Wolff arrives in the collection as if he owns it, opening the cupboards and running his fingers across the labels. Constance feels the urge to tell him to disappear but restrains herself, for Wolff is a useful creature who will acquire new samples for her.

When first she saw the collection, Constance had thought the room full, but now she sees the gaps where various birds and animals once stood. She has gone through the catalogues of animals, the lists of species native to the colony, and a new passion has lit up within her. She dreams of collecting in this room all the wildlife in Alaska, a freeze frame of all the life that she will never see but can gather here, within arm's reach. But in order to make this dream a reality, she needs help, and for this reason she decides to tolerate Martin Wolff.

Still, Constance cannot help but cause a little mischief, and in the taxidermist's presence she behaves even more gauchely than usual, she talks to herself, watches him as he examines the shelves, and lets out small, hiccoughing sounds. Martin Wolff – even his name amuses her! The taxidermist is more a rabbit than a wolf, he has long limbs and goggle eyes, warily staring here and there as Constance potters behind his back.

Wolff opens a box and lifts out a goose, a round-headed, short-necked bird whose white plumage is marked by two magnificent black tail feathers. This is Ross's goose, *anser rossii*, the newest addition to the governate's collection. Constance watches the taxidermist at work. She has examined the animals in the collection, scrutinised their seams, run her fingers along the stitching and gone through the birds, catalogue in hand. The great grey shrike appears in the catalogue twice, and Bonaparte's gull is missing altogether.

Constance examines the paperwork, looking for any note

that might tell her when the bird was added to the collection, but she finds nothing and decides to try and guess. This is not impossible, as she has learned to recognise certain taxidermists' handiwork. Some of the animals added to the collection at the beginning of the century have been stuffed immaculately. In the hands of this craftsman the creatures look vibrant and alive: the mink raises its head, disturbed while eating, the raven looks as if it is about to take flight, and Constance believes that Bonaparte's gull must be the work of the same man, so lively are its eyes as it stares at her.

She examines the Ross's goose. She knows that this irritates Wolff, and she turns the bird deliberately slowly, feeling the weight of its skin stuffed with rags. Its eyes have been skilfully attached, the edges of the eyelids preserved intact, the feathers are pristine, and she cannot even find the bullet hole, though she touches the skin beneath the feathers too. Wolff's work is clean, but he is no artist. Standing on its plinth, the goose looks stiff. Wolff has not considered how the bird stands and moves; he spends more time in the tavern than out in the wilds, and it shows: he has found a form and settled for it. But the seams are smooth, and Constance lifts the goose into her arms, places it between the northern shoveler and the king eider, and experiences the slow, solemn fulfilment of a true collector.

On evenings when Constance feels up to joining the rest of her family, Anna marvels at the change in her. Her usually quiet sister-in-law now babbles endlessly about birds and mammals, and there is a spark in her eyes that makes Anna concerned. If one did not know better, one might imagine she was smitten.

Anna asks her husband into the salon. Is it seemly for the taxidermist and the governor's sister to spend so much time together in that dim room without a chaperone – Constance, a girl so unaware of the ways of the world – but Hampus gives the briefest of smiles. This is Sitka, and Constance is Constance: two exceptions to the rule. What would be unimaginable in Dresden or St Petersburg is banal here, commonplace even – or would Anna prefer to have Constance back to assist her? Anna hurriedly shakes her head and tries to explain that it is not so much a question of what might happen but of what it looks like, that out here the officers' wives watch one another as closely as anywhere else, perhaps more so, because here they need something to pass the time, and a scandal can form at the drop of a hat. And when they finally uncover a sin great enough, it will sustain them for a long while.

Anna had barely stepped off the ship when she heard the first stories about the former pastor in Novo-Arkhangelsk, of how Uno Cygnaeus had hurriedly given his housekeeper's pretty daughter a gold ring, and before long everybody knew exactly why a promising man of the cloth had been sent away to the furthest corner of the earth. The words *maid* and *lovechild* started to spread around the town, and if Cygnaeus had imagined that the disapproval would not follow him to Novo-Arkhangelsk, he was soon to find out how wrong he was, for as a result he was forbidden to teach at the girls' school. Eventually, Cygnaeus judged that enough water had passed under the bridge, and he returned to Finland. Back home, he was finally able to put into practice certain thoughts on education that the people of Alaska were not yet ready to hear, but though the pastor is gone, the whispers will not abate, and Anna orders Ida Höerle to take Constance a cup of tea at unpredictable hours and to step into the room without knocking, just in case.

For a moment, Martin Wolff even wonders whether it might be beneficial to induce the governor's sister to fall in love with him. Normally, he would not even entertain the idea of such a thoroughly odd union, but for a sickly spinster he could make an exception. Constance notices that he has started combing his hair, and as he presents a harlequin duck that he has recently stuffed, he leans over towards her and brushes her hand so clumsily that there is no mistaking the gesture. Constance bursts into laughter. She chortles so much that spittle flies from her mouth, and for a brief moment she pities him. The things he has to do to keep himself afloat! Wolff decides it would be ignoble of him to try to woo such a simpleton – why would he be interested in an ugly, twitching woman when the town is full of Creoles who laugh so prettily?

Anna has got her Hampus back, and before long she is expecting again. The decidua and the villus begin to form inside her, and as she notices the first tell-tale signs, she slumps into bed once more. Children are a blessing, but do they have to come so soon? Annie is barely walking, and Anna again finds herself with child. She blames the doctor who did not have the good sense to tell her and Hampus to abstain from relations, but what can one expect of a man like that? Nothing, and now she no longer goes into the town even in Hampus's company. The stairs leading down the hill make her feel faint, and being so short of breath is dangerous in her condition. She does not go into the town and moves out of the blue salon. Her new room is small and dingy, but it is situated right beneath the governor's office, so she can hear when Hampus leaves his study. Otherwise, they might not see each other all day, and Anna only seldom leaves her own room, she never goes upstairs, blaming the stairs themselves, and declines to take luncheon with the officials. She must take care of herself, and to this end she maintains a strict diet: no raw vegetables at all, only soup, meat and some light puddings. She lies in bed and listens to her husband's footsteps on the office floor above as he paces around his desk. She learns to foretell bad news by the way his shoes touch the boards, and when the door creaks on its hinges, she rushes to the foot of the stairs. If she can catch Hampus before he disappears into his room, she might be able to lure him into the salon for a moment.

Then the worst happens, again. Hampus is drawn away on a new mission. He intends to open a mine and plans to oversee the initial work in person. It is naturally unfortunate that yet again he will miss the birth of his child, but his duty is clear, and he informs Anna of his decision, only this time she does not follow the advice of her books but opens her mouth and shrieks. Never before has she challenged her husband , but this time she has no choice. She must think about the child floating inside her, and if she remains here, she will surely die. This she knows with as much certainty as she knows that the sun will rise again in the morning. Hampus tries to reprimand his wife and remind her of her place, but Anna startles everyone by having such a fit that she has to spend several days in bed, and the doctor fears she may lose the child. Upon hearing this, Hampus relents. He cannot take Anna with him into the wilds, but he can take her to Kodiak Island.

It was on this island that the former governor had a villa constructed. In size and splendour, it bears no comparison with Kekoor Castle, but still Anna feels like a schoolgirl on holiday. She takes walks, goes outdoors for the first time in months and picks flowers on the hillsides in all imaginable colours. In addition to their own entourage, there are only a handful of fishermen on the island at most. Here there is no need to fear the Indians and she has no social duties, so she can spend long, perfect sunny days with Hampus and take little Annie out into the meadows. The girl examines the moss, the pebbles, and Anna watches Hampus scoop his daughter into his arms. He seems to like the girl more with every passing day.

They take Constance with them too. She seems peeved, reluctant to leave the collection behind, but when have they ever asked her opinion before, and she packs her few belongings and steps aboard the ship with a scowl. The island has its benefits, however. There are no social circles from which she needs to be hidden away, and she can wander outdoors to her heart's content, as long as she takes one of the servants with her in case she has a seizure. She goes out into the woods and tries to identify different species but finds it hard to see any similarity between her birds and the restless creatures fluttering in the trees.

Hampus spends a few happy days with them on the island, but then it is time for him to leave, and Anna notices that it is easier to cope with their separation here than at home. In a place like this, even longing assumes a romantic glow, and her sadness is tinged with a wistful pleasure. She is like the protagonist in a novel, pining for her beloved in the wilderness, surrounded by flowers, only now she has a child in tow. Annie is learning to speak, starting to call her mother, and Anna tries to believe that she might mean it after all.

On the island, even Constance seems a little easier to tolerate. In the evenings, they drink tea together on the veranda, the wind blowing in across the sea keeps the gnats away, and Anna chats to her sister-in-law. Constance's mind is damaged, sensible conversation is beyond her, but she certainly knows how to listen, and Anna can speak without having to guard her words – for who could a mute girl who only talks of skins and dead animals possibly tell about what she has heard? And on the evenings when Constance is in pain and does not join her, Anna feels surprisingly upset and lashes out at the servants.

The child in Anna's womb is growing, and Constance watches her changing body with fascination. In her room, she reads about mammals, she imagines the placenta and the two separate blood flows inside Anna, and when the time finally comes, she asks to be present at the birth. To her surprise, Anna agrees. As the contractions come and go, Anna grips Constance's hand and asks her to pray with her, and Constance prays and thanks the Lord that she has never known a man. Mammals have a tough lot: ruptured membranes, torn muscles, and blood. If she could decide, she would choose rhizomes, spores and pollination, but their lot is tough too, and she looks on as Anna pushes the child from inside her. The midwife swaddles the tiny, bloodied creature and hands it to Constance; she looks at Anna, startled, but Anna does not forbid her, just nods and drifts into sleep.

Soon after the boy's birth, Hampus returns from his excursion and takes the women home. Constance is happy to get back to her collections, but Anna feels like a prisoner stepping into a cell to resume a sentence. On the island, everything had gone as she had planned. This time the milk comes naturally and she feeds her son by herself, happy and proud. Otto Edvin is a lively, chubby baby, but Anna is worried that the fumes of Sitka may yet ruin her happiness, and she shuts herself away in the nursery and feeds her son until her nipples bleed.

*

Hampus summons Anna and Constance into his study. This is not out of the ordinary, sometimes he is keen to show them the items he has brought back from his trips – skins and Indian handicrafts, animals carved from bones that he brings as gifts for the children – but invitations to the study have been less frequent of late. Hampus has many things on his mind. British troops are massing in Canada, and the memory of their losses in the Crimea is still fresh. If the British decide to invade Alaska, it is far from certain that they will be able to defend the territory, and in St Petersburg there is even talk of selling off some of the empire's overseas colonies. Would it not be better to extract payment for them than to lose them by force? But Hampus is reluctant. Is his fate really to become the last governor of Alaska, the man after whose tenure the colony ceased to exist? He is keen to avoid such a humiliation, and to this end he pens letters beseeching his superiors, he will open mines and harbours, anything to turn their finances around.

Hampus invites his brother to head up the mining project, but this proves to be a grave mistake. Hjalmar takes after their father. He has grand notions and ideas, he writes clumsy poems exalting the natives and the majestic Alaskan landscape, he visits Indian villages and criticises the colony's activities – the Company has stolen this land from the savages, put them to work, then taken their innocence too, plundered their beautiful, Edenic environment. The natives refuse to work underground, and Hjalmar is forced to pay them a very handsome wage, yet when the first cart of coal is hauled up to the earth's surface, the disappointment is immense. The coal is of such low quality that they end up selling it at a loss, and eventually word reaches the governor: a delegation has been sent from St Petersburg to draw up an impartial assessment of the state of the colony. Hampus had hoped to be able to show his superiors a flourishing mining industry, but now he is terrified. What can he show them but ice and the gradually depleting forests?

In his sheer gawkishness, Hjalmar almost rivals Constance. To Anna's horror, her brother-in-law returns from one of his trips with a child, a small Yupik girl that he says he has adopted. Hjalmar claims to have saved the girl, explains that the tribe was planning to sacrifice her to their ancient gods, but it later transpires that he bought her from her parents in exchange for alcohol and gunpowder. Hampus is furious. Selling liquor and weapons to the Indians is strictly forbidden on pain of exile – how can he tell the others to obey the rules if his own brother cares not a jot for them? But Hjalmar simply laughs. He names the girl Aino Giulyanima, a double-barrelled moniker combining names from the Finnish and the Yupik traditions, for alongside his admiration of the Yupik, he has national-romantic stirrings in his breast, he admires the humble, resilient Finnish people and their ancient, sinewy language. Hjalmar parades around Kekoor Castle with the girl in tow, just as Anna has finally got rid of Annie's wetnurse – and not a moment too soon. Annie had started talking about spirits living in rocks and trees, and using soft, foreign words, though Anna had stressed that the wetnurse should not speak her own language to the girl. The woman simply had to go, but Annie has already picked up bad influences, and now she cries after her wetnurse, wails and sputters until her cheeks are covered in snot, and she is indifferent to her mother's arms but throws her toys around instead. Day after day, the wetnurse appears at their door, begging to see the child, until eventually they have to instruct the guards to keep her away from the town. Anna decides not to tell Hampus about any of this but instead proudly informs him that Annie has learned to locate Paris on the map.

Hjalmar suggests that Annie and Aino Giulyanima might play together, and Anna is at a loss. She does not want Annie to play with a heathen, and wicked tongues are already whispering that the native girl is in fact Hjalmar's bastard child, a half-caste brat born out of wedlock, here under their very roof. Anna takes to marvelling at how good-hearted Hjalmar is to take in this unknown girl and raise her as his own, though she knows very well what people are saying around the town.

Weeks have passed since their last invitation to the study, but today Hampus asks the women to join him. As they step inside, he can hardly conceal his glee. Several boxes stand piled up on the floor. Hampus asks Anna to choose one of them, which she does, then he tells her to open the lid. The room is filled with the smell of sawdust and seaweed. Hampus takes a bone out of the box, a triangular chunk of an animal, half a cubit wide. It is so heavy that he has to lift it with both hands, and he asks Anna and Constance to guess which animal it is from, then sets it to rest and picks up the skull without waiting for an answer. It is a peculiar head, one that does not resemble any of the other skulls in their collections, it is not long like that of a seal, a whale or a porpoise; this one is sturdy and has a wide brow. Its muzzle resembles a bird's beak, and right in the middle there is wide, smooth-edged hole. Hampus holds the skull in his hands as gently as if it were his own child, and suddenly Constance realises what it is.

*

The sea cow's skeleton was discovered by two Aleuts. We know nothing more about them because nobody thought to write down their names. The governor sent men to look for gold and coal, and in the hope of uncovering precious minerals he tells them to begin mining on the Aleutians' own islands too. Now seal hunters can earn an extra income by bringing back rock samples, and the men set off. They row out to the furthest tip of the chain of islands and come ashore on the same island as Steller and his comrades did over a century earlier. In their language, they had a name for this island long before anyone in Russia had ever thought of locating the remote coast of America, but that name is nowhere to be found on maps or in the annals of history, so let us simply note that these two mineral hunters arrived at Bering Island.

They come ashore on the same island as Bering and Steller, but the island they discover is no longer the same as it once was. The species living there have changed altogether. The shores and hillsides have been purged of mammals, and what was once the blue foxes' island is now the birds' island. And of those, the largest is gone too, the fifteen-pound spectacled cormorant – an impressive, black bird that had given up its ability to fly and concentrated instead on developing hydrodynamics suited to life at sea. It was a large and irascible creature that the foxes left well alone – why fight with a giant when the gull and ptarmigan fledglings made easy pickings on the hillsides – and when the *St Peter* first arrived, the spectacled cormorants, with their wingspan of more than three feet, dotted the craggy rock faces like ominous seamarks.

To its great misfortune, the spectacled cormorant was also delicious. Steller mentioned that some of his crew members were particularly partial to its meat. They would fight most ferociously over nesting grounds on the crags, and the more inexperienced birds were forced to build their nests on the shore, and if one could get between the cormorant and the sea, it was easy prey. In the water, the creature moved with exceptional speed, but on the ground, this nimble bird became slow and clumsy and quickly found itself roasting above an open fire. Their flesh was palatable to the fur hunters too, and they had no need to spare their bullets, and before long the penguin of the Bering Sea had been eaten to extinction.

Now different birds populate these same crags. As the mineral hunters row closer to the shore, the emperor goose, the northern shoveler and Steller's eider flap up into the air, and as the men pull their kayaks from the water, they happen upon the pits dug by Bering's expedition. Rain has collapsed their walls, grass has sprung up at the bottom, and soon afterwards, the wind and the sea will fill them with sand and gravel, but as these men arrive, they can still make out the deep, grave-like depressions in the shoreline. However, these men are not interested in the pits but in the cliffs, and they gaze up at the hillsides and look for any points where the rock changes colour.

Closer to the mainland, seals too are now few and far between, but here they laze along the shoreline in large herds. The cream-coloured hide of the northern fur seal makes beautiful shoes and clothes, and the men spend their time hunting them, skinning them, and chiselling samples from the rocks. In an *iqyax* made from stretched seal hide, they can canoe into coves that previous fur hunters could not reach in vessels with deeper draughts, and in the shallow waters of one of the bays a promising sight awaits them. A long, red-brown streak runs the length of the dark grey rockface. Red can be a sign of iron, so they haul their kayaks out of the water, but a surprise is waiting for them on the shore. At the foot of the hillside is a large rock, a boulder dislodged by an earthquake, and behind that they make out the shape of a boat. The vessel was clearly dragged behind the boulder to protect it from the elements, but it is apparent that it has rested here for a very long time. Its upturned hull has given way, and the rain has left its frame full of holes. A strange sight in a strange place – why would anyone leave a boat on a shore covered in gull droppings? – but as they come closer, they realise that the shape they see is not the work of human hands.

They make out the curve of a rib cage protruding from the rocky ground. The ribs form a vault rising out of the sand, but the spine, limbs and skull have long been buried underground. It is a curious sight. The men have skinned a walrus and cut a whale to pieces, but the creature lying before them is neither a walrus nor a whale. Hope flickers to life. Could this be the kelp-eater that the governor is looking for? They know about the sea cow, for though no living man has ever seen one with his own eyes, they have heard their grandparents' old stories. Hunting the sea cow was so easy that the creature was even dubbed "women's prey". The Aleuts did not need harpoons because they knew the sea cow's behaviour, they knew that in stormy weather it moved into shallower waters, and when the winds whipped up, all the hunters had to do was pick up their spears and wade out to the creatures huddling against the rocks.

Not only was it easy to kill, the sea cow made an excellent catch. Its hide was big enough to make a kayak twenty feet long and seven and a half feet wide, with enough room for twelve men, and all those who ate its liver gained incredible powers. This particular specimen could no longer be eaten, but with the bounty the governor had promised, they would be able to buy all the delicacies they could ever dream of. The men fall to their knees and start digging.

The sand retreats to reveal the large, thick bones and the sea cow's rugged skull. Yes, this is indeed the kelp-eater, the king of all marine animals, which the governor is so keen to get his hands on. And now the slow, painstaking work begins. They must dig up the bones, but the ground is hard and rocky. They dig at the earth, the sand eats into their fingers and cracks their nails, and they have to soak their aching hands in a stream running down the hillside, but they do not complain, just continue working. They know how an animal is constructed, how to look for bones that have been buried under the sand and mud. After pulling back the sand to reveal the animal in all its splendour, they cannot believe their luck. Everything is intact, every piece of the sea cow, just waiting to be discovered, there among the rocks.

Or rather, almost everything. The only bones they cannot find are the palms and the fingers, but otherwise it's all there, the whole creature there on the rocky shore, and they begin their journey back to Sitka. Their progress is slow. The sea cow's bones are large and long, and they cannot carry all of them at once, but have to row back and forth, one island at a time, slowly transporting the bones along the narrow chain of outcrops, until eventually they catch sight of the town squashed between the sea and the mountains. They seek out an official and ask him to inform the governor that they have what he has asked for.

The official instructs them to leave the bones at the harbour offices. The governor is busy, but he will be informed of this find. However, the men know the Company too well and have brought only the skull. The rest they will deliver only upon receipt of payment, and in this they were very wise indeed. Money and the natives, two concepts that in the minds of the officials do not belong together, but the governor has given explicit instructions regarding the matter: anyone claiming to be in possession of the bones of a sea cow is to be taken directly to the taxidermist. Eventually, the official relents and tells them to speak to Wolff.

The men knock on the taxidermist's door, but it is early in the morning. The sun has just risen across the bay, Wolff is still asleep, and the men must knock for a long while before he wrenches the door open and tells them to go to hell. But when he sees what these men have brought him, his slumber vanishes in an instant.

*

Wolff examines the skeleton and writes up his findings: forty-seven vertebrae, nineteen pairs of ribs, a sternum and a set of shoulder blades, but his hands are trembling, as the governor has been at pains to stress this creature's immeasurable value. Wolff is used to handling birds and deer, but now he has before him a being of whose form he has only a faint understanding, a vague idea of a large, rotund marine animal. He has been ordered to clean the bones and number them. Von Nordmann will have his sea cow, but before that the governor intends to present this rarity to the delegation arriving from St Petersburg, to demonstrate the kind of wonders that this corner of the world still holds.

The delegation will be here soon, leaving Wolff too little time to reconstruct the skeleton in full, but perhaps they can present only the skull, and Wolff gives a decisive nod, though in truth he is hesitant. He knows how to remove a hide from around a body, to stuff it with rags and sawdust to simulate real muscles, but skeletons are not his forte. The remains of the sea cow are old and fragile, this is a very different proposition from bones pulled still moist from a stag. Seagulls, crabs and insects have eaten away the flesh and broken down the cartilage and tendons, while algae, time and the weather have darkened the bones' surface. He must clean them, but he is afraid that they might not survive boiling, and he does not have enough phosphoric acid to bleach them all. He is at a loss, but he knows that if he were to make a single mistake, his wages would not be enough to cover the damage. Here there is no university whose library he can turn to for advice, no master from whom to learn the proper techniques, and he turns the bones in his hands and curses. Never has he longed for the Tierra del Fuego as much as he does right now.

Wolff scrubs the bones with a small brush dipped in water, going over them an inch at a time. He scrapes grains of sand and flecks of algae from the nooks and furrows worn into the bones' surface and cleans them as best he can, but his skills are limited. He knows how to make a deer's bones as white as Greek statues, but these remain darkened though he rubs them until his muscles ache. And his woes do not end there. Usually, he puts the animals together in his workshop on the outskirts of the town, but the governor will not allow the sea cow to leave Kekoor Castle. Many people would like to get their hands on its bones; Wolff too could use the skeleton to finance his next expedition, he could hire an assistant and still have enough money for a life of luxury. The governor trusts no-one, and suspects that the officials and servants will steal from him the minute he looks away, so Wolff is forced to work in Kekoor Castle, where, on top of everything else, he must put up with the governor's sister.

Wolff had imagined that Constance would make way for him, would leave the collection to his care and retire to her room the way a respectable spinster should, but in this he realises he was mistaken. Constance makes sure that he is unable to spend a single moment in the collection without her. She makes sure that she's there to meet him, no matter how early or late he arrives, and has instructed the servants to inform her every time the taxidermist's dishevelled figure begins walking up the steps to the castle. At first, she thought she would be able to continue her work regardless of him, dusting off the animals as though she were still alone, but she finds the sea cow an alluring distraction. If she must put up with Wolff from one day to the next, she might as well make the most of the inconvenience, and she sets her duster and pieces of paper aside and crouches down, picks up a shoulder blade and caresses its surface. She can tell that Wolff would dearly love to forbid her from doing so, but he does not.

Constance runs her fingers along the edge of the bone. She tries to imagine what this creature might have looked like while it was still breathing, but she finds it hard to form an image of a living being from the pile of bones on the floor, so she asks Wolff to find her a picture. But there is only one clumsy sketch of the sea cow in existence, hidden in the pages of Peter Simon Pallas's *Zoographia Rosso-Asiatica*. Pallas is remembered as the first to depict the notion of one creature descending from another as a tree of all known life, and his works presented the world with a total of 220 new species of plant, forty-five previously unseen mammals and seventy-eight new birds, the marvels of the Russian Empire, but Constance flicks impatiently through its pages; today she has no interest in birds or shrews.

Pallas's illustrator is talented indeed. He has drawn the animals skilfully, coloured them in clear, bright shades, but the drawing of the sea cow is very different from the rest. In fact, the difference is so great that it is clear it was drawn by someone else entirely – someone who was not accustomed to producing anatomical drawings. The sea cow has been sketched in nothing but a few trembling lines. The image does not even attempt to conjure up the idea of a creature in its natural habitat, the artist has not tried to create a sense of motion and spirit but has simply depicted his subject objectively in profile and left the sketch uncoloured so that the animal's contours are filled only with the cream of the parchment.

It has been suggested that the image reproduced in Pallas's book is by none other than Plenisner, a topographer on Bering's expedition. Perhaps he sketched the animal in the margins of his report for his own amusement, to remind himself of the creature, but his life-drawing was destined to become the one and only eyewitness sketch of the sea cow to survive to this day. The others were abandoned on the island and lost, left to rot along with Steller's samples, but the topographer's reports were packed for the return journey. It is in among these papers that the image of the sea cow finds its way to St Petersburg, and a century later Pallas, now elevated to the role of professor, publishes it in his own opus.

After this, a great many images of the sea cow are sketched, painted and modelled, images whose artistic merit exceeds Plenisner's jittery pencil strokes, but these have all been completed after the fact, without seeing the creature in the flesh, compiled using only skeletons and the imagination. The fur hunters did not have an artist with them, so the only immortalisation of the sea cow is the topographer's simple drawing in which it resembles a confused potato with a fish's tail.

Constance has at her disposal a figure sketched with a few pencil lines and a set of bones, and she must imagine the rest, but she needs more information to guide her imagination. She wants to learn, and she is thrilled at how thoroughly shocking Wolff finds the idea. She wants to learn the bones' names, to understand the strictures and structures hidden beneath feathers and skin, she wants to hear how guts are removed from a body, eyes from a skull. She wants to know how the sea cow is put together. Wolff is forced to introduce the governor's sister to an animal about which he knows nothing, and all the while she uses him like a dictionary. What is this bone, and that one, and Wolff sighs and thinks of the statue he once saw in a museum when such diversions were within easy reach. He does not usually care for the arts, but that sculpture spoke to him. He stood in front of it and looked on as demure, bare-chested creation revealed itself to the watchful eyes of science, undressing humbly but without shame. Nature's cloak was fashioned from beige marble, her fulsome breasts from even whiter stone, and as he gazed upon it, Wolff understood his calling: the slow, thrilling unveiling of nature's secrets. And now this imbecilic woman wants to unveil it with him! There is something untoward about it, something lewd, a woman undressing another woman, but he cannot refuse, she might complain to her brother the governor, and so Wolff meekly obeys but makes his displeasure plain for all to see.

The sea cow briefly cheers Hampus up. The bones that the Aleuts brought back are a rare piece of good news, and in the evening he joins his family for the first time in a long while. He asks Anna to report on the children: has Annie been behaving, is Otto Edvin's cough improving? Constance comes down to the salon too, and Anna notices how pleased she is to see her sister-in-law. She hardly sees Constance in Sitka, and if it weren't impossible she might imagine herself actually missing her company. She is worried about Hampus. He has begun to suffer from headaches, terrible migraines that make his eyes water and banish sleep and badly needed rest, and at nights Anna lies in bed listening to her husband dragging himself around his study, pacing in a circle like a restless animal. Meanwhile, Constance simply hides herself away with her collection and would rather stare at the bones of a marine mammal than support Anna in her tribulations.

Today, Hampus reads to his family. There are rumours that gold ore has been located in the north, and now he is obsessed with minerals and rocks. He reads from Chambers' geological treatise and enlightens his family regarding the structure and history of the Earth's crust. Anna cannot remember the last time she lost herself in a book. Before coming to Alaska, she used to spend her days reading, but nowadays she can manage no more than a few lines from the Bible or a recipe in a cookbook. As lady of the house, she has no time for novels, and she prays that the children will not inherit her love of music and poetry. A constant, practical mind would be best: a person with such a mind will not suffer upon ending up in a place like this.

Anna has never considered rocks. To her they are dead objects, they are already fully formed and, as such, unchanging, but Hampus reads aloud, Anna listens to Chambers' words, and the geologist shows them how even the smallest pebble in the garden reveals a story of great change. The minerals layered one upon another inside the stone tell of upheavals and cooling magma, of continents pushing against one another and of periods whose sheer length shrinks a human life into insignificance. Anna listens and pictures the animals and plants in their rocky graves, wing bones and the ribs of leaves preserved in layers of sediment as they are pressed deeper and deeper into the earth. She thinks of the dinosaurs she saw at the Crystal Palace, and for the first time she senses why Constance enjoys spending her time surrounded by dead animals, consumed with her catalogues. If so much can be contained within a mere rock, imagine how much must be hidden within a once living creature, a deer or a duck.

Hampus cannot remember the last time he succeeded in anything, but now the bones of the sea cow have found their way to him, and he is filled with a renewed sense of energy and purpose. He has found a lost animal, succeeded in an endeavour many had thought was doomed to failure, so why should he not succeed again? Perhaps the colony can yet be saved, if only he tries hard enough, works hard enough. He intends to present the sea cow to the delegation, for is its discovery not an indication that, given enough time and resources, he is capable of even the most demanding tasks?

He summons Wolff. He needs proper scientific evidence to enhance his presentation, and to this end he has asked the taxidermist to gather information about the sea cow. Wolff steps hesitantly into the study. He can tell that what he knows will not please the governor, but he does as he is told and puts together everything he has learned.

The illustrious Peter Simon Pallas added his description of the sea cow to the list of species found within the empire, though he hesitated to do so. The sea cow had not been seen for almost a century, so Pallas sent his young colleague Martin Sauer in search of these lost mammals. Sauer sailed the northern seas for almost a decade, but even he could not find the sea cows' famed island. Eventually, Sauer reached a grim conclusion: the fur hunters have brought the sea cow to an end. Upon hearing this, the governor is taken aback. Wolff is silent and glances furtively around, but Furuhjelm implores him to continue, and Wolff hurriedly adds how ludicrous he thinks such a claim to be. The governor may take comfort in the fact that Pallas did not believe his assistant either. The scope of his *Zoographia* reflects the scope of the empire, its list of species the empire's grandeur, therefore how could he possibly suggest that the greatest of the animals depicted in his work has been eradicated by the actions of the empire itself? This is a story that Pallas did not wish to tell, so he added the sea cow to the pages of his work and told Sauer to hold his tongue.

However, Sauer did not hold his tongue but published an account of his travels, and inspired by this, the *Encyclopaedia Britannica* dared to print the contested hypothesis that the sea cow had indeed become extinct. It is an extraordinary assertion – that man could be to other species as great a threat as an asteroid or a flood – and when he sees the governor's expression, Wolff stresses that researchers are far from agreed on the matter. In fact, the eminent dinosaur scholar Richard Owens himself refutes the claim as utter nonsense: the account of one incompetent assistant is not enough to upend our understanding of life and death, of man and beast. The governor nods: hardly a coincidence that it was the British who came up with such a claim, they are always more than eager to cast our colony in a bad light, and Wolff laughs along with him.

Furuhjelm thanks the taxidermist for his report, but Wolff does not yet take his leave and remains standing in the study, nervously fidgeting. Furuhjelm is filled with an ominous foreboding. Is there still something he should know about the matter? Wolff curses to himself. Why is he the one who must bring the governor such bad tidings? Why is he not leading an expedition in the Tierra del Fuego, but instead standing in this stuffy study like a schoolboy brought before his master? He pulls himself together and spits it out: Sauer did not hold his tongue, and now he is suggesting that the next creature to meet the fate of the sea cow will be the otter.

Furuhjelm waits until the taxidermist's footsteps have faded down the stairs and holds his head in his hands. As Wolff was speaking, that familiar tingling returned to his temples. Now the pain is throbbing behind his eyes and for a moment he gasps for air like a dying fish. He has sent men to seek out the otters, forced them to scour ever more distant coastlines, ever more inhospitable wilderness, but they have always returned empty-handed, and now he no longer knows where to search, what to do. All he can do is pray that Sauer is mistaken. Did not Linnaeus himself once write that animals are like the tide, at times in short supply in any given place, at others plentiful, but that ultimately the population is stable? This must be true, for if the otters and the walruses do not return, their colony will be doomed.

*

Wolff eventually completes his work. The sea cow's bones have all been measured, cleaned and catalogued. Finally, he can return to his workshop, his birds and pine martens, their familiar bones and hides, forms that he knows and understands. Wolff asks Constance to inform her brother that his wishes have been fulfilled, then he rushes off. He wants to get as far away from Constance and the beast she guards so closely as he can, and heads to the tavern for a well-earned drink.

Constance slumps. She was keen not to show Wolff quite how exhausted she was or how great an effort it required to come to the workshop on bad days when her body was crying out for darkness and sleep, but now she has finally got her collection back, finer than ever before. Von Nordmann will get his sea cow, but until the arrival of the delegation, it will remain here for their amusement. Hampus has asked the carpenter to construct a plinth, and Constance arranges the bones on top of it. The plinth is positioned in the middle of the room so that the other animals look as though they have gathered round the sea cow to admire it, and Constance fetches the collection catalogue and adds the great mammal to the list, writing its name in Swedish, Russian and Latin, careful not to smudge the ink, and in doing so she experiences something warm and heavy, something for which she does not have a name.

She opens the glass cabinets, takes the birds and mammals from their shelves one at a time, first the water birds, the gulls, swans and geese, and only then notices her cold sweat. She is not even close to the mammals. Bad days, one after the other. She closes her eyes and continues, the surf scoter and the blue-winged teal, then the birds of prey, but then she senses a metallic taste on her tongue. She leaves the birds and heads straight for the sea cow, wipes the pock marks gathering dust on the skull.

*

A servant wakes Anna in the night. One word, Constance, and Anna knows. A massive fit has befallen her, and Anna wraps a shawl around her shoulders and hurries to her sister-in-law's side. The sight is every bit as horrific as she had feared. The spasms seem almost to rip her limbs from their sockets, her mouth is frothing, but Anna holds her sister-in-law's head, and her hands are neither sweating nor trembling. She does not know where her fear has gone, but there's no trace of it; when Constance loses consciousness, Anna drops water into her mouth with a spoon, and as the terrified doctor prepares to perform the bloodletting, Anna rolls up her sleeves. She keeps watch over Constance, but Hampus cannot bear to see his sister like this and heads into town, telling them that he will not return until later that evening or perhaps even the following morning. Anna kisses Constance's sweaty brow, sings and prays and feels the girl's racing pulse in her fingertips. The doctor lets her blood again. Constance's lips turn blue, her hands become cold, and in the early morning her life comes to an end.

Anna does not abandon Constance to Sitka's austere, sodden graveyard and the stink of rotting crosses riddled with mould.

No, Constance will be buried somewhere beautiful, lowered into a rich, green grove in the shade of the willows. It is so early in the spring that they cannot find any flowers for the grave, but Anna fills the vases with branches, and when given water they sprout tiny leaves, and they place the branches under Constance's head.

Two weeks have passed, but Anna still sees her sister-in-law, still hears her footsteps behind the closed door of the collection, and she orders a wrought-iron fence to be erected around the grave. At first, she plans to lock the gate – she does not want the Indians to visit the grave and incant their godless words, sing of a raven that flies between the realms of the living and the dead, but she begins to wonder whether the thought of a soul bird might please Constance, her strange, wondrous sister-in-law. She leaves the gate open and weeps for the woman who was always in her way, but who leaves behind an endless grief now that she is gone.

*

Though it is midday, the sky is dim. The sun only barely squeezes between the cloud curtain, and they have had to light the lamps first thing in the morning. Twelve days of unrelenting rain, and Governor Johan Hampus Furuhjelm is standing amid his zoological collection. He has just bidden farewell to the delegation, and all he was able to show the inspectors was a crumbling village in decline and forests devoid of animals. Their report will be damning. He spoke truthfully, presented all the correct figures, though he knows this will not give a favourable impression of his tenure. He also explained that there are rumours that gold has been discovered in the north and says that he believes the earth still contains unknown riches, that one can learn to live alongside the natives. He even suggested that they could commandeer Alaska's great woodlands, start foresting and shipping timber to America, but in St Petersburg people are tired of the colony's constant demands and dwindling returns. The governor stands amid his collection and looks at the sea cow. In the yellow light of the lamp, the creature appears to shimmer quietly, and he places a hand on its forehead and strokes it. So much promise – a creature that was supposed to feed Siberia, a colony that was supposed to produce endless riches – and all that is left of both are some tall tales and a skeleton.

Anna has already ordered clothes for the children for their return journey. She is finally going home where she can live the life she has always dreamed of: five children, a beautiful manor house, and an enviable societal position.

She dies at the respectable age of fifty-eight, surrounded by family and friends, and in that same year Kekoor Castle burns to the ground, taking the governate's collection with it.

A group of polite but nervous men have gathered in the room. Through the door we catch a glimpse of an opulent ballroom, but more important is this study, the mahogany desk and the maps laid out upon it. Hanging from the ceiling are the star-spangled banner of the United States and the two-headed eagle of Russia, and at the left-hand side of the painting a worried-looking man proffers a piece of paper to a self-assured gentleman. The worried-looking man is one Frederick Seward. He has just offered to buy Alaska, and listening to his offer is the Russian diplomat Eduard Andreevich Stoeckl. Stoeckl is about to place his hand on a great atlas, his hand casts a shadow over the north, and the men reach a deal. Russia sells Alaska and the Aleutian Islands to the United States for a total price of $7.2 million, four cents per hectare. After reaching this deal, Stoeckl receives Tzar Alexander II's personal thanks, a significant reward and a pension, and after this he moves to Paris, where he lives a most pleasant life. Seward, however, is the butt of much derision. The deal is nicknamed "Seward's folly" – and what a folly indeed, to buy but snow and ice, a land devoid of furs.

Professor Alexander von Nordmann picks up his letter opener and slices open the envelope. The letter is dated in December, but in Helsinki it is already July, the swallows are nesting in the eaves, swooping down from their nests and flying past his windows. The letter has taken a long time to arrive, but it was well worth the wait. The Governor of Alaska has granted the professor's wish: he has acquired a full skeleton of a Steller's Sea Cow. The governor has sent it to the professor together with some other specimens, reserving space for them aboard the ship of Capt. Lars Krogius, due to arrive in Helsinki in August. The professor reads the letter, closes his eyes for a moment, then instructs his assistant to fetch a bottle of the finest champagne.

List of specimens bequeathed to the Imperial Alexander University in Finland by Johan Hampus Furuhjelm:

- Two skeletons of the white-tailed deer, one male, one female; female removed from the collection on 3rd July 1960, male leathered and stuffed in 1955
- Two North American porcupines, one stuffed, one skeleton (sex unknown)
- One Steller's Sea Lion, stuffed (sex unknown)
- One Dall sheep, stuffed ram, declared missing in 2016
- One mountain goat, stuffed (sex unknown)
- One American marten, male, stuffed, upon arrival erroneously listed as a sable
- One Steller's Sea Cow, skeleton (sex undetermined)

III

Hic locus est ubi mors gaudet succurrere vitae
This is a place where death rejoices in serving life

Inscription on the door of the anatomy hall,
University of Helsinki

*

In recent years, fascination for the natural world has grown, particularly among the younger generations. [...] Many enthusiasts in this field have developed a strong desire to keep and preserve the objects they find in nature [...] How many wanderers, upon snaring a beautiful bird or a small, smooth-coated mammal, wished they had the skills to immortalise this beautiful piece of nature for posterity?

Aarne Hellemaa, *Taxidermy as Hobby and Art*, 1950

60°10'31"N, 24°57'13"E

IMPERIAL ALEXANDER UNIVERSITY

DEPARTMENT OF ANATOMY

PROFESSOR BONSDORFF'S SKELETON COLLECTION

HELSINKI, 1861

Hilda Olson is concentrating on a vertebra. She can feel the gazes on her neck, but shuts them out and focuses on examining the bone. This will be different from her earlier work. She is used to making the small larger, to increasing the size of her subject, until a spider reveals itself in all its beauty, but with this creature there is no need for a microscope. No, now she has to reduce the size of her subject so much that the vertebra will fit onto a single sheet of paper, and she makes the appropriate calculations, searching for just the right scale. The university's drawing master leans over her work, and Olson nods politely, though the situation is distinctly odd. She is used to drawing her subjects in the wild, in forests and meadows, first sketching the landscape before gently sliding the arthropods under the lenses of her microscope. Today, however, she is not in the wetlands of Opukskii but in her anatomy professor's study, surrounded by statues of Antiquity, renowned academics, and dark wood –and even if she can hear the rapid beating of her heart in her ears, she does not let her nerves show, but lowers her pencil to the paper and begins to draw.

The drawing master Magnus von Wright leans over her,

carefully scrutinising the lines she sketches. When Prof. von Nordmann started looking for an illustrator, he asked if he might find himself an assistant among the students at the drawing school, but to his disappointment von Wright could not recommend any of them. They are students, future scientists that he is instructing in the art of seeing, but in the boys' home schooling not enough attention is paid to the artistry of the hand. As artists, they are hapless, unskilled, they step into the drawing hall without knowing how to prepare a canvas or make a stitch in leather, he has to teach them everything, even the most rudimentary skills. If it were anyone else, he might have suggested one of the younger boys, still wet behind the ears, but not for von Nordmann, for he has seen the sketches this great man produced in his youth.

*

In the past, von Nordmann used to illustrate his own research, and his skill and precision were equal to that of even the deftest nature illustrators. His paintings of fish garnered praise from all those who saw them, but the print run was small because the professor only used the most valuable paints in his illustrations. The volume became so expensive that universities could not afford to acquire it for their libraries, but those who had seen the images lauded the professor's skill. His works were made all the more special by the fact that he painted the fish while they were alive. A dead fish lies on the researcher's slab, flat and lifeless, its fins retracted, though the very word animal means a creature that is animated! It is a living, breathing thing, and he documented his fish as they moved and lived, though this entailed taking an aquarium everywhere he went. In arduous terrain, the glass vessel had to be carried by his assistants, so that vibrations felt as the carriage's wheels drove over stones and roots did not cause its fragile glass walls to crack. Maintaining an aquarium in the wilderness required care, but when a fish plopped into its waters, von Nordmann forgot all the trouble involved.

Von Nordmann was the foremost nature illustrator of his day, but time has dimmed the lenses in his eyes. Initially, he noticed that he needed a little more light while drawing and scheduled his work for the brightest hours of the day. Whose eyes do not grow tired from time to time, staring at fish scales in the dusk? But gradually the details began to evade him even in the brightest of lights, and his illustrations became sloppy. One scale becomes smudged into the next, and before long he must admit the truth: he needs another pair of eyes to help him.

But where can he possibly find such an artist, someone with a mastery of observation who can also withstand the discomfort of research expeditions? This is a problem indeed, and he asks his colleagues to spread the word: the professor of zoology and botany is looking for an assistant with excellent illustration skills. He interviews a number of young men recommended to him, but none of them meets his requirements. He cannot imagine spending weeks travelling with anyone who waxes lyrical about Darwin's madcap theories or who out of sheer carelessness draws the wrong number of eyes on a lynx spider.

None of them is good enough, for none of them is Arthur.

His son was a promising illustrator. Arthur had a good eye for nature, its little idiosyncrasies and the minute differences between species, and though his greatest passion was for birds, he was an avid illustrator of beetles and harvestmen too. With a little practice, he would have developed into an artist every bit as skilled as his father, perhaps even more so. The professor looks at the canvas above his desk, Arthur's painting of the Eurasian nuthatch. He refuses to take it down, though every time he looks at it, it feels as though the world were about to run out of air.

Arthur had travelled to Siberia to conduct an investigation into the local birds. Von Nordmann was waiting for a parcel containing his son's drawings, perhaps revealing fascinating new discoveries, but instead a courier brought the most dreadful news to his door. A silly, drunken argument over a gambling debt, and now his son is gone, murdered in a Siberian tavern. He inspects the boys turning up at his study and cannot imagine any of them taking Arthur's place.

He was about to give up, but then his luck took a turn for the better. He was invited to dinner – a most tedious, inconsequential affair – and he'd even considered staying at home, spending the evening cataloguing the specimens that had found their way into the corners of his study, but his daughter forced him to attend. It would do her dear father a world of good to spend time not just with insects and mosses but with members of his own species too. He agreed, reluctantly, but Matilda's commands proved fortuitous indeed, as at dinner he was seated next to none other than Zacharias Topelius, general secretary of the Finnish Art Society. The professor bemoaned his situation to Topelius, complained of how difficult it was to find an assistant who knew how to hold a pencil and whose head had not been filled with nonsense. To his great surprise, Topelius breaks into a smile: he knows just the right illustrator.

The Art Society's competition recently gave a prize to a young lady with an exceptionally deft hand. Miss Hilda Olson's winning entry was such a detailed copy of Löfgren's painting *Girl with Flowers in Hand* that the painter could not tell his own work from the copy, and to Topelius's delight, he can vouch not only for Miss Olson's skills but for her character too. The Olson family used to spend their summers in the same area as the Topelius family, and Miss Olson herself used to play with his own children. She was a quiet, serious child who never complained about wet petticoats if it started raining but thanked the Lord for taking care of her thirsty plants.

A woman for an assistant. A remarkable thought, though not entirely out of the question, and von Nordmann is happy to admit that in the art of illustration women's work is often more precise and detailed than that of their male colleagues. His daughters are all skilled with a pencil and paintbrush, and if the world were different, their gifts would have carried them into careers as nature illustrators just as Arthur's should have done. It wasn't an altogether impossible thought. Of course, the subjects of women's paintings are often different to those of scientists, but if Miss Olson could paint children and flowers, there was nothing to suggest she could not turn her attention to insects too.

*

The botanical gardens in Helsinki can be a bleak, barren place on January mornings: the pathways lined with hesitant young trees, hay blackened by the winter jutting here and there through the snow. Von Nordmann takes in the view in front of him and sighs. Helsinki is certainly no Yalta, though Miss Olson does not appear to notice the Gardens' modesty and studies the greenhouses most keenly. The professor notes her demeanour. If the lady so wishes, we can visit the palm house, he begins, but only if you do not care too much for your attire: in the frozen weather, the gardeners have to keep a fire burning in the boiler rooms around the clock, lest the palms and vines shrivel and shed their leaves. The hot smoke is then channelled into the palm house through a complex system of flues. This ingenious system creates artificial tropical conditions within the glass walls, keeping the plants alive through the cold, dark winter months, but the system is not perfect. The palms remain alive, but anyone visiting them must put up with the smoke, which makes one's eyes sting and leaves an unpleasant smell on one's clothes. Olson glances at her simple skirt and laughs in amusement: she would be only too happy to see the palms.

The professor shows her the Gardens' rarities, their exotic, long-leaved plants, the like of which she has never seen before, and after walking around the greenhouses they retire indoors for a hot drink. She stirs honey into her tea and savours its sweetness. Her own honey ran out before Christmas, and she cannot afford to buy any more. Work has been hard to come by, and since Topelius passed on the message that the professor might have some work for her, she has been sitting at home waiting for word to come.

Word eventually did come, and here she is, sitting on the professor's couch with a cup in her hands. Von Nordmann tells her of his plans to develop the Gardens, he talks about the weather and Olson tells him about her family and work. The professor's tone is jovial, but she notes how carefully he weighs up her every word, and she does her best to give a good impression. Yes, she did study at the drawing school, but it is hard to find work as an artist. She has designed a few board games for Edlund's publishing house, which he sells in his bookshop, and which earn her a modest income, but for the most part she makes a living by teaching English and translating short stories and articles from England and the United States. She learned the language from her father, who was a sea captain and spoke many tongues, a skill that he passed on to his children.

When talking about her father, her voice quavers slightly, but she continues, explains that her skills as an artist come from him too. Captain Olson understood not only ships but beauty too, and when he returned from his journeys, he showed the children sketches of far-off towns and lands in his notebook. While her father was away, the family hung his drawings on the wall in the children's room and imagined themselves on mountainsides, dreamed of his life in bustling squares. In return, they drew their father pictures of events in the home, and when she heard the familiar steps coming from the porch, Hilda would run to meet him, notebook in hand, and show him drawings of the kittens that had been born under the stairs and the birds nesting in the eaves.

Von Nordmann likes the fact that Miss Olson sits so calmly. Many would be nervous at an invitation to see the professor, but she looks him in the eye and answers his questions directly and without any fuss. It makes the professor think of his own wife. Anna Helena's father was a jeweller, a man whose clients were among the highest-ranking noblemen in the land. He too learned the ways of the nobility and gave his children an excellent education: Anna Helena understood etiquette, she dressed impeccably and spoke more languages than many a scientist or man of letters, though there are always those to whose mind no amount of style or learning can ever remove the shame of being a craftsman's daughter. But von Nordmann did not allow such condescension to disturb him. Anna Helena knew she was a better wife to her husband than any finicky noblewoman who would have had conniptions at the thought of a long and bothersome expedition, and when her shoe sank into the mud on an unknown path in the Crimea, they giggled like children, and von Nordmann knew that he had taken the only possible woman as his wife.

Anna Helena's father taught her to recognise precious rocks and the wonders hidden within them, and she saw the same beauty in her husband's work too. She was not repelled by the contents of fish guts, and when von Nordmann showed her the *Diplozoon paradoxum* she gripped his hand, and he knew that she understood what he was trying to say.

The *Diplozoon paradoxum* is an extraordinary creature. The flatworm begins its life alone, but once it finds a mate, the functions of the two individuals become conjoined. From that moment, they continue their lives as one, fusing together so that separation is no longer possible. When one dies, the other cannot go on living, and when Anna Helena left this world, von Nordmann lay down in his bed and waited for death to come. He remained there for four days and four nights, but on the morning of the fifth day there came a knock at the door, and to his astonishment he realised he was still alive. A confused courier stood timidly at the threshold, apologised for disturbing the house during this period of mourning, but explained that von Nordmann's publisher had asked him to deliver the plates he had promised, and he got up and, admonishing himself, began to mix his paints: as a husband, he was not worthy of the flatworm.

Anna Helena's last wish was that their children be brought back to Finland. To that end, von Nordmann accepted the invitation that the Imperial Alexander University had extended many times and took up the professorship in zoology and botany, turned his back on the university libraries and scientific palaces of the great metropolises and returned to Finland. Never again will he be happy, of that he is certain, but this notwithstanding, life in Helsinki is a pleasant surprise. He is given the practical, comfortable house designed by Engels in the grounds of the botanical gardens in Kaisaniemi, where he can escape his grief by delving into work. Some thirty years earlier, the great fire of Turku destroyed the work of previous generations, and he must begin putting his collections together from scratch, laying the foundations upon which to build a new garden. He undertakes fundraising trips, writes to his colleagues and acquires seeds and saplings, classifies and catalogues them, and gazing into his microscope, he momentarily forgets all about human sorrows.

Miss Olson places her cup on the saucer, and the clink of porcelain brings von Nordmann back to the salon. He has to force himself to shake off his woes – these days they seem to stalk him like a needy cat – but she takes another sip of tea and allows the professor to compose himself. She recognises her own sadness in his eyes, allows him to linger in his memories, and does the same.

When Hilda realised that she wanted to draw, to study, to learn how to construct images and to mix colours, her father was not unduly shocked, he did not start talking about the benefits of marriage or a woman's duty, and instead he paid for her art studies. But alas he did not live to witness Hilda's joy when she was accepted into the drawing school. Tuberculosis cut his life short, too quickly and yet too slowly, and she tries to banish the images that begin to appear in her mind, his skeletal, emaciated figure, the sheets spattered with blood.

The pause in their conversation has lasted too long. Miss Olson's attention is inevitably drawn to the silence, but she does not glance furtively around, trying to find an exit or a way back to their original conversation, and instead remains in her chair, calm and alert. The moment does not feel awkward and, grateful for this, von Nordmann decides to get to the point.

What does Miss Olson think about spiders? The professor's expression is expectant, and she realises that the question is an important one, that much depends on her answer, but she has never given spiders much thought. She dusts their webs from her room, but their life and character are a mystery to her. Eventually, she simply states that all God's creatures are interesting and beautiful. This appears to suffice, as the professor stands up and beckons for her to follow him.

The professor's study smells of mahogany and plants pressed between sheets of paper. Lining the walls is a series of glass cabinets containing insect charts and catalogues of plants, and hanging above them are brightly coloured maps with the winding routes of expeditions marked across the continents. A room full of the strange and fascinating, the weird and wonderful, but Olson's attention is drawn to a contraption on the desk. The professor notes her gaze and is thrilled: his microscope is truly the finest in the realm.

As a young researcher, von Nordmann financed his studies by illustrating other people's work. He examined the creatures that researchers had brought back from their expeditions and replicated them through the glass walls of preserving jars, trying to bring their faded colours back to life. The Russian ambassador himself commissioned some illustrations from him, and when he saw von Nordmann's plates, von Alopaeus was so thrilled that he gave the young researcher a very rare gift indeed.

The Chevalier microscope is a miraculous contraption, a device whose mirrors have been sanded and smoothed by a renowned family of Parisian opticians to make them thinner and sharper than was ever thought possible. Von Nordmann could scarce believe his luck: he had managed to acquire the *Microscope Achromatique Universel*. He placed a perch under the lenses, and all of a sudden he saw other animals within this animal, worms, shellfish and spores clinging to the gills and to the inside of the guts, and whenever he opened up a fish, the microscope revealed new, tiny beings, nature within nature. Von Nordmann picked up his pen, started writing and later published a study featuring illustrations with a level of detail that had never been seen before, revealing to his readers the wonders of the egg pouches of water fleas, the double-tailed spores of the *Henneguya zschokkei* endoparasite and the hooks of the *Diplozoon paradoxum*, which it uses to latch onto its host's gills.

But time is cruel. Living matter degrades, and retinas are no exception. Von Nordmann turns the cogs and cleans the mirrors to bring his subjects into focus, but the images remain blurred. The colours become fainter all the while, and before long the eyepiece shows nothing but a thick, soupy fog. The microscopic world disappears, scarpers out of reach, but he cannot stop now, he has taken it upon himself to classify all the spiders in Finland, to present to the world the arthropods hiding in the forests and ditches and their tiny, extraordinary bodies. There is much to do, but try as he might, the fog will not lift.

The brass tubes of the *Microscope Achromatique Universel*

gleam in the pale afternoon light, and Hilda Olson steps closer inquisitively. She admires the device, it is like a jewel or a strange statue, and when the professor asks whether she would like to try it out, she does not hesitate but sits down and waits for instructions. Von Nordmann shows her how to adjust the magnification and prepares a sample for her. He places a dish under the eyepiece, and Miss Olson grips the dial and turns.

She looks at the body of the money spider. The professor lets her get used to the sight, allows her to enjoy the moment when small becomes large for the first time, but he cannot contain himself for long and fetches some drawing equipment. Miss Olson nods and picks up the pencil, looks into the microscope then at the paper in turn, and von Nordmann watches as she sketches the spinnerets and the chelicerae, traces the marbling across the spider's abdomen, its tiny dark eyes, and when she lowers her pencil, every last cilium is just as it should be.

Von Nordmann has Miss Olson's grey irises and sharp pupils at his disposal, and not a moment too soon. A scintillating letter is waiting on his desk. The botanist Christian von Steven has written, saying that he is ready to bequeath his personal plant collection to the Imperial Alexander University. Von Nordmann has seen von Steven's study, its flower presses and leather-bound trunks containing the vascular plants of entire continents, almost one hundred thousand specimens in total, another scientist's life's work now just within reach. All he has to do is fetch the specimens and transport them to Finland, a long and expensive trip, but he has already applied for funding and plans to put the time to good use by examining the spiders of the Ukraine and southern Russia on the way. In order to do so, he will need the help of an illustrator. They must set off very soon, lest somebody else snatch the opportunity from under their noses, and as he watches the money spider come into view on the paper, he puts his doubts to one side. He comes up with a contract, and to his relief Miss Olson's salary requirements are eminently reasonable. All in all, the day has surpassed all his expectations, and when he goes to bed that evening and waits for grief to return, it does not, and he falls asleep with a grin on his face as he thinks of all the consternation his new assistant will surely cause.

History is replete with scientists who have enlisted the help of a wife or daughter, but to take on an unknown woman as an assistant – that is quite something. If von Nordmann were less renowned, many might think his decision unseemly, but his reputation is pre-eminent enough to keep wagging tongues at bay, and any conversations along the corridors of the university are held only in whispers. Meanwhile, the professor's daughters are left shaking their heads. They love their father dearly, but at times he is inappropriate to the point of exasperation, though the melancholy he has suffered since Arthur's death would leave even the most discerning of men susceptible to reckless decisions. But what's done is done, and now they can do nothing more than show him that the family supports him in his decision.

The professor's daughters invite Miss Olson for a visit. Matilda and Maria await the meeting in a mood of distinct trepidation, but when Miss Olson steps through the door, their burden is lightened. She is dressed in a practical black frock and greets the professor's daughters courteously but amiably. Miss Olson, too, is nervous about the meeting. If they wanted to, the professor's daughters could make her life very difficult and might even implore their father to rescind his offer. Miss Olson greets the women cordially, nervously fidgeting with her skirt.

By the time they have drunk their coffee, she has won the daughters over. She is a down-to-earth woman, there is no doubt about her honour, and it turns out that she is exceptionally good company too. She gives Matilda's children a game she has designed, and as Matilda examines the playing board, Hilda notices that she has the same joviality as her father. Maria's horses get stuck at Foul-Mile Hill. She has to return to the start of the board, but the die favours Matilda. She climbs aboard a steam ship, travels all the way to Tornio and is the first to get back to Helsinki. Matilda is giddy with excitement as she moves her piece over the finish line. Hilda congratulates her on her victory, and they agree to another round once she returns from her expedition.

Work takes Miss Olson and von Nordmann to Yekaterinoslav and Simferopol, then through Serbia, Turkey, Bulgaria, Moldova and Odesa, though they are less interested in cities and cathedrals than in what can be found beneath the rocks and leaves. Von Nordmann teaches Miss Olson to find the webs of garden spiders and the crab spiders hiding in among flower petals. First, they shut these arthropods into glass jars, then Miss Olson places the jars in a holder attached to her easel and waits. Initially, the spider cowers at the bottom of the jar, gathers its legs beneath its body and plays dead, but when no predators appear it becomes curious, stretches out its legs and starts exploring the walls of its glass prison. And at that moment, Miss Olson makes a quick sketch. She records the spider's shape and colours, reproduces any patterning, and once the drawing is ready, she removes the lid, fills the jar with ethanol, and the arthropod's life comes to an end.

In the evening, she draws the spiders for a second time. She pulls the deceased creature from the liquid and pins it out in something approximating a natural position, just as the professor taught her. Von Nordmann sets up his microscope, and Miss Olson uses it to draw another image, this time a detailed anatomical enlargement. She draws the tubular heart that only a moment ago was pushing colourless blood through microscopic arteries, she sketches the differences between the sexes, the palpal bulbs and the epigyna, and when the sketch is ready, she colours it using the drawing she made from the live animal as a model. The dead and the living merge into a single, detailed image on the paper, and through her eyes von Nordmann can once again see the spider in all its grandeur.

*

The sun is slowly setting, dyeing the hillsides overlooking the garden. Miss Olson tries to commit the view to memory. Surely this is what Paradise is like, five hundred fruit trees, vineyards as far as the eye can see, thousands upon thousands of flowers. Von

Steven's garden is the most beautiful thing she has ever seen. The elderly botanist smiles broadly upon hearing her praise. When von Steven first arrived at Nikita, it was a small scrap of a village, but he has conducted one sample-gathering expedition after another. His rickety carriage and shabby horse are a familiar sight to the local villagers, who gently tease him about his dishevelled appearance. He does not own a proper pair of boots, though even the lowliest farmhand has such things, but the villagers' laughter merely warms him, and he leaves them to gather their harvest in peace. He has collected the rarest and most fascinating plants from Russia and the Caucasus, and now his own garden is beyond compare.

Von Steven's garden and manor house have become a Mecca and a guesthouse for botanists, and now he finally has the pleasure of hosting his old, long-awaited friend. He invites von Nordmann and his assistant for a delicious dinner in his arboretum, and after the meal von Nordmann shows his friend the spider drawings from their journey. Von Steven admires the images, and when he hears that it was Miss Olson who painted them, he proposes a toast to her, and the professor raises his glass too. Hilda shakes her head in amusement, and she is filled with a warm, bubbling joy.

She has loved every moment of this journey. For once, she can concentrate solely on her drawings; the professor has bought her a quire of thick rag paper that will not curl at the edges or yellow in the sunshine, a set of excellent watercolours, brushes with tips of pine-marten fur, making her work an absolute pleasure. More importantly, her paintings are useful. With her brushes, she can make visible that which normally goes unnoticed, and she is proud at the notion that with her help the professor will add another small stitch to the great fabric of science.

It has been a hot day. The warmth lingers under the trees, and though it has been a long journey, von Nordmann and Miss Olson are in no hurry to retire for the evening. If one goes to bed too early here, the heat will make anyone longing for sleep toss and turn in their sheets, so they wait until the evening has cooled, sit beneath the trees and enjoy some chilled drinks. Von Steven shares some of the latest botanical advances with von Nordmann, and as he is talking, a spider lowers itself from a branch and lands on his jacket shoulder. He asks Miss Olson to identify the species, and to her satisfaction she correctly identifies it as the European garden spider; she remembers copying its white marbling onto paper. Von Steven congratulates von Nordmann on his assistant, then turns to Miss Olson. The young lady knows her spiders, but does she know how the arthropods first came into being? Miss Olson shakes her head, and von Steven assumes a comfortable position and begins his story.

Arachne was the finest weaver in the land. Her tapestries were so exquisite that word of her skills reached the gods themselves. However, Minerva, the goddess of crafts, was envious that a mortal should receive such praise and challenged the young woman to a weaving competition. The two weave, but even the gods cannot find a single flaw in Arachne's tapestry. However, this skill does not bring her happiness, as the goddess will not settle for a draw and attacks the young weaver. Arachne is shocked at the goddess's wrath, and when she sees the girl's sadness, Minerva relents. She saves Arachne from death and gives her eight limbs with which to weave her fabrics. Now she can weave perfect creations in peace until the end of time, remaining invisible and innominate, hidden in dark corners and the notches of trees, for such is the price of boastfulness, the fate of all those who seek a position that is not theirs to take.

*

As the expedition nears its end, von Nordmann is content. He will return with von Steven's plants and his impressive collection of spiders, a collection including several species hitherto unknown to science. The collaboration with Miss Olson has exceeded all his expectations. His assistant has shown herself to be a most excellent microscopic illustrator, and perhaps more surprisingly, a skilled collector too. Miss Olson can survive in the field – better than the professor, in fact, as von Nordmann is plagued by an injury he sustained in childhood. She clambers across the rocks alongside him, swatting away mosquitoes, and shows exceptional aptitude for learning. Watching the way she stretches out the many-jointed limbs of the wasp spider and pins them to the chart, he makes up his mind: the expedition is coming to an end, but their collaboration will continue. Next they will document the spiders of the forests, bogs and shores of Finland, many of which are still waiting to be named.

*

Upon returning from the Crimea, the professor grants Miss Olson a short holiday. Von Nordmann must go through the specimens he took from von Steven and write up the notes from their trip, so Miss Olson travels back to Ostrobothnia to visit her sister, but even on holiday she cannot forget about the spiders. She is used to training her eyes on arthropods, and suddenly she sees them everywhere. In the past, she was able to work at her desk without paying any attention to the creatures buzzing about, but now there is no place where she cannot find a spider. She learns to sense the domestic house spider under her washstand and to spot the zebra spider wandering across the ceiling. This is her favourite spider, a lively, nimble creature that upon seeing her raises its upper body and shakes its limbs, as though waving at her, and as her sister looks on in amazement, she carries jars of soapy water out into the garden. In the morning, she collects her rewards, the spiders and insects that have crawled into her slippery jar overnight. Upon coming across a species that she does not recognise, she submerses it in ethanol, wraps the test tubes in cotton wool and sends her discoveries to the professor: *here for your consideration are some of the species I encountered, which I was unable to identify and which I thought you may appreciate.*

In total, Hilda Olson paints more than four hundred spiders for the professor, four hundred reproductions of arthropods drawn with microscopic precision, and von Nordmann is so happy with his assistant that he makes the bold gesture of naming one of these species not only after himself but after Miss Olson too. The creature is christened *Olsonia pilifera Nordmann*, a long-limbed testament to their collaboration. It later transpires that the same spider has in fact already been named elsewhere, and the name that von Nordmann gave it does not live on, but Miss Olson does not know this and immortalises the creature on paper with jubilant strokes of the brush.

*

Miss Olson and von Nordmann usually meet in the grounds of the botanical gardens, but today the professor has asked her to come to the university. He has been waiting for the arrival of this animal for a long time – a magnificent, long-awaited beast of the sea – so Miss Olson climbs the stone steps up to the university's main building and walks in between the white columns framing the entrance. The janitor is taken aback at the sight of a young lady stepping through the doors and asks quite what she is doing there. The University of Zürich has recently taken a revolutionary step in opening some of their programmes to women, but as yet there are no womenfolk gracing the corridors of the Imperial Alexander University. Here the only feminine presence is the alabaster Artemis standing in the foyer. Miss Olson was prepared for this befuddlement, and she tries to remain calm and composed, though the stares of the passing students make her distinctly uncomfortable. She is unaccustomed to drawing attention to herself, but now she stands out from the crowd like a bright-red velvet mite in a collection of spiders. She takes a breath and explains that she is here at the express request of the professor of botany and zoology, and with that the janitor swallows his objections and shows her to Bonsdorff's collections. Miss Olson steps inside, and the befuddlement follows with her. Of course, everyone has already heard about von Nordmann's assistant – after they set off for the Crimea, the university gossips spoke of little else – but seeing her here in the flesh is another matter entirely, and upon seeing how satisfied von Nordmann looks watching Bonsdorff wonder how best to greet the woman who has just entered his study, the professor of anatomy cannot escape the thought that his old friend might be playing some kind of prank on him.

"Now, look at this, Miss Olson! Here we have a creature whose anatomical survey is sure to arouse international interest!" Von Nordmann dashes from one bone to the next, and Miss Olson looks at the pieces of the animal laid out on the floor: ribs, vertebrae and, on the table, a skull in two parts: the crown and the jawbone lying next to each other. She looks at the bones, but they mean nothing to her. She is not acquainted with skeletons, nor does she understand anything about this animal other than that it is enormous, but she does not let this trouble her. She is an illustrator. She does not need to know; all she has to do is see, her skills are in the art of looking closely and reproducing, so she remains unperturbed at the creature's strangeness and begins instead to scrutinise its bones, assessing their texture and examining the joins along the skull.

The sea cow is a magnificent specimen, though few researchers will ever find themselves up here in the coldest, remotest corner of Europe. But the postal service works, and von Nordmann has already agreed to give a lecture on the animal and for this lecture to be published in a large print edition. Scientists may not be able to view his specimen in person, so the specimen must travel to them in printed form, and for this, precise drawings of the bones are essential. For a moment, von Nordmann considers drawing them himself. Even his eyes are good enough to reproduce the sea cow, but he is short of time. He only received the bones yesterday, but he has already agreed to hold his lecture at the beginning of the semester, in only three weeks' time, when the animal will become the focus of everyone's unwavering attention. His time will be spent writing, so let Miss Olson do the drawings.

Von Nordmann wants the lecture hall to be so full that the slowest will be left without a seat, but for that he needs more than learned words. He needs drawings too, the whole animal, so that those enthusiastic souls who have gathered to hear his lecture can leave the lecture hall and walk to the collections to witness his story for themselves. He and Miss Olson must reconstruct the sea cow for people to see, put the bones together, and when the master in charge of the bone collection complains about the short notice, the professor dismisses him with a wave of the hand. Surely von Wright understands that what they have before them is a quite unique creature, and if two professors of zoology and their assistants cannot put one vertebrate together in three weeks, something is surely amiss.

*

When selecting a new home for the sea cow, Bonsdorff's collection is by no means the only option. For though Helsinki is a small, provincial town, the bickering among its scientific community rivals that of any seat of learning. This is why Helsinki contains not one but three natural history collections, and von Nordmann must choose between them. Clearly, he cannot keep the animal for himself. He does not have a bone collection of his own, and though he briefly toys with the idea of reconstructing the skeleton in his salon for his own amusement, the notion soon evaporates. The sea cow is too significant to serve as one man's private entertainment.

The collection of the Imperial Alexander University is out of the question. The masterful illustrator von Wright, who was appointed the collection's first official curator, could barely conceal his astonishment upon seeing the state of the exhibits. They have been cared for in the shoddiest manner, with assorted remains and hides piled up in corners and left at the mercy of time and the beetles, and von Nordmann has no intention of leaving his treasure in a dusty warehouse alongside untidy heaps of unidentified bones.

The collections of the Flora and Fauna Society, meanwhile, are of the highest order – after all, von Nordmann oversaw their curation himself – but these days he does not even deign to spit in their direction. He was once an esteemed member of the society, at one point even its chairman, until he attracted the ire of the young Fennomans, who scrutinised his expeditions, his choice of guest lecturers, and the bursaries he awarded. They accused him of being too cosmopolitan and neglecting the needs of the fatherland. Von Nordmann cannot understand their stance: roaches and spiders do not have a fatherland, bones and flesh do not demand one take a position on acts of russification, and blood flows through the veins of a Russian scientist just as it does a Swede. But the young continued their polemics, and eventually the professor left the annual meeting, slamming the door behind him. The scoundrels of the Flora Society will not get their hands on his skeleton.

And thus, the sea cow shall go to his friend Bonsdorff, the professor of anatomy. Bonsdorff and von Nordmann first became acquainted while on research expeditions. They have spent numerous fascinating hours exploring what can be found under a stone and inside rotten trees. Few people think of insects as anything more than a nuisance, but the two naturalists are united by their appreciation of the beauty of a web spinner or an angel insect. They pluck these buzzing, humming creatures up with their tweezers, and when a mosquito sinks its slender proboscis into their skin, they do not raise their other hand to squash it but watch its body, pulsing red, then let a second mosquito land next to the first and compare their wings and the disposition of their legs.

Professor of anatomy Evert Julius Bonsdorff examines von Nordmann's beast contentedly. A glorious gift indeed, and by way of thanks, he invites von Nordmann for an exquisite dinner. They too have their differences: von Nordmann believes that in order to fully understand an animal one must examine it alive, observe a spider in its web, a plant in blossom. Naturally, it is impossible to keep alive all the natural life one studies, and his rooms too are filled with pressed flowers and insects pinned to charts in meticulous order, but from the safety of its aquarium, a fish can tell us things that will be missed once it is lying on the anatomist's slab. Only by watching the living creature can one divine, for instance, how the common dragonet uses its fanlike fins, how its eyes dart from side to side, how the gills open and close, but Bonsdorff shakes his head. The oxygen flowing through an animal's cells does not change its structure, and with scalpel in hand he becomes more intimately acquainted with an animal than any poet or illustrator, even if they were to draw a fish's each and every scale. The two men have their differences, but these they discuss in a brotherly, scholarly manner, and if a debate threatens to escalate into a full-blown argument, they refill their glasses of cognac, change the subject and talk instead about the young and their fanciful notions.

Von Nordmann berates the hotheads of the Flora Society and Bonsdorff complains about his nephew, Johan Axel. The boy is destined to become an excellent scientist, and it is clear that once he graduates from the lyceum, he will go on to read zoology at the university. Bonsdorff has already presented the boy to von Nordmann, and the professor thought him a pleasant and knowledgeable young man. But nowadays he seems enamoured with Darwin's theories and likes to hold forth to his uncle about the origin of species, though Bonsdorff is careful not to take a stance on the Englishman's hypotheses.

It is true that a scientist should always be prepared to question the theories of his predecessors. Even the greatest scientific mind is fallible: in his valedictory lecture before his retirement, the great Linnaeus himself continued to advance the notion that swallows hibernate underwater, slumbering in nests beneath the ice until the sun makes them shoot up to the surface like nimble fish, though anyone who has cut open a swallow's breast can see that its lungs were designed to breathe air. Yet another reason a scientist ought not to try to imagine the past or the future but should instead concentrate on what he can see with his own eyes, trusting only that which can be proven and placed under a microscope. Bonsdorff urges his nephew to be judicious in his opinions. One should not be taken in by every new-fangled idea or anger one's professors by clinging to an assertion that may yet prove nothing but wishful thinking, a young man's folly and ruin.

Bonsdorff is careful in his opinions, but when something appears right, he does not hesitate. He is the first anatomist at the university to give his students dissection assignments. Doctors studying under his tutelage must learn to identify a damaged lung, a fatty liver and an exhausted heart. His methods meet with scepticism among the older generation. A gentleman should not get his hands dirty but should trust in tradition, he should read the conclusions of his forebears and base his understanding on scientific treatises and educated debate. In the beginning, perhaps he too thought like this, he wrote his doctoral thesis on natural philosophy and contemplated the nature of life and organisms.

After gaining his doctorate, he set off for Europe to continue his studies, and it was there that he encountered a new kind of science, the rigorous, reassuring principles of empiricism. At the

Karolinska Institute, he sat down in front of a microscope, and the concept of life began to open up to him. It was a universe of interlinked cells and membranes, nerves, muscles and blood vessels that a scientist can press between two plates of glass. He picked up his scalpel and charted the circulatory system of toads and examined the complex nervous system of rays.

Eventually, Bonsdorff secured a professorship in Helsinki. It was only a matter of time. He comes from a family in which having a professorship is as natural as breathing: one may choose the field, but an academic career is a foregone conclusion, and after taking up his position he imposed a set of reforms, introduced dissection into the curriculum and founded the department of comparative anatomy. Every self-respecting university has a bone collection, but the Imperial Alexander University was still lacking one, so Bonsdorff acquired the skeletons of a horse and a snake and opened a bony exhibition with which to enthral and instruct his students. Now they can walk through the history of the animal kingdom and learn how life is structured, and how those structures repeat throughout creation.

Bonsdorff carefully follows European scientific developments, and when the great anatomists added human skeletons to their collections, he did the same. If we can learn more about animals by comparing their bones, should not the human bone tell us something about its bearer? Bonsdorff did not intend to lag behind his colleagues, and to this end he entered into a curious correspondence: an Egyptian scholar sent him the skull of a local farmer, and Bonsdorff posted him a Finnish skull in return. Two anatomists, sending each other skulls wrapped in brown paper, rattling their way across continents, unbeknownst to their couriers. Acquiring such skulls nonetheless presents challenges for the researcher. People are unwilling to give up the heads of their loved ones to be displayed in the glass cabinets of a university, but luckily there are the poor, the Sámi, the vagrants and criminals, those whose heads nobody would miss or ask after, and curator von Wright even notes the deceased's misdemeanours on their foreheads: drunkard, adulterer, murderer, Lappish.

The crowning glory of Bonsdorff's skull collection is undoubtedly the head of the Vesivehmaa Ripper, the serial killer Juhani Aataminpoika. If a man's evil accumulates in his skull, what better skull to put on display than that of a man nicknamed the Executioner, a man who killed twelve innocent women and who is said to have gorged on the hearts of their unborn babies? If any skull can show small bumps that indicate a propensity for cruelty, then surely it must be that of a man who could commit such atrocities. But Bonsdorff is not interested in the constitution of people's souls, but rather in the neurological messages passing through their nervous system. He has no time to examine the skulls, but he amasses a collection for future scholars, and now the skull of the Executioner resides there among all the others, staring at students from its shelf with empty eyes, reminding them that behind every face is a shared structure of thick, white bone, waiting to be revealed.

*

Hilda Olson finds the skulls gathered on the shelves hideous, but she tries not to think about the people to whom they once belonged and instead focuses her attention on the task at hand. She has never worked with bones or mammals before, and to her eyes the remains that the professor has laid out in the room look disproportionate and alien. She is more used to spiders, to tiny creatures that only give up their secrets once they are placed under the ocular lens, but this animal's bones are large and thick, and she is unsure quite where to start. What does von Nordmann want her to do? Is there some kind of etiquette when it comes to drawing a skeleton, an order in which the bones should be committed to paper, an unspoken rule that is clear to anatomists but unknown to the daughter of a sea captain? She does not know where to start, but neither does she wish to show them her hesitation. She has already seen Bonsdorff's sceptical glances, von Wright's expectant expression, but von Nordmann does not leave her high and dry, and hands her a sheet of paper. He has come up with a list of the images he wants: first she is to draw the skull from above, then from beneath and behind, making sure to include the internal structures of the head. After this, she is to draw the principal vertebrae from different angles, then move on to the shoulder blades, the bones of the arms, the sternum and ribs.

A concentrated murmur ripples through Bonsdorff's study. Von Wright sketches a suitable frame to hold the skeleton, Hacklin the janitor writes a list of all the materials they will need, calculates the prices and begins carrying in tools and sacks of gypsum. Von Nordmann and Bonsdorff examine the bones and compare observations, discuss qualities specific to this species, and Miss Olson sits down by the window and starts to draw.

Von Nordmann has placed the sea cow's skull on the table in front of her. He has turned it upside down, and she examines it, the vessel that once contained the sea cow's brain, eyes and fleshy tongue. Now all that is left is an empty space between the bones, and she considers the best way to represent the skull's joins and porous surfaces.

Be it a spider or a bone, she examines her subjects like a sculpture or a bust to be reproduced, for were she to think of the creature itself, she would have to think of its death too, the traps, the nets, ropes and bullets, and then the anatomy professor's collection would seem an unfathomable, cruel mausoleum. But as she walks behind von Nordmann through Bonsdorff's exhibits, she does not think of a living human or creature but imagines herself wandering through an illustrated encyclopaedia without returning to the moment when within this rib cage, now held together with bolts, was once a heart, still beating, and a set of lungs filling with air.

Von Nordmann is disappointed. Furuhjelm claimed to have found a complete skeleton, but this set of bones is incomplete: it is missing its hands and fingers. Half of each front limb is also missing, and if they were to erect the skeleton in its current state, it would look as though it were groping at the air with blunt, inelegant stumps. It is true that Steller wrote in his notes that the sea cow lacked bones in its hands, but this claim has since been dismissed. All marine mammals have fingerbones hidden inside their flippers. This is the case for whales, seals and porpoises, so why would the sea cow be an exception? It is easier to assume the naturalist must have been mistaken. It would hardly be surprising if a man on the verge of starvation had not noticed the slender bones hidden inside the sea cow's rigid flippers, and his equipment and the prevailing conditions left much to be desired. The sea cow's fingers have not been preserved, but that doesn't mean they did not exist. The lack of these bones is down to the ineptness of those who discovered the skeleton, and carpenters and preparators across Europe begin to imagine what the sea cow's limbs must have been like. The sea cow is imagined with long fingers, short fingers, broad hands, small hands, and von Nordmann recalls the specimen he saw in Cuvier's collection in Paris, its skeleton adorned with fists cast from gypsum, and he asks von Wright to examine Bonsdorff's collection of marine mammals, seals and walruses, and to design the sea cow some beautiful wooden prostheses.

The carpenter fashions a pair of hands, which the professors attach to the sea cow's elbows, inserting pieces of wood to replace the decomposed cartilage so that the creature's barrel-like chest opens up in front of them in all its beauty. The sight is nothing short of majestic. Hacklin the janitor has built a brass trellis to support the skeleton. A single skeleton usually requires only one or two brass pipes underneath it, but this one requires five supporting pillars, so heavy are its bones, so long its chain of vertebrae. Upon these pillars, the professors assemble the sea cow, tying the spine together with strong metal wire and attaching the head to the atlas vertebra. Miss Olson soon completes her own work too. All that is missing is the final image, the complete skeleton viewed from the side, but for this she must wait until the scientists have erected the animal in full. She has spent three weeks staring at various parts of the sea cow, concentrating her efforts on the vertebrae and the ribs, and now the parts all come together and the whole animal comes into view in front of her, one piece at a time.

With that, her work is done. She collects all the drawings she has made and takes them to the professor for approval. Von Nordmann goes through the sketches and nods with satisfaction. He truly has an excellent assistant, as skilled with bones as she is with insects, and he sends the sketches off to the publisher. But there is a problem. Miss Olson has chosen to draw the complete sea cow at a scale of 1:15, but this means the image is too big to fit on the page. There is no time to make another drawing, so the printers attach a larger page at the end of the book on which they reproduce the drawing of the complete sea cow, and this page is then folded neatly inside. Von Nordmann smiles to himself. He could not have imagined a better way to remind readers of the sheer magnitude of the animal they are reading about, so large that it does not fit onto the pages of a book – even after being considerably shrunk. Now scholars from far-off lands can read his presentation and flick through the skeleton like a book. First the individual parts, the vertebrae, the ribs and skull, then finally they can unfold the page at the back and see the sea cow in full, spread the image out in front of them, imagine its scale and admire the enormous, beautiful creature that Hilda Olson has drawn for them.

In his presentation of the sea cow, von Nordmann introduced the Finnish scientific community to the notion of human-driven extinction. Unlike so many others, he believed Sauer's account of what had happened. To von Nordmann, the idea of species disappearing was familiar and natural. In his younger days, he had run the botanical gardens in Odesa, and during his tenure a fascinating system of caves was discovered underneath the city. Von Nordmann ventured deep into the earth, crawling along damp, dusty tunnels, and these caves, which had lain untouched for millennia, revealed thousands of animal bones. And what animals they were! He uncovered one creature after another and carried the remains of these forgotten beasts up to the surface, the long-toothed skulls of cave hyenas, lions and bears. He published a study on the fossils of the Ukraine, remnants of species that had long since ceased to exist, and he cannot think of any reason why the possibility of such destruction should be limited to prehistory. Nature does not change its habits. He does not hold out hope. As he sees it, the sea cow is gone forever, just like the mammoth and the woolly rhinoceros before it.

But many people are not yet ready to believe that human beings could drive another species to extinction. A full three decades after von Nordmann's study was published, Rudyard Kipling includes in The Jungle Book *a story about a white seal that finds a sea cow on a secret island, a safe haven where the two have fled to avoid human contact. Not an altogether unreasonable idea. In what remains of the isthmus of Beringia, the mammoth survives long after its conspecifics have headed elsewhere, and while humans erect the Pyramids, the woolly mammoth continues to graze, cut off on its islands. The sea cow lives on in its sanctuary for millennia after the mammoths are gone, but gradually it becomes clear that man has discovered their island, that their hiding place was revealed the moment Bering and his crew set their boots in the sand of the blue foxes' island.*

Hilda Olson is walking along one of the sandy paths running through the botanical gardens. The burnet roses are in full bloom, and she enjoys the fragrances, the hum of bumblebees visiting the flowers. She has been putting the finishing touches to her most recent sketches of spiders native to the Åland Islands and has come to the gardens to bring the professor her work, but it is not the housekeeper who opens the door but the professor's daughter. She can see the news on Matilda's face before she even opens her mouth.

The professor had spent the evening organising a newly acquired collection of insects – the beetles gathered by Count Mannerheim – and examining their chitinous shells, but he had complained of tiredness and went to bed early. In the morning, the housekeeper found him in bed, already cold. His heart had taken its final beat. Hilda looks up at an elm swaying in the wind, and Matilda takes the folder of drawings from her friend's arms, lest her tears smudge the pictures of the arthropods.

Their collaboration lasted six years and took in four hundred and fifty-four spiders and one sea cow, but now von Nordmann has gone the way of all living creatures.

*

Rain lashes down from the sky. It has been a cold, wet summer, the potatoes and crops are rotting in the ground and the earth gives off a sweet, sickly smell. Hilda Olson walks until the city turns to fields, the fields to thickets, and there are no people in sight. She heads in among the trees and kneels down. The rain has filled her trap. Muddy water spills over the edges, but there are a few shrivelled creatures at the bottom, and these she plucks out and stores. She collects the spiders and submerges them in ethanol, though she is unsure who will look at her discoveries now. The professor is gone, and she will be unable to take part in the expeditions of the naturalists' society or play any part in putting together their exhibitions. She is not a naturalist, and she will never become one. She can no longer draw her own discoveries, not like before. The Chevalier microscope has been gifted to Bonsdorff's nephew, Johan Axel Palmén. Now he can examine these tiny beings under the lens, and she will be left with the inadequate powers of the naked eye.

After von Nordmann's death, she grieves for her mentor, for the friend he had become. She takes to visiting Matilda on Sundays, and together they reminisce about her wise, cheerful father. At times, Hilda tells Matilda about her own father and misses both men in equal measure, vehemently, viscerally. She is in mourning, but she would like to continue drawing, and asks Bonsdorff to spread the word to his colleagues that she is available and keen to work for them. But the naturalists would rather hire the young men from von Wright's drawing school as their assistants. With young men, they need not consider the mores of social etiquette nor worry that their assistant will suddenly marry.

The naturalists have no use for her, so she offers her services as a map sketcher and an illustrator for magazines and publishers, but even then nobody responds.

Perhaps she will simply have to make a name for herself as an artist, she thinks, and she decides to send her most beautiful spiders to an exhibition of the Art Society. Her drawings are accepted, but in the exhibition hall a terrible disappointment awaits her. Her work has been hidden away in the furthest corner of the room in light so bad that it cannot possibly do justice to the detail of her spiders, and to add insult to injury she cannot find her name in the exhibition catalogue. She studies the brochure in bewilderment until she finds the professor's name: *Councillor of State v. Nordmann*. The Society has credited her drawings to the professor, and she marches out of the exhibition without speaking to a single patron.

Hilda does not find work as an illustrator and does not marry, but her landlord still demands the rent, so she accepts a position writing up notes for the magistrate. Now she spends her days reproducing letters, original documents, builders' certificates, passports and debt notices. The work is monotonous and the pay dismal, but even she must eat, though she yearns to go back to her work as an illustrator so much that it hurts. But she does not come from a wealthy family, she has no benefactor to take care of her living costs, so she grits her teeth and writes up one document after another.

She spends the daytime copying receipts from the city's debt payment plans, and in the evenings she feels as though nothing has any meaning anymore. She muddles up her words, and the hand holding her pen aches. At times like this, she retrieves her spiders. This she does almost daily, regardless of the weather and the smell of damp laundry that fills her small room when her clothes get wet in the rain. She does this because, kneeling down by her trap, she can imagine that when she returns there will a letter from von Nordmann waiting for her in the letterbox: *Miss Olson, pack your things, we are going on a trip!*

She has finished copying the city's tax-base report, delivered the papers to the magistrate and picked up a new pile of papers covered in the officials' smudged shorthand. The wad of paper feels heavy in her bag, leaving her in low spirits. When she gets home, she checks her letterbox. She has stopped waiting for a response to her many applications, but sometimes she receives a letter from her siblings with news of her sister's children and her brothers' greetings from all corners of the world. They have set off to sea, just like their father, and Hilda reads their letters with a pang of envy. Only a moment ago, she too could write to them about her exciting adventures in faraway lands, but what could she possibly tell her family now? Her life has become small and tedious. No expeditions, no research trips to Åland and Lapland nor journeys to Odesa and the Crimea, just endless documents and her small, stuffy room. But one day she opens the letterbox lid, and her gloom evaporates in an instant.

In Finland, her applications had been dismissed out of hand, but she did not give in. She switched language and sent examples of her work around Europe. Now, waiting for her in the letterbox is a letter with a stamp bearing the imposing profile of Queen Victoria. She tears open the envelope, and after reading the words she hurries indoors, sits down at her desk without even taking off her coat, and picks up her pen: yes, yes, yes, she will take the job!

*

Flowers seem to burst through the image. Hilda has positioned the leaves and petals of the meadow flowers to form a most pleasing pattern. She has visited Kew Gardens and Epping Forest, drawing her surroundings, sketching snowdrops and enchanter's nightshade, and now she has transferred everything she has learned onto wallpaper. It took her a while to find the right rhythm, but now the plants have settled, and she is pleased with the result. The work as a wallpaper designer allows her to spend her days drawing once again, and though she sometimes yearns for the past, her microscope and the strict, systematic nature of scientific work, she cannot complain. And she has found herself a good friend in London. Miss Witherwick creates wallpaper designs too, and now the two share both a job and a room, and on weekends they pack up their easels and head out to the countryside.

The image is ready, and before Hilda sends it off to be transferred onto printing plates and entered into the machine that will reproduce her design on wallpaper, she makes one last-minute addition. On the leaf of the flower at the very edge of the pattern, she draws a tiny spider, so tiny that it will barely be noticed unless one were to examine the image very carefully indeed. But she knows it is there. A minuscule creature on a primrose leaf, a creature very nearly named after her. She moves on to the next one, arranges the plants and animals into images that people will use to decorate the walls of their salons without ever learning the name of the young lady who helped enrich their quotidian lives.

Professor of anatomy Evert Bonsdorff sits pensively amid his collections and loosens his collar. He has just seen his friend and colleague off on his final journey, looked on as von Nordmann was lowered into the earth, and he instinctively thinks about his own death. He is an anatomist and knows his own fate all too well: soon, his cells will divide for the last time, the carefully balanced system of molecules will begin to break down and his writings will be forgotten. This is how science works. New generations make new discoveries, write new studies, and it won't be long before nobody will even remember his ground-breaking study of the human sympathetic nervous system. But he has something that time cannot erode. His body may turn to dust and his writings age, but his bones will remain and carry his name forever.

Bonsdorff leaves his bone collection to the university, but there is one condition in his will: the collection must never be merged with those of any other museum or society. Bonsdorff's nervous system stops sending messages, blood ceases to circulate in his veins, but his anatomical museum will endure and will move into a new, beautiful space. The medical students of the future will need modern classrooms in which to observe autopsies and practise their procedures, and on the hill at Siltavuorenpenger a grand, new building is opened, the eggshell-blue Athena. The building contains microscope laboratories, morgues and a chapel where the dead can be blessed before their bodies are committed to the service of science. In time, Bonsdorff's collection of skeletons makes its way to Athena too.

Bones are all that is left of the sea cow too. Some of them find their way to Paris. Cuvier has erected a sea cow skeleton in his museum, as part of the great march of creation. Visitors think they are seeing one sea cow, a whole being, but this is in fact not one but many sea cows, assembled from the pieces found on the shores of Bering Island: a female's head on a male's shoulders, bones from the entire herd making up the spine. As such, it is still a rare and precious sight, one of only fourteen composite sea cows, put together in museums like enormous jigsaw puzzles. In addition to these, there are seven incomplete Steller's Sea Cows languishing in the drawers and cabinets of universities, twenty-seven skulls, fifteen ribs, seven shoulders, ten ulnas, eight shoulder blades, thirteen lower jaws, forty-one assorted vertebrae, one sternum and a radius, some skull bones and the row of teeth that Steller managed to smuggle off the island. And, most valuable of all, three complete skeletons of Steller's Sea Cow: one in Kyiv, one in Moscow and the third in Prof. Bonsdorff's collection in Helsinki.

The Helsinki sea cow is assembled in Athena, where it joins a group of skeletons left to teach the living. It is placed above a glass cabinet containing a row of other marine mammals: the ringed seal, the grey seal and the common seal, pinnipeds one after the other, frozen inside a glass coffin. The sea cow floats above its smaller cousins, its wooden hands outstretched like a stocky patron saint that the medical students must run past as they hurry to the autopsy room.

The years pass. Old disagreements are forgotten, and researchers begin to wonder why a city the size of Helsinki has a full three natural history collections. The university and the Flora and Fauna Society are the first to find each other. The hides, bones and insects of these two collections are brought together, creating the Museum of Zoology. Initially, the specimens were pieced together within the walls of the university, but the department of zoology did not have any exhibition spaces of its own, and the animals were stored as best as could be. The collections were scattered, with one animal here, another there, but in the 1920s the university acquired a whole residential block on Arkadiankatu. The purchase included the Alexander Lyceum, a large neo-Baroque building that the animals will soon have to themselves.

Crowds gather to behold a magnificent sight. Giraffes, elephants and lions on the back of trucks, travelling through the city to their new home, but Bonsdorff's collection does not join the others. The weight of his last will and testament can still be felt, and when the other animals begin to take their leave, his skeletons remain obstinately in place. The Steller's Sea Cow stays at Siltavuorenpenger, but the medical students no longer study animals, they do not compare species to learn about the structures hidden within them. Now they concentrate their efforts on humans, they cut open a body, weigh its heart and liver, and Bonsdorff's museum turns from a place of learning to a curiosity taking up space that could be put to better use. And once ninety years have passed, nobody remembers the demands laid out in his will.

The doctors will not miss all those dead animals, but the curators at the Museum of Zoology are ecstatic. In terms of sheer scope, Bonsdorff's collection is a significant addition to the museum's collection, but its breadth creates another problem: the professor had amassed a thousand skeletons belonging to almost six hundred species. The rarest and most fascinating of these the museum plans to display for the public to admire – but where? The museum occupies a small space, and the walls of its exhibition rooms are already lined with dioramas. There is no room, so they will have to invent some. And so, the ballroom on the second level of the building is split in two. A concrete floor is constructed across its width, and with that the museum acquires a new floor dedicated to bones.

Moving the collection is a beautiful, tiresome spectacle. The curators offload one animal after another from the trucks: a humpback whale, a giraffe and a tiger, and one vehicle even comes bearing the faded skulls of one thousand five hundred human beings, which the museum staff hide in the attic, confused and embarrassed. Up there, the skulls can resume their eternal slumber, hidden in their boxes, their crimes still scrawled across their foreheads. But the staff's embarrassment is quickly forgotten, as the next truck arrives with the most hotly anticipated of all the specimens, and with that, Steller's Sea Cow finally arrives at the natural history museum.

The sea cow is put on display in pride of place. It is a rarity in the collection, an enormous discovery of world renown, destined to become the star of the exhibition, but before this it must be put together once again. The sea cow was first assembled almost a century earlier. Its bones need care and maintenance, its wooden limbs and cartilage have shrunk and cracked in the cold, dry air of the university corridors. The skeleton must be taken apart and put together again, and this task is given to a man with fingers whose dexterity is unrivalled.

60°10'16"N, 24°55'52"E

MUSEUM OF ZOOLOGY

HELSINKI

1950S

John Grönvall has spent all day painting canvasses, sketching mountains and fells, capturing the winter light behind the willow grouse and Arctic foxes. At six o'clock, he rinses his brushes and hangs his overalls on the coat stand, gives his colleagues a nod and takes the steps up to his lodgings, a small room above the exhibition halls in the Museum of Zoology. But once home, he doesn't open a book or put his feet up, but pulls on his coat, hurries out into the street and jumps on a tram.

He rides all the way to Munkkiniemi. He takes a shortcut through the park at the manor house. In the summer, the gardens are beautiful, but now the plants have wilted, the greenery replaced with a flat wasteland offering no protection from the wind blowing in across the sea. Grönvall quickens his step, pulls his coat tighter. By the time he arrives at the door of the oology museum, the sun has dipped behind the horizon, making the trees in the yard cast long shadows over him, but the lights in the magnate's window glow bright, as always. He doesn't know when Kreuger ever sleeps. He can't see Kreuger in the window, but out of habit he waves at it before taking the keys from his pocket, then steps inside and into the dim, its odour of wood and metal.

The darkness in the oology museum isn't the soft, gentle half-light that the sunset leaves behind: this is an eternal, impenetrable night. The space was designed to store birds' eggs, and the only windows in the room are narrow slits at the top of the walls. Building regulations wouldn't allow an entirely windowless space, so small hatches were added to the walls, but they have been covered from the inside to make sure sunlight cannot get inside and destroy the museum's collections. To an egg collector, the sun is the greatest enemy of all. In a matter of days, a blackbird's egg, laid in among the hay, will lose its beguiling colour, the blue will fade and sunlight will singe the dotted patterning from the shells' surface – but here they are safe.

Sensation gradually returns to Grönvall's fingers, blue from the cold, the blood tingling as it forces its way through his contracted veins. He flicks the switch, and an electric light reveals the glass cabinets running across the room, the sketches of birds displayed on the rafters and the bureaus leaning against the walls containing a great and magnificent treasure that the average passer-by will never see.

If this were any other evening, Grönvall would walk straight to the bureaus, pull out a drawer and check the condition of the specimens inside it, decide whether to change the cotton-wool padding for fresh, check whether dust has begun to harden on the surface of the shells, but today he heads directly to his workshop, for the magnate has sent word: their hotly anticipated delivery has finally arrived.

The egg is oval, a creamy off-white, its shell dappled with streaks and spots that remind him of Japanese ink sketches, but this work of art wasn't drawn with a brush held in a human hand but by pigments secreted in the bird's fallopian tubes that the auk's body pressed into the calcium shell one hundred and fifty years ago, as the egg popped out of the bird and into the world.

The precise location of the rugged North Atlantic outcrop upon which the egg in front of him was laid, and the identity of the collector who climbed in among the rocks to claim it, remain a mystery. History has forgotten what happened before the egg was placed on the table at a London auction house and Viscount de Barde raised his hand. The known provenance of this egg begins at the moment when it became private property, as the auctioneer's gavel came down on the table in the Year of our Lord 1795.

Now that very same egg is lying in a box on Grönvall's desk, but a hundred and fifty years ago it was the happy nobleman who held it in his hands. Viscount de Barde is thrilled at his purchase, though the price rose higher than he would have liked. The great auk's eggs are valuable indeed because they are things of such rare beauty, some with dark spots, others with wavy lines, each of them unique. Auk's eggs are fascinating in their own right, and the auk itself is a fascinating creature, a strange bird whose body, standing three feet tall, features atrophied limbs, more like flippers than wings, meaning that the auk doesn't fly but swims instead, and its Welsh name *pen gwyn,* "white head", gradually gave rise to the standard name for the black-and-white inhabitants of Antarctica. There has been a shortage of auk's eggs recently, the birds have retreated to ever more remote islands, and the prices have gone through the roof, but de Barde raises his hand irrespective. He wants this egg because it is so beautiful, and de Barde isn't just a collector; he is a renowned painter too. He has resolved to visually record the contents of his natural history collection, and to this end he fills canvases with arrangements of minerals, conch shells and vases from Antiquity, and in the corner of one of his paintings depicting the avian world, he immortalises the auk's egg.

In de Barde's painting, the auk's egg rests under various stuffed birds, leaning against the breathtaking eggs of the cassowary and the ostrich, but soon after completing the canvas, the viscount shakes off his mortal coil, and his collection is acquired by the natural history museum of Boulogne. And because de Barde had the extraordinary good fortune to own not one, not two but three great auk eggs, the museum is willing to barter and exchange one of the eggs for an ostrich skin. The ostrich or "camel crane" is delivered to the museum by one Thomas Henry Potts, the son of an arms manufacturer who is more interested in birds and lizards than in calibres and gunpowder. He bequeaths the museum an ostrich, accepting an auk's egg as payment, but Potts cannot enjoy his acquisition for long as, shortly after sealing the deal, he leaves England and settles in New Zealand. There he can forget the stink of the arms factory and his father's hopes that he might one day take it over, and instead devote himself to the study of nature, though alas he is forced to leave his collection behind.

And so the egg finds itself on an auctioneer's table once again, and this time it is Lord Garvagh who bids the highest. Grönvall shudders with empathy as he thinks of Lord Garvagh's footman. Perhaps he was dusting his master's collection, and this was why he lifted the egg from its velvet cushion. Perhaps the footman wanted to examine it against the light filtering in through the library window – this miniature work of art, shaped like a pear – and for a brief moment he understood the folly that had made the nobleman pay the price of a house for a single egg, but as he recalled the egg's value, he rushed to return it to its rightful place.

It's as though he sees the accident before it happens. First, he walks in the wrong direction. The effect is evident before the cause, and the footman sees the egg rolling out of his hand long before the lid of the glass cabinet slips from his fingers, he watches it falling through the air and witnesses the moment its fragile calcium shell strikes the lacquered, hardwood floor.

From this moment onwards, the egg is known for this man's clumsiness. History has forgotten the bird that laid this egg and the name of the man who plucked it from its nest, but it will not forget the hands that let it slip. The egg becomes known as Lord Garvagh's Footman's Egg, and the footman lost his job because of it. We don't know what happened to him after he was fired, but we can be sure he didn't come away with a glowing recommendation. The loss he caused is immeasurable, for while this particular egg travelled between the collections of three men, the species that laid it departed this world for good.

There was a time when the great auk dotted the shores around the North Atlantic. It was a tasty bird, its feathers made plump pillows, its body was so oily that it burned like a lantern, and where there was a shortage of wood, a canny fisherman would set an auk ablaze on the fire. Fishing and coastal communities had used the auk and its eggs for food through the centuries, until a new continent was discovered, the miraculous Americas, making longer and more difficult sea journeys necessary. Crossing the Atlantic required great stores of provisions, and this great wingless bird was easy prey: in his memoirs, the explorer Jacques Cartier mentions that, in barely the space of half an hour, an expedition off Newfoundland succeeded in hunting so many auks that they needed two longboats to carry their carcasses.

But these days of plenty did not last forever. After a few hundred years of crossing the Atlantic, the great auk is already a rarity, and this is when collectors become interested in the auk and its eggs. Curators begin to compete with fishermen for the few birds that remain. The auk lays only one egg every summer, and if that egg ends up in the hands of a poacher, the bird will leave its nest and return to the sea without any offspring. In 1844, a group of fishermen come across a pair of auks on a small island off the Icelandic coast. They wring the delicious birds' necks, and with that the auks are gone, so abruptly that not a single naturalist has a chance to publish a comprehensive study of the species, and suddenly nobody can remember how the auk called out to its young.

The great auk joins the sea cow in that unenviable group of species extinguished by human hands, and even if, by some miracle, the footman could repay Lord Garvagh the sum he had paid for the egg, that too would be cold comfort. No amount of gold can recreate the egg of an extinct bird, and Lord Garvagh kneels on the floor and gathers up the scattered fragments, swallowing back the tears and rage.

The egg in front of Grönvall is cracked. Someone has tried to repair it, but the work is so cack-handed that, rather than hide what happened, the repair job serves only to emphasise the accident that once befell the egg. Time has yellowed the glue used to put the pieces back together. The shell's surface is smeared in thick adhesive, suggesting that the conservator summoned by Lord Garvagh wasn't used to restoring eggs. Few people are, as putting eggs back together is a troublesome job requiring careful fingers, steady hands and endless reserves of patience, all qualities that this particular conservator clearly lacked, and after the accident the egg loses most of its value. Nonetheless, it still attracts interest on the market as the great auk left behind only seventy-five eggs, all blown empty, a finite corpus over which collectors can outbid each other, and as prices rise, even the footman's egg finds a buyer.

The industrial magnate Ragnar Kreuger, a most enthusiastic collector of rare eggs, finally acquires one of those seventy-five specimens for his collection. What a purchase! One hundred and seventy-five pounds sterling for the egg of an extinct bird, whereas a great auk's egg in pristine condition recently achieved the dizzying price of $180,000 at auction. Kreuger might even have paid such an amount, but the Americans got there first, and he settles for the footman's egg, and while rival collectors might scoff at his purchase, Kreuger's smile does not fade, for in his employ he has a man who knows how to make a broken egg immaculate once again.

Kreuger began by buying up the most significant Finnish egg collections. Soon he had acquired examples of all domestic species, their beautiful, fragile eggs, though he doesn't stop there, but picks up the bird atlas, lists the species still missing from his collection, and sends letters to the relevant collectors and merchants. His collection begins to grow, but he is a busy man. He acquires more eggs but doesn't have the time to get his acquisitions in order. He must make water flow beneath the city, design drainage systems and filtration plants, oversee extensive infrastructure projects around the country and the world. He might not have time, but he certainly has plenty of money, and this he uses to buy even more birds' eggs, and his drawers and cabinets fill with evidence of trees scaled, swamps traversed, jungles conquered. The shelves sag with parcels sent from all corners of the globe, their contents still waiting to be catalogued: he needs a curator for his collection, and he wants the best that money can buy.

Kreuger writes to the ornithological association to ask, who is the best egg collector and conservator in the business? The secretary does not hesitate: when it comes to restoring eggs, the preparator John Grönvall is second to none. The Museum of Zoology hired him to paint dioramas and mend equipment, but it soon transpires that his true calling lies in restoring delicate specimens. He has an excellent eye and precise hands. He can take birds worn away over the decades and return the gleam to their feathers, the yellow hue to a blackbird's beak, and when it comes to working with brittle eggshells, he is more skilled than anyone else.

Grönvall sits in the oology museum and inspects the egg of this extinct creature. He imagines the bird that laid it, the curious northern penguin, and a sadness descends upon him. Might the auk have been saved if the collectors had stopped for a moment to think about why the birds' numbers were dwindling? But the disappearance of one bird doesn't arouse much interest. It is true that bird species die out in every corner of the globe – the great auk on the shores of Europe, Steller's spectacled cormorant in the Bering Sea – but collectors don't seem concerned, one swallow does not a summer make, the great flightless birds were exceptions, a melancholy anomaly in a thriving world of birds, and the hunters and collectors carry on their work without a care in the world.

Collecting rare eggs is a gentleman's pursuit, a refined pastime through the annals of natural history. Generations of schoolmasters have taught children to find and revere eggshells, and the ranks of eminent egg collectors continue to swell, for few can walk past an egg resting in its nest without admiration and a desire to possess it. But collectors very quickly tick off the most common species. Then their attention turns to rarities, birds that live in the wilderness and avoid human contact, birds whose nesting places are a closely guarded secret. They forget about gulls and thrushes. They want to acquire the eggs of gyrfalcons and snowy owls, auks and tropical parrots, and they are prepared to pay good money for them, and where there is money, there is always someone willing to sell. Farmers and hunters scale remote promontories and climb high into the boughs of trees, then deliver the eggs to the middlemen, and auctioneers sell the nobility happiness plucked from a nest. In the farmer's hand, the egg becomes a currency, food for his hungry children, while in the gentlemen's salons carpenters build cabinets to house the wonders of the avian world. The collections grow, and the harder it becomes to find a gyrfalcon's egg, the more collectors are willing to pay.

Over time, the first notes of discord begin to sound – does the choir of birds sound fainter in the spring, do flocks of migratory birds in the autumn look smaller, thinner, maybe boys shouldn't be taught how to find their nests – but people laugh at such concerns, do you really think the quick fingers of a few rascals can drive a species to extinction, and catalogues of ever greater selections of birds' eggs continue to fall through the letterboxes of those for whom money is no object.

Eventually, the birds disappear, which brings a tear to the eye of even the most nonchalant watchers of the skies. The passenger pigeon was deemed to be the most abundant bird in America, perhaps in the whole world. You will have heard the stories: a flock of passenger pigeons might take fourteen hours to pass, even an amateur would be able to spear a dozen of them, while a skilled hunter could take out up to sixty birds with a single shot, and three and a half thousand birds could end up in the hunter's nets in a single session. What a banquet, what a bacchanal! But then such feasts come to an end. The last wild passenger pigeon is shot dead in Illinois on a rainy day in November 1901, and suddenly the skies are empty, a supposedly infinite bird has been hunted to extinction.

The passenger pigeon is gone, and the discord escalates. If

a bird like that can disappear, are any of them safe? Nature has its limits, and people's blitheness is slowly replaced with fears of a time of scarcity, of dwindling reserves, but the egg market continues to rattle along regardless. For traders, the idea that the age of plenty may soon be coming to an end is the best possible news: the rarer the species, the more they can ask, and prices for auk's eggs and fragments of the sea cow's bones continue to rise. In Finland, hunters and collectors shrug their shoulders – surely we're nothing compared to the insatiable Americans – but gradually the evidence becomes irrefutable: the birds of the north are disappearing too, and it isn't fate or disease that is claiming them but the greedy hand of man, and confronted with this fact is none other than the preparator John Grönvall.

*

John sketches the horizon in his jotter. It is his and Gio's turn to be lazy. Frecko and Harald are taking care of steering the boat, and Gio has a jotter in his lap too. All four brothers are skilled illustrators, competing with one another to be the best, watching to see which of them can make the finest drawing of the birds and plants in the yard, though the winner is rarely clear. Gio's pictures are the most beautiful, John's the most accurate, and at some point Frecko gives up and turns his attention to photography, gets his hands on a large, heavy machine and records light on glass, but today they are not competing. They have set out early in the morning, gathering up their equipment as soon as the sun peered above the horizon and heading down to the shore. The brothers' belongings are heavy, but their minds are light. School is closed, their father is at sea and their mother spends all day washing guests' backs at the bathhouse, it is summer, and they have a boat; they are free. The wind catches their sails, Gio starts to sing, his voice mingling with the calls of the seagulls.

Their destination is Aspskär, a cluster of four islands, a miniature world out in the open water. They choose Aspskär because it is home to an old fishing hut that Estonian fishermen once built to offer protection from the elements. Nowadays, the hut is nothing but a battered old shack, but it will give them shelter for the night, and they have brought timber to mend the new holes that winter has left in the roof. After a little bit of renovation, the hut will provide them with some perfectly decent lodgings, and when rough winds whistle through the walls, they will huddle under their blankets, light the storm lanterns and boil water for tea, and nothing could be more perfect.

They approach the island, and razorbills greet their boat. The birds land amid the waves with a squawk, and the boys note down their numbers. They are adept at identifying the species living on the island, razorbills, great cormorants, black guillemots, nimble skuas, they learn their Latin names and test one another on them, and as summer draws on, the birds get to know them too. The first time the boys step ashore, they take flight, swoop above the boys' heads, trying to draw their attention away from the fledglings waddling among the rocks, but they leave the nests and the young in peace, and soon the birds learn not to fear them.

On their excursions, they only ever shoot a few birds and gather a few eggs. The four mostly live on fish and the provisions they have brought with them, preserves and crispbread, and any birds they shoot, they use most carefully. They keep the skins, and during the long winter months they use their prey for practice – every self-respecting artist should know how to reconstruct a bird – arranging a frame under the feathers to imitate a living creature. And when the sea is cold and the birds have flown away, they sketch the cormorants and seagulls posing on their windowsill. It is the only way to see a bird up close. No living winged creature would allow an artist near enough to draw the feather patterns around the beak or the streaks running along the sides.

All four of them have learned how to collect and blow eggs at school, but when it comes to these finds, John is more competent and diligent than anyone else, and when Harald throws away a Eurasian oystercatcher egg after it cracked when he was trying to drill a hole in it, John picks up the pieces and patiently puts them together again, restoring the specimen to its former glory. He joins the fragments together with a set of pincers, a magnifying glass and endless reserves of patience, and once the fragile jigsaw is finally ready, he hides the cracks where two pieces have been joined together. There is no glue in the world quite the same colour as the oystercatcher's brown eggs, but John mixes colours together until he finds just the right hue, so that his handiwork can no longer be distinguished from nature's own perfection.

The boat glides closer to the island's shore, and their

excitement is great. They have been waiting for this day since the last time they left Aspskär: their first summer's day on the island. They carefully steer their boat towards land and tie the ropes to the rings sunk into the rock. The weather is glorious: a south-easterly wind pushes scum towards the shoreline, the ryegrass sways in the breeze and the chive flowers gleam against the stones. A day like this will give John enough energy to carry him through the black winter mornings; but now, as he stands on the rocks along the shoreline, happiness will not come. They haven't had time to count the nests, but they can see right away that there are only a handful, fewer with every visit. The island should be full of sounds, squawks and feathers, but now there are only a couple of nervous seagulls swooping above them. John runs his shoe back and forth across the bullet shells left scattered on the ground. Brass scratches against rock.

Fishermen have always hunted birds, gathered eggs for their pans and feathers to pad their coats. Local crofters aren't allowed to hunt on private landowners' grounds, but if it's only a spot of shooting, the gamekeepers tend to look the other way. Now the gamekeepers are gone too. The lords of the manor move to the cities and sell off their land, and suddenly anyone can get their hands on a motorboat and head out to the islands with a gleaming new rifle. Aspskär was always renowned for the abundance of its bird life, and now that abundance has attracted the hunters. The results are appalling. They count the remaining birds, and the numbers committed to their jotters make for sombre reading. Worse still, their island is no exception. More and more hunters have discovered the easy prey on these islands, and with each passing autumn fewer fledglings take flight from these rugged outcrops.

They return from the island quiet and downcast. John is sitting in the kitchen, fresh migratory statistics from the ornithological association in his hands. He looks at the numbers, then glances up at the stuffed birds on the windowsill, the great cormorant he immortalised and Gio's guillemot, and places his cup on the table. The coffee has turned bitter in his mouth. Frecko invites him out for a spot of fishing, but he shakes his head and concentrates on his plans, and when his brothers return with a pike, he beckons them into the kitchen. These last few days John has been quieter than usual, spent his time alone, thinking, rummaging in boxes, but now he picks up a beautiful black bound folder bearing the ominous words *Bird Protection on Aspskär* and places it on the table.

That evening, they form an association. John has no need to coax his brothers into it. They each felt the same anxiety upon seeing the nests kicked to pieces. Frecko collects all the photographs he took on the island, Harald reads up on legal matters and Gio, who has a way with words, writes to newspapers and meets with local leaders and politicians. And each of them goes door to door with the folder that John compiled, showing the residents of Loviisa the islands of Aspskär and the beauty of its resident birds.

The campaign is a success. The fishermen find it within their hearts to protect the islands. Their love of birds is all the greater because so many of them make a little money selling moonshine on the side. In the dark hours of the night, Finnish and Estonian fishermen meet one another far out at sea, and boxes change hands. The fishermen would be more than happy if the coastguard were to turn their attention from the bootleggers to the sawmills, from the factories to the hooligans and their rifles, and they sign the brothers' petition without a moment's hesitation.

The residents of Loviisa are amenable to their project and donate funds, but Harald has scrutinised the letter of the law, and he has bad news for his brothers. The President can decide that any part of state land can be cordoned off and turned into a nature reserve to keep its flora and fauna untouched. But Aspskär is not state land. The landowner could apply for permission to protect his own land too, but a private decision to protect the land needs the permission of the local governor, and it is widely known that the governor upon whose desk this application would arrive is a keen rambler and a fervent opponent of hunting restrictions. Even if they could get Aspskär's landowners to file this complex application, the chances of success would be vanishingly small. The brothers listen to Harald's explanation in a mood of resignation: not even the law can protect the birds.

In the evening, John gathers all the money they have collected. He counts it up, does some quick calculations, and the following morning he calls his brothers into the kitchen. The residents of Loviisa have donated a total of 4,445 marks towards the protection of the island. It isn't quite enough to purchase Aspskär outright, but it will be enough to rent it, then they can start protecting it themselves.

This means they will have to live on the island right through the long nesting season to protect the birds and their offspring. When he realises this, Harald hesitates. He has recently secured a job at a local printer with responsibility for their garden, where he has planted fruit trees and berry bushes alongside beautiful, delicate flowers that require his attention throughout the season. He can't spend all summer looking after the birds. Frecko and Gio, however, are thrilled. They have grown up reading boys' books full of stories of adventures and expeditions, and they are forever bemoaning the timid world into which they were born by a cruel turn of fate. Now they can become heroes, defend the innocent inhabitants of the island against human evils! Frecko and Gio's excitement makes John laugh, and he promises to take care of Harald's share of guard duty.

The landowners with the deeds to Aspskär look favourably upon the brothers' suggestion. They have nothing against the protection of the birds, so long as they can continue to fish in the waters around the island and harvest the long grass growing around the rocks once the nesting season is over. They draw up a rental agreement lasting fifteen years. With the remaining money, the brothers buy an old pump room from the city authorities. The fishermen's hut on Aspskär will provide adequate accommodation during the summer, but the nesting season begins during the cold months of the spring, and they must start their guard duties as soon as the first goldeneyes return from the south and land in the shallow waters by the island's shores. They load the pump room onto a sled and pull it across the brittle sea ice to the island.

For the next few years, they spend all spring and summer on the island, keeping watch and making sure the birds are never left unsupervised. John takes the longest shifts. His brothers gradually grow into adulthood, and with that comes adult concerns, wives, children and work, but John spends his time sitting on the steps outside the pump room, drawing, listening to the shipping forecast and the birds, and whenever he sees an approaching boat, he quickly strides down to the shore. He always greets the new arrivals with a smile and tells them that hunting and gathering eggs is forbidden on the island. His words and demeanour are pleasant, but he always has a rifle slung over his shoulder.

*

A gull is building a nest in the roof of the pump room. It plucks twigs and branches from the shore, carefully weaves them together and opens its beak in a long mating call. The squawk startles John. He steps outside, sits on the steps, and the gull continues its work without paying him the slightest attention. He is shaking off the remnants of sleep and watching the bird go about its business, when the sea carries a sound all the way to the steps of the hut. The roar of the approaching motor cuts through the birds' cries, and he soon sees a boat approaching from the north-west. Its course shows it is heading right towards the island, and before long he can make out four men sitting on board. He doesn't recognise the boat, and he pulls on his shirt and trousers and quickly heads down to the shoreline.

The wind brings with it a whole host of new sounds. One of the men is singing, braying so raucously that it is clear the group has been drinking more than just water. John can see the rifles propped between the thwarts and begins to fear the worst but raises his hand and calls out a hello. Upon noticing him, the men fall silent, one of them quickly hiding a bottle in the folds of his jacket. They don't reply to his greeting, but John wishes them a pleasant day and tells them that hunting on the island is forbidden. When he hears this, the man who hid the bottle bursts into an ugly laugh. He will hunt wherever he likes, and people should think twice before trying to stop him. His comrades egg him on with a volley of cheers.

John doesn't take the bait but explains that he can direct them to many excellent islands in the waters off Loviisa where there are plenty of birds, but that here they will have to leave empty-handed. In response, he is met with a slew of curses, and one of the men hands the spokesman a rifle. The man raises the rifle and asks whether Grönvall would still like to tell him what to do. He is drunk and unpredictable, but John continues talking as though he hadn't noticed the weapon in the man's hand.

He thinks about his own rifle in the pump room. He was in such a hurry to get down to the shore that he forgot to take it with him, so he'll simply have to do without it. The seagulls have noticed the intruders, their warning calls are ringing out across the island. John listens to the gulls, takes a deep breath and doesn't even flinch when the man fires a warning shot. The bullet strikes a boulder, sending fragments of rock into the air, and the men give a cheer, but John stands firm, though it is all he can do not to let the fear show. We could shoot you right here on this island and nobody would ever know. We could put you full of holes and leave the police to work it out, the drunkard threatens him. John nods: if you want to hunt on this island, that's what you'll have to do. For a moment, the men exchange confused glances, then the drunkard throws the rifle from his hand – no point wasting bullets on this bastard – and they steer their boat back out to sea.

John waits until the boat has disappeared over the horizon before slumping to the ground. The shaking lasts a long time. He sits on the rocks, trembling, and the seagull nesting on the roof of the pump room flies down and lands next to him. He looks at the bird, and it nods, raises it beak then lowers it again, and John nods back. He will not betray his birds.

*

John Grönvall is accepted to the drawing school of the Ateneum art gallery. All the Grönvall brothers are skilled illustrators, and John would happily spend all day drawing. But he is the son of a sea captain and a backwasher and does what is expected of him: he gets himself a proper job. He secures a position at the Loviisa cardboard factory, but after two years of stripping spruce trees he makes up his mind and walks up the fossil-dappled steps of the Ateneum with a portfolio under his arm. He swaps the factory floor for the drawing ateliers of the opulent palace and spends his days sketching gypsum, tracing people and animals.

John graduates, his teacher Bruno Tuukkanen hires him as an assistant, and the two work on decorating churches. John isn't perhaps the most imaginative of his peers, but he is diligent and a pleasure to work with, not remotely predisposed to the emotional outbursts so typical of young artists, and his eye for colour is second to none. He is able to reproduce the suggested patterns with such attention to detail that Tuukkanen cannot tell his student's work from his own, and they spend the summer on raised platforms under the vast arched ceilings, painting high above the life going on around them. John learns to unveil the work of the old masters from beneath a layer of whitewash. He reinvents the colours they used, grinding pigments until oxide green and earthy ochre come together to form just the right shade.

In his spare time, he collects eggs. Hidden in the boughs of an old spruce, he finds a goldcrest's nest, woven together from cobwebs and lichen, and gathers its tiny eggs, wraps them in cottonwool and takes them home. Once at his desk, he carefully picks up one of the eggs, which weighs but a fraction of an ounce, drills a hole in it, blows, and his breath replaces the life hidden inside the shell. He realises that his timing was just right. He climbed up to the nest shortly after the eggs had emerged from inside the bird. The yolk dribbles out of the hole, wet and sloppy, the embryo inside hasn't yet begun to take shape. It is possible to blow an egg even once this process has started, but tugging the foetus out via the tiny hole is difficult and unpleasant work. He wipes the emptied egg with a chamois leather, moves on to the next, tries and fails, but continues until he is able to open his cabinet, pull out a drawer and place in it a glass tube containing a row of brittle, brown-dotted eggshells.

From time to time, he attends meetings of the ornithological society. He doesn't take part in the scientists' conversations but listens intently and offers to help maintain the cabinets used to store the eggs, and when the Museum of Zoology advertises for an assistant who knows how to use both a chisel and a paintbrush, he gets the job. Tuukkanen loses his assistant to the birds, and John swaps the churches for the museum.

*

John spends the daytime at the Museum of Zoology and his evenings with Kreuger's egg collection. These days he only rarely gets out to Aspskär, but their work there has borne fruit. Every spring, more fledglings hatch from their eggs. Many species that had abandoned the island have found their way back, and when the first couple of common guillemots choose to nest there, the brothers' joy and pride know no bounds. Aspskär has got its birds back, and the brothers are replaced by the next generation of bird lovers, new inquisitive youngsters who take up residence in the pump room.

The birds return to Aspskär, but elsewhere numbers continue to fall, and nesting charts reveal that breeding pairs are dwindling year upon year. Marine-bird populations collapse, and there are ever fewer birds of prey. Hunters are rewarded for culling "detrimental pests and predators", and their eggs are once again in high demand among collectors. The forests and rocky shores fall silent, and ornithological societies begin to demand hunting restrictions and measures to protect the birds, but the notion of restricting the collection of eggs is one they raise with some trepidation. It is easy to condemn the mindless slaughter of birds of prey in the hope of generous rewards, but collecting eggs is the cherished hobby of naturalists the world over. Of course, science is different from mere hunting, and how can one study birds without gathering samples, skins, eggs and nests? How can we kindle a love of birds among the youth, if the joy of collecting eggs and experiencing the beauty of egg collections is taken away?

The debate is heated. Those present fail to reach a decision, and John Grönvall leaves the meeting somewhat confused. After all, he too has cocked his shotgun and allowed pellets to pierce a ptarmigan's heart. He too has climbed a spruce and emptied a goldcrest's nest, but his motives were pure. He killed those birds and took their eggs out of scientific curiosity, artistic ambition, he harbours nothing but love for birds. All those countless hours dedicated to his winged friends – could this really be evil disguised as love, had he in fact harmed the thing he most wanted to save? He can't relax in his bed but heads off to the one place that will calm his mind.

Fifty thousand eggs, eighteen thousand nests, three thousand two hundred species of bird, all packed into a single room.

Imagine what kind of flock they would have made – ostriches, ducks, chickens, grebes, doves, cuckoos, spinners, cranes, owls, sparrows, penguins, storks, birds of prey – a whole aviary packed away in cabinets, tens of thousands of fledglings pushing free of their shells with a dizzying squawk. But the collection around him is neat and silent. Where once there were living, breathing, straggly creatures, now there are rows of empty, beautifully arranged shells, eggs from which the possibility of life was blown away before the beak could form and tap its way to freedom. Grönvall stands surrounded by cabinets, lists the species and numbers in his head, and for the first time, the collection's silence feels ear-splitting.

Kreuger doesn't wait for public opinion to change but sets to work. The time for private collections has passed, but he has an idea to make sure that his treasures are never seen as mere hunting trophies. He enters negotiations with the Museum of Zoology: he is prepared to offer his collection for the benefit of science. The museum is thrilled at the offer. Kreuger's collection is magnificent, an almost complete catalogue of European nesting birds, only missing the eggs of two species, the wallcreeper and the white-winged snowfinch. It includes four hundred species that are so rare that they can only be found in the industrial magnate's boxes. The museum board accepts the donation and can hardly believe their luck.

In its comprehensiveness, Kreuger's collection is stunning, but its sheer scope brings with it a number of challenges. An egg is a demanding exhibit requiring stable conditions, a space designed especially to preserve the shells. Where can they possibly house 50,000 eggs? But Kreuger has thought of everything. It's clear that the Museum of Zoology doesn't have enough room to house his collection. To that end, a new space is planned specifically for the eggs. He has already selected a suitable plot of land and has begun negotiations with the architects, and all city hall and the museum have to do is sign the paperwork.

When the university's collections moved into the Museum of Zoology, the process was a public spectacle. People gathered on the streets, took their children along to wave at the stuffed animals as they travelled through the city. The egg collection, however, moves to its new premises in secret. The new building doesn't draw much attention either, and many people walk right past without realising what is held inside it, they don't notice the dark slate next to the door bearing the mysterious engraving OOLOGICUM R. KREUGER.

Kreuger gets his museum, and it truly is his museum, for it never opens its doors to the public. The staff at the Museum of Zoology worry that the specimens on display might prove irresistible, that the eggs might rekindle a passion for the very kind of egg collecting that they are trying so hard to snuff out, and their concern is not entirely unfounded.

One day, an English researcher pays a visit to the museum. Under normal circumstances, nobody is allowed inside unsupervised, as Kreuger has taken it upon himself to be present whenever an expert is given access to the collection, but a rare twist of fate makes this visit very different. Though usually in fine health, Kreuger is bedridden with such a fever that even he must admit that he won't be much of a guide, but since the visitor is one of the most respected oologists in the field, Kreuger makes an exception and allows the man into the collection without supervision.

The following day, Grönvall appears at the magnate's door, beside himself. On the desk he found a note left by the researcher explaining that he had borrowed a few of the rarer eggs from Kreuger's collection to compare them to those in British collections. The eggs were never returned.

Kreuger's collection can turn even a researcher into a thief. Mercifully, Kreuger himself is not there to witness the greatest misfortune to befall his specimens, as this occurs many decades after his death. The magnate is spared the knowledge that his magnificent collection gave rise to one of the most scandalous environmental crimes in Finnish history. The Museum of Zoology employs a young intern to look after the eggs. He shows a great interest in oology, asks insightful, educated questions about the location of certain nesting sites and the process of gathering eggs. In fact, he asks so many questions that the senior researchers begin to the fear the worst. Once the intern's tenure comes to an end, he is no longer allowed access to the collection.

Some years later, the police knock on the door of a detached house in rural Närpiö. A customs office has opened a parcel addressed to the young man containing the eggs of several rare birds. The police are duly informed of the illegal shipment and drive to Närpiö to raid the man's house, but nothing can prepare them for the sight that awaits them.

The intern has put together an egg collection of his own. He has taught himself how to find nests, engaged in secret correspondence with other collectors, exchanged one rarity for another, and over the years his collection has grown so much that the police find more than nine thousand eggs in the house. In court, the man is asked what drove him to do this, but he can't give any rationale for his actions. His only explanation is that he found it impossible to resist the beauty of the eggs, that they consumed him, took over his mind, and he couldn't stop himself, though he knew that what he was doing was wrong. Kreuger's collection is too beguiling, too dangerous, and for this reason it becomes a shrine, a place where mere mortals have no business.

*

The magnate is lying in bed, staring at the wall. His mind is a flurry of thoughts – drainage systems, contracts, negotiations. He is hunting for rest, but sleep eludes him, and eventually he gives up, gets dressed, walks downstairs and opens the door to the egg collection. He had an apartment built in conjunction with the collection's new home and asked the architects to add a door directly from his home into the museum. A strange decision, but Kreuger is paying for such a large chunk of the costs that he can have whatever he wants, and now he opens the door and steps from his living room right into John Grönvall's workshop. Grönvall has done a hard day's work – Kreuger didn't hear the door close until gone midnight, and he looks at the preparator's desk. John has everything he needs in his workshop, and more, because he never throws anything away. He even saves the greasy paper bags in which he brings fresh cinnamon buns from a local bakery, and the workshop is home to a glorious clutter that would seem more fitting for an alchemist than a pedantic servant of the natural sciences. Every surface is covered in equipment: tools, pots of paint and ink, packaging, drawing paper, notes, pens, brushes, glass jars full of pigment – the antithesis of Kreuger's own study, where every piece of paper is in its rightful place, but because he has never found fault with Grönvall's work, the magnate sees no reason to complain about the state of the workshop and looks instead at the sketchbook left open on the table.

Grönvall has been experimenting with different stencils, cutting different-shaped holes in pieces of cardboard and blowing ink through them to reproduce the patterns of the eggs he is restoring. He has spent his evening developing just the right paint, making one version after another, and continuing only once he has made a stencil that will leave brown speckles on the peregrine falcon's egg. He has forgotten to turn off his desk lamp; Kreuger flicks the switch, and the light disappears. For a moment he can't see anything, but gradually the forms of the trees in the garden begin to take shape, the last leaves clinging to their branches. The next gust of wind will separate them from their moorings and send them shimmering down to the withered lawn, but for now the air is still and the leaves remain where they are, the garden and the workshop, both so motionless that the magnate's heartbeat is the only sign that time is marching onwards. He steps from the workshop through into the museum hall. He doesn't switch on the lights but allows his eyes to become accustomed to the dark in the windowless room, walks to one of the display cases and places his hand against the glass. On their velvet cushions, the eggs appear as distinct blotches in the darkness, but he doesn't need light to see their shapes and patterns, or the porous surface of an elephant bird's egg. He spends his nights watching over his treasures, and the agony of those sleepless hours turns to a silent euphoria.

Egg collecting is eventually made illegal, but John Grönvall continues his work. He repairs shells and restores colours, carefully and precisely, and when it's ready his work is hidden away in a cabinet to protect it from light and dust, in a museum that nobody is allowed to visit. Very few people ever see his work, but that doesn't stop his reputation from spreading, because he has become the last of his kind. One country after another outlaws the collection of birds' eggs. From now on, researchers and responsible enthusiasts no longer gather eggs but fill out a form where they log the number of eggs, the location of the nest and any other relevant information, and over time paper records replace physical eggshells. Birding books no longer teach readers how to blow an egg or stuff a bird's skin, and teachers stop showing children how to find nests.

The delicate and curious skill of egg restoration gradually wanes, and museums including the British Museum and the Smithsonian Institute turn to Grönvall, sending their most precious eggs to the son of a Loviisa sea captain for restoration.

Stepping into the museum has begun to feel like stepping into the past, a time when a collector might pluck the eggs right from their nest, imagining he is recording one tiny piece of an unchanging world in the belief that a scientist cannot possibly affect his subject, but beyond the walls of the egg museum, such a world is already gone.

*

Now John Grönvall has been given the task of putting together the first of the disappeared species that forced humans to look at themselves in the mirror. The skeleton of Steller's Sea Cow was first assembled ninety years earlier. Now it is being examined by the eyes of researchers a century younger, and in its construction they see a number of incorrect assumptions and outdated notions. The people who first assembled the sea cow weren't very familiar with its evolutionary family – and how could they be? Professors and illustrators from a country on the Baltic coastline, they were acquainted with different types of seals, the skeletons of the various whales and porpoises on display in local collections, but they had only a superficial understanding of sirenians, and though von Nordmann had seen the Paris sea cow, all he had at his disposal was his imagination and a general idea of how this mammal fits together.

The sea cow they built is beautiful and impressive. They did painstaking work, but mistakes were made nonetheless: the skeleton's posture is strange, the head is too elevated and the wooden cartilages holding the ribs together too broad – and then there is the matter of the sea cow's hands. At first, they assumed that the men who had recovered the skeleton must have been careless, that the small bones of the palm had simply gone unnoticed, but since then a lot of effort has gone into trying to locate the sea cow's fingers. Nordenskiöld offered a handsome reward for anyone who could find them, and on Bering Island the Aleutians dug up all manner of finger bones belonging to foxes and seals, but they couldn't find the sea cow's hands. Additionally, there is Steller's testimony that the sea cow's flippers contained shrivelled, hoof-like structures that it used to wander along the ocean floor like a bull in a paddock. The sea cow's hands are never found, and the skeleton loses its pianist's fingers, for a researcher should not complete nature based on assumptions alone, should not make the image more perfect than it already is, and Grönvall dismantles the professors' old joins, separates the bone from the wood and places the prostheses on his bookshelf as a reminder that science is about knowledge, not imagination.

Grönvall removes the screws and metal wires. He organises the bones and numbers them, his handwriting like a palimpsest above the professors' already faded numbers. The sea cow's bones are old and weather-beaten. Nobody knows how long the skeleton lay on the island before it was found, whether it had been waiting, hidden in the sands, for decades, centuries or even millennia, buried by the wind and the water in layers of silt and sediment, so slowly that its sinking motion evaded the beady eye of birds and humans, but sure enough it was buried, one grain of sand at a time. The vertebrae and the skull disappeared from view, and before long the sea cow would have disappeared completely, slipping into the sand where it could continue to decompose in peace.

An egg is designed to break, to endure only those few short days that the embryo needs to develop into a bird in the warmth underneath its mother. After this, its purpose is to allow the fledgling to tap its way through the shell. An egg exists only for a moment, while bones are designed to persist beneath muscles and tendons for years, decades, but ultimately the difference is negligible. Bone and eggshell are made of the same material, and over time a bone too will degrade and disappear, but that is not the fate of this skeleton. The sea cow was exhumed from its grave, and now it is here, halfway around the world from its island, in a small northern museum in a small northern capital, having its bones examined by the preparator John Grönvall.

He scrutinises the sea cow one bone at a time, cleans them, repairs their surfaces, but some are in poor condition, particularly one pair of ribs and the vertebrae of the lower spine and tail. To protect them, John casts replacements out of gypsum and reads up on methods for how best to make the material resemble the animal's porous bones, striving for just the right colour, faded by time and the sea.

He tries to acquaint himself with the creature he is reconstructing, but there is only scant information available. The bones reveal that this was a young sea cow that was still growing; its growth plates were yet to reach full epiphyseal closure. Its age and sex, however, remain a mystery. We don't know how quickly or slowly the sea cow grew or how long it took to reach the majestic dimensions of adulthood. Nobody was able to observe them long enough to watch the young achieve their full stature. The encounter between man and sea cow was brief and brutal, and none of the calves that Steller saw had the chance to die of old age.

Grönvall constructs the sea cow during the day, and in the evenings he turns his attention to restoring the great auk's egg. It is slow work. Restoring an egg that has already been repaired once before is harder than repairing it for the first time, just as a skeleton that has already been reconstructed requires a very different approach from an animal freshly skinned and gutted. This time, he has to dismantle someone else's handiwork, assess its traits, the qualities of its materials and joins, he must learn how hard or softly to tap a seam for the glue to give way without further damaging the shell.

Grönvall spends his days in the company of the lost. The animals are gone, but he keeps their memory alive, stopping the degradation of the shells and bones so that those who come after him will be able to pause at their remnants and see their own time reflected back at them. In the sea cow, Steller saw the hand of God, a link in the great chain of creation, another part of a beautiful, unchanging system, and perhaps he slit open the sea cow's belly and cracked open its skull without any sense of guilt or concern. For Furuhjelm, the sea cow's bones were a frustrating mystery, its disappearance an ominous twist of fate, but for Grönvall it reflects a possibility born out of loss, and the idea that his own species could drive another to destruction has turned from an inkling to a pattern that repeats itself over and over. But the traces that Grönvall leaves on the bones are gentle and meticulous. He repairs hairline fractures in the *processus spinosus,* casts new vertebrae to replace broken ones and gives the sea cow a new, more curved posture. Von Nordmann and Bonsdorff set the sea cow's head in a proud, upward aspect, but it is more likely that it swam with its eyes and head angled downwards. It was less interested in the sky than in the strips of kelp rising from the ocean floor.

*

In the museum hall, John Grönvall stands examining the metal wire wound around the ribs, the arches that he has bent into shape to keep the skeleton together. He checks the joins one last time and finds everything in order. He takes a step back, inspects the animal and gives a nod of approval upon seeing that his gypsum replacements blend in with the originals so well that the average visitor will never realise that some of these bones were not created in a sea cow's womb but in the hands of a preparator.

The sea cow is intact once again. Grönvall wonders how he might celebrate its completion and decides to start by smoking a cigarette. He steps into the courtyard and watches the wagtails bobbing across the lawn. He wonders where they have built their nests, but the possibilities are endless. The wagtail isn't a fussy bird; it will build its nest almost anywhere. He leans against the museum wall and waits, but the birds don't reveal the location of their nest and simply dive here and there across the lawn hunting invertebrates that he cannot see. The janitor opens the door and the birds flutter away. He comes bringing a message. Grönvall unfolds the telegram, reads it, and a broad smile spreads across his face. He couldn't have imagined a better way to celebrate.

*

A gust of wind catches the sheets of paper, and John holds them against his chest to stop them flying off across the island. The seagulls let the wind carry them high up into the air, screeching as they rise, and he gathers his sketches and steps into the pump room before the rain starts. He boils some water, makes a pot of tea and tastes the words in his mouth: Aspskär Nature Reserve. Twenty-seven hectares of land and 342 hectares of protected water. Their association has taken care of the island for thirty years, but now the birds are protected by the letter of the law, and the brothers' shifts on guard duty can finally come to an end.

*

A bolt of lightning strikes the rocks, and the whole island trembles. John wakes with a start. He rolls over in his bed but still can't get to sleep, so he gets up, places a chair next to the window and gazes out at the rain lashing down upon the sea. Lightning illuminates the sky, and all at once he can just discern a dark shape far out at sea, something large and round among the waves. He waits for the next flash, but when it comes the shape has gone and doesn't return. The downpour settles into a drizzle, and the sea is calm once more. John returns to his bed, and as he sleeps the sea cows surround the island, herds of them, quietly grazing, and John Grönvall smiles. Here they are safe, with 342 hectares of water to protect them.

*

The industrial magnate Kreuger keeps the great auk's egg for himself; the museum only receives it after his death. He keeps it because, for him, the egg of an extinct bird is not a story of greed and destruction but one of skill and love. When, at the fine age of 97, Kreuger closes his eyes for the final time, the auk's egg is at last inducted into the collection at the Museum of Zoology. A label is added to it indicating that it has been repaired, as the cracks are invisible to the naked eye.

In 2017 the egg collection closes its doors. The university decides to streamline its activities and eventually gives up its Munkkiniemi campus. Kreuger's bespoke cabinets and glass cases are dismantled, and the eggs housed within them are moved to the basement of what is now known as the Natural History Museum, which boasts storage facilities meeting modern standards. The building that once housed the egg collection is now home to a gym and a massage parlour, but before leaving for the last time, museum manager Stjernberg collects all the papers Grönvall left in the workshop, all the jotters, photographs and grease-stained paper bags with which he created his unique world of colour. Then he opens the desk drawer and picks up the old cigarette packets on whose unfolded cardboard John Grönvall inscribed his notes about the sea cow's bones in a beautiful, semi-legible hand.

*

The sea cow is assembled and displayed in the great hall at the Museum of Zoology. It is the most splendid of rarities, but in the great seats of scientific learning, researchers focus their efforts on other species, other specimens. Museum visitors pause in front of the sea cow for a moment, marvel at its large, bony form, but otherwise it is left to slumber in peace for decades until a curious incident is revealed by one of the museum's assistants in a naturalist magazine a full four decades later.

The assistant is presenting the skeleton of Steller's Sea Cow to a group of biology students. As he is describing the animal's structure, he gently taps one of the spinous processes and is taken aback: the bone responds to his touch and rings against his finger. He continues his presentation, but he cannot forget the sound made by the vertebra, and once the students have left, he hurries back to the sea cow. After checking to make sure he is alone, he starts tapping the creature's bones and realises he was right: spinous processes of different lengths produce a scale of different pitches. Thus begins a unique hobby. Once the museum is closed for the day, the assistant returns to the sea cow's skeleton and practises until he is ready.

Eventually, he invites his colleagues to gather around the skeleton. As they look on in bewilderment, the assistant performs the *poco allegretto* theme from Brahm's third symphony, which Yves Montand later borrowed in a wistful song of his own. He raps and taps the bones, and the conservators and janitors gathered for the occasion listen as the sound of an extinct animal echoes through the hall.

Steller's Sea Cow is gone, but in the world's oceans its extinction continues to this day. At the Great Barrier Reef, the seabed is vacuumed by its cousin, the last of the sea cows. The dugong is a shy creature about which we know very little. It shuns human contact, and unlike its larger relative, it is a skilled diver and spends most of its time underwater. We have the dugong and three manatees: the Amazonian manatee grazing on water grass in the flood plains along the Amazon; the West Indian manatee, which prefers the warm waters around Florida and the Caribbean; and the African manatee living among the mangroves of West Africa. Four sirenians still carry the memory of their lost relative in their genes, though their future is far from certain.

But the dugong doesn't bemoan its fate. It sinks its lips into the sands of the seabed and tugs the grass into its mouth, constantly followed by a shoal of sprightly yellow fish. They shelter underneath the dugong and nibble at the tiny beings that its tail whips up from the sand. The sea cow rolls over, turns its wrinkly belly towards the sky, and as it turns its iris makes out the lights shimmering on the water's surface. It leans on its tail for support, then pushes off, rising slowly through the bright water until its head pierces the surface. It doesn't look at the heavenly bodies above, pays no attention to the birds swooping overhead or the ship barely visible on the horizon, but fills its lungs and dives back down into the depths.

60°10'16"N, 24°55'52"E

NATURAL HISTORY MUSEUM

HELSINKI

Today the museum is quiet, only a few visitors wander absent-mindedly among the dead, examining labels and bones, the quiet drum of the rain filling the hall. An elderly woman stops in front of the sea cow, looks up and down its remains, sees the centuries of deeds they contain, the cracked vertebrae, the handiwork, a creature that is no more.

The sea cow is gone, but hasn't everyone dreamed of being able to look the past in the eye? Each generation comes up with its own ways of honouring the dead. Now researchers are reconstructing a mammoth in their laboratories, boring a hole into a rock dove's egg, cutting off the inheritance of the embryo inside it and refilling it with genetic material from an extinct bird. One day, a dove will hatch from that egg. It will grow, mate and lay its own eggs – and then we'll be in for a surprise. Instead of a common rock dove, the fledgling that hatches from that egg will grow up to develop the distinctive red plumage of the passenger pigeon. Now researchers' attention turns to other species carrying another relative in their genetic constitution, the female Asian elephants from whose wombs the mammoth could be born again. What a comforting thought! Perhaps our loss isn't permanent after all, perhaps we can correct the mistakes of the past and reverse extinction. But even this resurrection is a compromise: what the Asian elephant will push from her womb will not be a mammoth but a barely credible chimera, an elephant whose genes have been imbued with a long coat and the ability to withstand the cold. The new fledgling might look like a passenger pigeon, but half of its genetic inheritance will still be that of the rock dove, and what hatches from the egg is but more proof of man's scientific prowess, beckoned from the underworld. What has died cannot be brought back to life, but a thought can, a hope, a realistic copy. Maybe that is enough.

The woman continues on her way. Her footsteps echo through the galleries, merging with the sound of whale song coming from one of the rooms, and all of a sudden everything stops. The rain pauses, Steller's quill freezes above his notebook, Constance lowers the chamois in her hand, Grönvall's paintbrush stops on the paper and the poisonous spiders hiding inside the museum walls stand stock-still, all breath holds a brief hiatus, then everything resumes, but for a fleeting moment it is here, a faint, all-consuming sorrow upon beholding this creature, so large and so meek, so irrevocably departed.

ACKNOWLEDGEMENTS

I would like to thank the species that have been declared extinct during the writing of this novel:

Thank you to *Sympterichthys unipennis,* that strange handfish; thank you to *Pristimantis anotis, Atelopus pinangoi* and the twenty-two other species of tropical frog that were never even given a Finnish name; thank you to the countless species of mite that have been disappearing more quickly than researchers have been able to classify them; thank you to seventeen species of fish in Lake Lanao in the Philippines; thank you to *Chitala lopis,* which used to swim in the forest streams of Indonesia and to *Schizothorax saltans,* now forever lost from the rivers of Kazakhstan; thank you to the lesser stick-nest rat, *Leporillus apicalis,* which, as the name suggests, lived in enormous nests made of sticks; thank you to the Christmas Island forest skink, *Emoia nativitatis;* thank you *Bettongia anhydra,* a small marsupial that once hopped across the deserts of Australia; and thank you to the bats, to the Japanese *Pipistrellus sturdeei,* to *Nyctophilus howensis,* which lived on the island of Tasmania, and to *Pipistrellus murrayi,* another resident of Christmas Island; thank you, *Sus bucculentis,* the Vietnamese warty pig; thank you to the Bramble Cay mosaic-tailed rat *Melomys rubicola,* a tiny rodent living near the Great Barrier Reef whose fate was sealed by increased ocean flooding; thank you to the Australian great hopping mouse *Notomys robustus;* thank you to the small dwarf mantis *Ameles fasciipennis;* thank you to the Jalpa false brook salamander *Pseudoeurycea exspectata* from Guatemala; thank you, *Achatinella apexfulva,* a yellow-tipped snail from the Hawaiian island of O'ahu that crept among the boughs of the trees; thank you, *Carcharhinus obsoletus,* the large-eyed, long-nosed tiger shark; thank you and farewell to *Partula faba,* the oval-shaped snail from the islands of French Polynesia that, according to Captain James Cook, a zoologist on the expedition by the name of Thomas Martyn decided to call a bean snail, though nobody really knew why; and thank you to the other 374 living creatures that were declared extinct during the writing of this novel.

I would also like to thank the numerous researchers – of the humanities and the natural sciences alike – whose findings and scholarship made this book possible. Particular thanks go to Janne Granroth, head curator of the Helsinki Natural History Museum, and to its manager Torsten Stjernberg, whose knowledge and expertise were not only of invaluable help in the writing of this book but brought immense pleasure too.

Any potential mistakes, inaccuracies or misunderstandings are my own. Where definitive information was unavailable or I was unable to access such, I have taken the liberty to use my imagination.

IIDA TURPEINEN's short stories exploring the relationship between humans and animals won the J. H. Erkko Young Writers' Competition in 2014. Her debut novel, *Beasts of the Sea,* published after seven years of research, was awarded the Helsingin Sanomat Prize and shortlisted for the Finlandia Prize. Translation rights were quickly sold across the world, along with record-breaking sales in Finland, leading it to be acknowledged as the most successful Finnish fiction debut of all time.

DAVID HACKSTON is a British translator of Finnish and Swedish literature and drama. Notable publications include Laura Lindstedt's *My Friend Natalia,* Petra Rautiainen's WWII thriller *Land of Snow and Ashes,* and Kari Hukkila's *One Thousand and One.* In 2020 he was awarded the Oxford-Weidenfeld Prize for his translation of Pajtim Statovci's *Crossing.*

RAISING READERS

Books Build Bright Futures

Thank you for reading this book and for being a reader of books in general. We are so grateful to share being part of a community of readers with you, and we hope you will join us in passing our love of books on to the next generation of readers.

Did you know that reading for enjoyment is the single biggest predictor of a child's future happiness and success?

More than family circumstances, parents' educational background, or income, reading impacts a child's future academic performance, emotional well-being, communication skills, economic security, ambition, and happiness.

Studies show that kids reading for enjoyment in the US is in rapid decline:

- In 2012, 53% of 9-year-olds read almost every day. Just 10 years later, in 2022, the number had fallen to 39%.
- In 2012, 27% of 13-year-olds read for fun daily. By 2023, that number was just 14%.

Together, we can commit to **Raising Readers** and change this trend. How?

- Read to children in your life daily.
- Model reading as a fun activity.
- Reduce screen time.
- Start a family, school, or community book club.
- Visit bookstores and libraries regularly.
- Listen to audiobooks.
- Read the book before you see the movie.
- Encourage your child to read aloud to a pet or stuffed animal.
- Give books as gifts.
- Donate books to families and communities in need.

BOB1217

Books build bright futures, and **Raising Readers** is our shared responsibility.

For more information, visit **JoinRaisingReaders.com**

Sources: National Endowment for the Arts, National Assessment of Educational Progress, WorldBookDay.org, Nielsen BookData's 2023 "Understanding the Children's Book Consumer"